LIFE
AND
DEATH
ON
10 WEST

LIFE
AND
DEATH
ON
10 WEST

ERIC LAX

Times
BOOKS

Portions of this book appeared in somewhat different form
in *New West* magazine.

Published by TIMES BOOKS,
The New York Times Book Co., Inc.
Three Park Avenue, New York, N.Y. 10016

Published simultaneously in Canada by
Fitzhenry & Whiteside, Ltd., Toronto

Library of Congress Cataloging in Publication Data

Lax, Eric.
  Life and death on 10 West.

    1. Galbraith, Linda. 2. Myelocytic leukemia — Patients —
California — Biography. 3. Marrow — Transplantation.
I. Title. II. Title: Life and death on ten West.
RC643.L35   1984   616.99'419   82-40360
ISBN 0-8129-1037-0

Designed by Doris Borowsky

Manufactured in the United States of America

84 85 86 87 88 5 4 3 2 1

Prologue

Most of the activity described in this book takes place on ward 10 West of the UCLA Medical Center, the location of the bone marrow transplantation unit. The seven patient rooms and the nurses' station that comprise the unit are in many ways a world of their own. Ten West is a place where young people with almost assuredly fatal diseases subject themselves to an extraordinarily difficult and life-threatening medical procedure in the hope that by surviving this ordeal they will be able to enjoy what most everyone takes for granted—the expectation of a long life. The patients who come to this place and the doctors and nurses who treat them are a determined and exceptional group. I went there to be merely an observer, but that is impossible in such an environment. I went intending to stay a month but stayed seven. I spent ten or twelve and sometimes more hours a day, six or seven days a week on 10 West, watching, listening, and talking with doctors and nurses, patients, their families, and researchers. At the outset, the doctors and nurses warned me that anyone who comes to the ward must maintain a safe emotional distance from patients lest he be overwhelmed by the intensity of their struggle. Each of them, though, had stories of the times when that distance could not be kept, and of the pain they felt when a patient they grew close to died. I felt that pain, too. No one goes to 10 West and leaves it unaffected.

I was, of course, very drawn to Linda Galbraith, whose story is the basis of this book. But because statistically she had a very good chance for recovery and because a reporter's notebook provides a certain shield, she did not, at least at first, wrap herself around my emotions the way Nellie Tapia did. Nellie figures only peripherally in my recounting of Linda's story, but in the seven months I knew her, she became like a member of my family. Her prognosis when she arrived on the ward was very unpromising. She was eighteen, and she had a form of leukemia that is very difficult to put into the remission that is necessary before a bone marrow transplant can be attempted. She was someone I could not but be drawn to. She was brave and sweet and funny. She worried, as every teen-ager does, about the way she looked and the way she dressed, and she played her cassette player often and loud; her favorite singer was Jackson Browne, and she often wore a green sweat shirt commemorating one of his tours. But in facing almost certain death, she displayed only calm and determination and a sense that each day was to be taken for itself alone. She husbanded her strength and kept her optimism fired. One can only marvel at such grace.

Moreover, her family lived in a small town in southern Arizona and did not have the means to visit her often. Thus, because of her personality and her circumstances, she caught the attention of the 10 West staff and mine as well. I spent an hour or two every day with her, doing jigsaw puzzles or watching football on television or passing the time in some other way. She seldom spoke about what she was going through, and when she did, it was casually; I learned only by an offhand remark that before coming to UCLA, she was in a coma and near death for ten days from the attempt to muscle her disease into control. In her room were only two things that could be called inspirational, that she turned to for strength: a poem sent by a friend, the last lines of which are, "There is *no* tomorrow, there is just now/ And I'll make the best of it, somehow"; and a bookmark inscribed, "You have failed only when you have failed to try." If 10 West were ever to have a motto, either of those would do.

Nellie's fight for life and her eventual death, and the lives and deaths of many other patients I grew to know, carried my involvement in this story well beyond simple observation. It is more than two years since Nellie died. I still think of her every day, and I think, too, of the many patients who walked away after their transplants and today lead lives they otherwise would have lost had they not come to 10 West.

My choice of UCLA was not accidental. It has a reputation for being one of the foremost medical research centers in the world. It also has someone I could call on for help. I went to college with Dr. Robert Gale, the director of the bone marrow transplantation unit. Although I had not seen or talked with him in nearly fifteen years, a writer with no medical training needs all the help he can find just to get in the front door. When he explained at our first meeting what he and his staff did, I was immediately enmeshed. We had several subsequent meetings to discuss how I might properly gather the information I needed. Happily, our concerns and demands were similar. We both felt that I could not adequately cover the issue without full access to the ward, the doctors, and the nurses, and that I should follow one patient through the weeks of treatment and recovery that are entailed in a bone marrow transplant. We also agreed that it was my responsibility to present the medical issues in depth. Gale would help me all he could, but it was my job to get not only the human story but the medical one as well. That took over a year.

Having access is one thing, staying out of the way is another. Gale and I met with the 10 West nurses, and it was agreed that with proper care I would not interfere with their work. If I did, I would have to leave. I spent the first week getting used to the routine of the ward. My presence was explained, and patients and their families were assured that I would not intrude on them; only if they wanted to talk with me would I talk with them. Interestingly, everyone was willing, even eager, to talk because they felt it was time that someone explained their disease and what they were going through, so that not only friends but also patients to come would know as much as possible about what they had experienced and what lay ahead.

At the end of that first week, a nurse came to me and said that the perfect patient for me to follow had just checked in. She was, the nurse said, articulate, introspective, good-humored, and positive, and she had a good chance of doing well. As soon as I met Linda Galbraith I knew the nurse was right. Here was a remarkable woman. And she was eager, she said, to tell her story in the hope that it would help others. We struck a simple agreement: I would talk with her only when she wanted to see me, and she and her family would check the finished manuscript for facts but not for content. She was on 10 West for two months, and I spent, on average, two hours a day with her.

This book, however, begins four months before Linda or I came to 10 West. All quotes and details of that time are from the recollections of Linda, her family, and the hospital staff. Medical facts are from her hospital record. By circumstantial and emotional necessity, I became part of her story after she came to the ward, and thus, beginning in Part Three, I am a participant as well as the narrator. I was party to all dialogue I've recorded here, which took place on the day and at the time stated in the text; nothing has been altered or moved around for the sake of enhancing the story. Other than the few exceptions I point out, all names are real. Where the names have been changed, the facts are accurate.

I have felt from the day I set foot on 10 West that I experienced a part of life that is by turns horrifying and hopeful and that is outside the realm of normal living. I watched many people die terrible deaths, because leukemia is a hideous disease. I also saw people escape that death which would have come to them without a bone marrow transplant. It is still an uncertain process, but it is often better than the alternative. Life is anything but fair, as the stories here amply show. But they also show that just because it is unfair, not everyone has to lose. Linda and Dan Galbraith picked an apposite middle name for their daughter, Angela: Hope. This book is written with that spirit, and it is dedicated to her.

ONE

Linda and Dan Galbraith spent the early part of 1980 getting ready for the birth of their first child. They had been married nearly five years and, at twenty-six and twenty-nine, were ready to start a family. They had decided at the outset of their life together to wait until they were professionally and financially stable enough to properly assume the responsibility, and it had proved a wise choice. Like most young couples, they began their marriage with little money. Their home was a small apartment near Dan's job; Linda spent their first year commuting seven hundred miles a week to finish college, where they had met. Then she went to work, too. They were capable, and their firms rewarded them. By their fourth anniversary, Linda had become accounting supervisor of the Petoseed Company, an agricultural seed firm, and Dan was assistant general ranch manager of The Samuel Edwards Associates, a large citrus, avocado, and vegetable concern. Both companies are in the fertile and largely undeveloped valleys inland from Ventura, California, about midway between Los Angeles and Santa Barbara. They lived only an hour and a half's drive from the heart of California's

urban sprawl, but in atmosphere and even values it was dec-
ades away, a pocket of the California of forty years ago, filled
with citrus trees and open space, the roads lined with pepper
trees and stately sixty-foot-tall eucalyptus.

A few months before Linda became pregnant, they bought
their first home, a two-bedroom house in Oak View, a town of
a few hundred people that lives up to its name: There was a
large oak tree in their yard and a lovely view of the countryside
from their living-room window. It was an exciting time for
them.

They were an active couple. Each put in long hours at work,
but they made time for parties and doing things with friends.
And both were good athletes. Dan—six-foot-one and strap-
pingly built—was the one who looked the part, but it was Linda—nine inches shorter and physically compact—who had the
real brawn. She looked like almost any pretty brunette, at least
until she got on a horse. She was an expert rider and for years
competed around the country in trail-riding events that test the
stamina of both the horse and rider. One she liked in particular
was a twenty-four-hour, hundred-mile ride across the Sierra
Nevada Mountains that form the Nevada-California border.
But with the baby coming she was off the trail for a while. It
was about the only concession to her pregnancy. She was an
ambitious woman with high expectations for herself, expectations that were reinforced by a lifetime of succeeding at what
she set out to do.

In July, when she was six months pregnant, Linda went to see
her doctor. It was a routine monthly checkup, but she was glad
to be going. She had been feeling weak for some time; even simple tasks now tired her. Of late she'd had to rest while doing the
dishes. Still, she insisted on putting in her usual ten-hour day at
work and on doing jobs around the house. She intended to go on
as she always had right up to the time she went to the delivery
room. She had first noticed the weakness two months earlier.

The blood tests that her doctor took then showed that she was a little anemic, as expectant mothers often are, and he prescribed iron and folacin pills to counteract it. The tests he ran on this visit showed the anemia was persisting in spite of the treatment, and, feeling a specialist ought to check her, he referred her to a hematologist. Linda and Dan drove the twenty miles to his office on July 16. Neither of them was anxious about the anemia, only curious. The hematologist examined her, drew blood for further tests, and said he'd call them the next day with the results.

Dan's job requires that he spend much of his day driving between the various fields that are scattered around an area within a fifteen-mile radius of the Samuel Edwards offices in Santa Paula, an agricultural town of 21,000 where Dan grew up and which hasn't changed much in his lifetime. The building is one story of medium size just off the main street. Dan's office is simple and comfortable. On one wall are several needlepoint copies done by Linda of the colorful labels that until recently adorned the ends of California and Florida fruit boxes. In a corner, two dozen baseball caps with various company and team logos hang all over a coat rack.

By chance he was in the office rather than on the road when the hematologist called on the morning of the seventeenth. He asked Dan to call Linda and for the two of them to come to his office as quickly as they could.

"Linda," he said in a shaky voice, "has leukemia."

Dan was dumbstruck, then nauseous. He felt as if he would pass out. This was something that happened in movies, he thought, but it didn't happen in real life. After a few minutes he was able to get up from his desk and walk next door to the general ranch manager's office. Someone said something to Dan in the reception area as he passed by, but it was as if he couldn't hear. He continued into the office. As soon as he closed the door behind him, he broke down crying and spilled out the story to his astonished friend. When he had finished, and after he had pulled himself together, Dan went back to his office and called Linda, who worked twenty minutes away in Saticoy, a town even smaller than Santa Paula. The Petoseed offices and warehouse take up several acres, and Linda's office, in the long, narrow, two-story executive building, had her close to the company's treasurer and controller and the cost accountants she dealt with every day.

She was at her desk when Dan called, struggling to keep his voice as calm as he could.

"The doctor wants us to come and see him," he said.

"I can't," Linda told him. "I have too much stuff to do today. Ask him to make it some other time."

"He wants to see us right away. We have to go." Dan was insistent but managed not to sound alarmed.

"What's the matter?" Linda asked, more annoyed than concerned.

"I'll tell you when I get there."

On the drive over, Dan tried to make some sense out of what had happened, but there was none. When he went to work that morning, it had been a normal day. Now he felt his world had exploded like a hand grenade. As he drove, he asked himself if he could handle this tragedy, and he wondered what would happen to their baby, and especially what would happen to his wife. He tried to decide how best to tell her what was wrong, but he could not think of how to do it.

"What is it?" Linda asked him when they were by his car in the Petoseed parking lot.

"You have leukemia," he said simply.

Linda just looked at him. "Well, they're curing that nowadays," she said matter-of-factly.

Dan looked back at her in surprise and said, "They are?"

They talked about what had happened as they drove to the doctor's office. Dan was terribly upset, but Linda wasn't, perhaps in part because such devastating news takes time to sink in and because she felt the disease could be overcome, but also because all her life she had met any crisis head on. Dan's distress affected her as well, in fact was even something of a help. She felt she had to be strong so that he would not be even more upset by her tears. Dan marveled at her cool. She acted, he thought, as if she were going to the doctor for only a vaccination.

What the doctor told them, however, was like a needle in Dan's heart. Linda had acute myelogenous leukemia (AML), he said, and she had at best eighteen months to live. Both the doctor and Dan were in tears; but still Linda remained calm, looking for whatever hope she could find. She rattled off questions like an ired district attorney: Do you mean *no one* has lived longer than eighteen months? What forms of treatment are there? What about the baby? The doctor offered little solace except to say that leukemia is not passed from mother to fetus and that it was possible she could have the child. He said that under normal circumstances, a person should begin treatment for leukemia as soon as it is diagnosed. But since Linda was close enough to term that the child might be saved by early induction of birth, and since the disease was still in its early stages, the doctor suggested that they could buy some time for the baby to mature in the womb by postponing treatment until the disease made its next move.

The doctor's prognosis left Linda very concerned but still in control of her emotions. The one desire clear in her manner and her thoughts was that her baby have every chance to live.

"If I don't make it," she told Dan and the doctor, "I at least want to leave something behind."

Linda and Dan stayed up most of the night, talking about what to do and trying to understand what had happened to them. Linda ate a little food, but Dan had no appetite. He was overcome with a feeling of helplessness.

* * *

When she was eight, Linda wanted a horse for Christmas. Unlike most eight-year-olds, she asked neither Santa nor her parents for one. She simply wasn't a child who asked for things. She wanted a four-poster canopied bed, too, but no one knew it. About the only time she ever let on that she did want something was when she was four and she came home with a little tea set in a paper bag. It actually belonged to her girl friend down the street, but when Linda saw it, she picked it up and put it in the bag and walked off with it. After her parents explained why she had to take it back, she did, but it didn't prompt her to make her desires known. She remained overtly cool about the things she really wanted, a young woman who kept her own counsel. Which made Christmas and birthdays something of a guessing game for her parents. But when they noticed that she loved all the Marguerite Henry books on horses, and *The Black Stallion*, and that she had amassed a collection of plastic horses, even though she had said nothing, they knew what she would like. On Christmas morning, 1963, Linda opened up a jewelry box and found a statue of a black horse. A ribbon was tied around its neck, a ribbon, she discovered, that led from the living room out to the barn of her family's home just outside Atlanta. At the end of the ribbon was a real horse, black with a white star on its forehead. She called it Black Magic.

Linda was the first child of John and Jackie Peters. Two girls and two boys followed, but as is often the case with firstborns, she was special. They called her "our love child" because she was born in the first year of their marriage, and when she was twenty-six they still remembered that there was a knot that looked like a baby's face in the board over the bed in Miami where she was conceived.

She was by every measure a good child: bright, polite, self-reliant, good with her siblings, and she was mature beyond her years. By the time she was six or seven, she had developed a sense about her, as her father put it, of having read tomorrow's paper. And she was good at sorting things out. The family camped a lot, in a twelve-by-eighteen-foot tent from Sears. John and Linda were the erecting crew, mostly at night, generally in the rain, because she was the only one in the family who could remember which frame pipe fit where.

She liked camping, but like her mother, she loved horses. By 1970, when she was fifteen, Linda had become an accomplished rider. The family moved that year to a home near Newhall, California, about forty-five minutes northeast of Los Angeles, into a huge house on a large tract of land ideal for keeping horses. They had sold Black Magic before leaving Georgia and bought three new horses in Newhall. Linda's was named Dagger because of a long blaze down its nose. He was two years old but untrained, and liked to come out of the stall with his hind feet kicking. He also had habits such as falling over backward and jerking back that were detrimental to the rider's health and to his. He pulled two-by-fours out of the barn, broke halters. Linda worked with him without much success, but finally, with the help of a professional trainer, she channeled his high spirit into good discipline. They became a pair. By then Linda had become a very attractive teen-ager, a brown-eyed brunette with a warm smile and a composed look not often seen on an adolescent's face. She was a good student and was a member of the highland dance group, which performed during halftime at school football games. In 1971 and again in 1972 she was queen of the Newhall Trail Riders.

A competitive trail ride is much like a sports-car rally, except on horseback. There are rides of generally thirty to thirty-five miles a day with a minimum and maximum time between points. Riders are judged on horsemanship, horses are judged by vets on fitness and soundness and manner. For several years Linda and Jackie drove 20,000 miles or more a year around the Southwest, their horses in tow, competing. Linda won rides all over the country and in 1973 won the President's Cup of the North American Trail Riding Conference, awarded to the rider and horse with the most total points.

She was as good with numbers as she was with horses, and in high school Linda began to help her father keep the books for his business. It was something she enjoyed, and, when she graduated from high school, she decided to go into accounting.

In 1973, after two years at a local community college, she enrolled at the California State Polytechnic University in Pomona. It was about an hour and a half's drive from Newhall, and Linda often came home on weekends in her old red Volkswagen station wagon. It was not the most reliable of cars, and on occasional Monday mornings John Peters would find Linda at the door of his San Fernando Valley office, telling him that yet another thing had gone wrong with the car and that she had a class in an hour. No problem, he would say. He had owned and piloted his own four-passenger plane for years, and he kept it at a nearby field. There was a field near Cal Poly, and he would have her there and be back at his desk in almost no time.

Even when Linda's car did run, it didn't go very fast, and she was often passed on the freeway. On some of her trips she noticed a white Camaro that passed her more quickly than other cars. It was Dan's. He was a junior who lived in the same co-ed dorm. Dan had never noticed Linda's VW but he had noticed her. They had met casually at a Monte Carlo night thrown by the dorm soon after she enrolled, but he hoped for a better chance to see her. He found it when he discovered that she studied every night in the lounge off her wing of the dorm. One night in January 1974, he was there when she arrived, and he started a conversation with her. They talked for three or four hours about all the things two college students who are attracted to each other talk about. His major was agriculture, and his home in Santa Paula was about half an hour west of Newhall. Linda told him she had seen his car zipping by her on occasion and chided him on his speeding. He learned about her horsemanship and her family and her hopes, and she about his. By the end of the evening each had met the expectations of the other, and they agreed to go on a date. Before they said good night Linda straightforwardly asked Dan what he thought their relationship would lead to.

"Probably marriage," he said.

Once they began going out, they went out only with each other. During that school term they stayed some weekends at one of their parents' homes. Linda even began including Dan's laundry in with her own, which no doubt pleased his mother; he had been taking it home on his visits. They went to movies and Los Angeles Dodgers games, and Linda got Dan interested in trail riding. He accompanied her to nearby rides, helped prepare meals, and worked as one of the officials who took the pulse and respiration rate of competing horses.

Dan graduated in June 1975, and in September they were married. Just as Linda had predicted to herself after their first talk in the dorm, she told him later.

They set up house in a two-bedroom apartment in Santa Paula. Dan's first job was as the assistant pest-control supervisor for an agricultural company. Linda still had another year to go for her college degree, so she drove Dan's Camaro to and from Pomona to finish her courses. The drive was time-consuming, but it had some advantages. The highway went alongside the San Gabriel Mountains, and Linda enjoyed watching the colors change as the sun glinted off them.

The first couple of years of their romance had been easy, if only because the demands of college life aren't as rigorous as the demands of establishing a life afterward. Also, a life together with a common commitment was a wholly new enterprise for them. In the words of each, Linda and Dan were "two young people in love," but they weren't prepared for having fewer individual freedoms than they had had when they were single. Like most young couples, they had much to learn. Sometimes the lessons were difficult, even if eventually helpful.

For instance, one day Linda fell from a horse and broke her right wrist. She was accustomed to doing most of the work around the house, but with a cast on one arm she found usually easy chores hard and annoying. Dan was slow to pick up on Linda's discomfort, in part because she tried to cover it but also because he wasn't paying attention as he should have. When that happened, Linda laid into him for his lack of help.

"Poor Dan," a friend of theirs recalled with a laugh after Linda had healed. "By the end of it, it was the worst time in his life." But he learned a good lesson, and long regretted not doing more to help her.

The first year of their marriage was tough financially, too. Dan was paid every other Friday. After the rent and other bills were paid and the groceries bought, they'd sometimes have literally a dollar to last them until the next payday. They were not in debt, however. Dan refused to buy anything he couldn't pay for in cash. Consequently, going to an occasional movie was about all they did for entertainment or relaxation, and that frustrated them.

Their money problems eased after Linda graduated. She received her degree in accounting and was offered a job with Main-LaFrantz, a large accounting company. She had met several of their representatives during the yearly audit on her father's books, and they had been impressed by the quality of the work Linda did on them. But the job was in Los Angeles, and Linda was tired of daily long-distance driving after her year of commuting to school. The job didn't quite suit her ambition, either. She wanted to get her CPA qualification and to have experience working within a company. She found that chance at Petoseed, which does $25 million a year in sales worldwide. The offices in Saticoy were only a short drive away. Linda signed on as an accounting clerk in September 1976. She worked on the payroll, did a little cost analysis, and quickly proved so able that she was made a cost accountant. By 1979, when she was twenty-five, she had become manager of the accounting department, with ten women working for her, and it was predicted that she would become the firm's first woman in high-level management.

In much the same way that her parents never knew what things she really wanted, her co-workers could never tell whether Linda was up against small or large problems; she was equanimous in the face of either. Her ability to conceal her emotions was something her co-workers marveled at. She was not cold, however. In fact she developed good friendships at work. She just kept her eye on her job and made sure she did it well. This reserve and self-reliance had another benefit: She had a great poker face and did well in games with friends.

Until the onset of her leukemia Linda had been remarkably healthy, and the occasional illnesses she had had were never serious. In some instances they were barely noticeable. Before a ballet performance when she was eight or nine her mother noticed what appeared to be a pimple on her chin and covered it with a little makeup before Linda went to the recital. Only a week or ten days later, when one of her sisters came down with chicken pox, did Jackie realize that that was what Linda had had. As an adult she took good care of herself, and while that was good for her, Linda wasn't necessarily the best person to eat with. She enjoyed a good meal and carried a few extra pounds, but she watched what she ate, tending toward fresh vegetables, homemade breads, and the like. A friend at work liked lunching with Linda but also had some mixed feelings. "Half the time I'd say let's have lunch, and she'd say, 'No, I'm on a diet.' The other times she'd look at the junk food that I like and shake her head. She'd ask me why I ate that stuff and try to reform me."

Although the financial stress that had constrained their lives at the beginning of their marriage was relaxed as they both received promotions and raises, other stresses developed. However much Dan and Linda loved each other, they had two quite different personalities, and those differences widened as they matured. Linda was a woman of action who spoke her piece and who attacked problems. Confronting problems, however, was a problem itself for Dan. His reaction to arguments or difficulties was to be quiet and do nothing in the hope they would go away. As the years passed they also found that they were not doing the same things or sharing the same interests that they had had while they were in college, something they needed to do to strengthen their marriage. The resulting strains were so great that in the third year Linda often wondered aloud whether the marriage would last. Dan continued to try to smooth things over by saying nothing after the outbursts, but he came to realize that that was precisely the wrong thing to do with her. One day after an argument in which Linda had again speculated on their separating, Dan, who was just as distressed as she was, decided to take another tack. He walked into the bedroom, took a suitcase out of the closet, and began packing it. Linda was astonished.

"What are you doing?" she asked in disbelief.

"Leaving," he said.

It was an unexpected move, and it made Linda realize that Dan was serious and that they were both responsible for their problems.

"Wait a minute," she told him. "Let's talk about this."

The shield that had grown between them fell, and for the first time in a long while they were able to talk things out. Dan had learned a lesson when Linda had the broken wrist; it was Linda who learned one this time. It didn't stop them from having other problems, but it did allow them to resolve them better than they had before. By their fourth anniversary they were on better ground than they had ever been, and they decided to try to have a child. They made a few attempts in the fall to time everything right, but when nothing happened, neither of them minded. Then suddenly in December Linda became adamant.

"I've got to get pregnant, and it's got to happen quickly," she told Dan. "The time is now."

Dan had never seen her this way before, but he didn't mind; he was eager to have a child, too. Linda was pregnant in January, and for the next few months, it looked as though their troubles were behind them.

Leukemia is a Greek word that means, literally, "white blood" —although in fact the blood of a leukemia victim looks no different to the naked eye than the blood of anyone else. But when someone has leukemia, a cancer of the blood, his blood-making system produces huge numbers of abnormal, immature white cells. Mature white blood cells form the body's defense system. They move through the blood independent of its flow, squeezing through capillaries into tissues. They ward off infection, fight colds, and identify and attack bacteria, viruses, and other foreign elements that invade the body. Leukemic cells, however, do nothing but occupy space. In the advanced stages of leukemia, the malignant cells become so numerous that they crowd out production of the normal, working bone marrow cells.

Blood is produced by the bone marrow, which is the spongy tissue that occupies the cavities in the larger bones—the sternum, ribs, pelvis, and backbone. The bone marrow is the body's largest organ. The blood cells it makes are constantly renewed and replaced in a very orderly fashion. All blood cells go through several stages of growth and maturation. They are programmed to go through those stages, and to die, at a specific time—the information for their birth, function, and death is stored in the DNA that is the core of their genetic makeup.

Eric Lax

For instance, a granulocyte, one form of white cell, is derived from precursor cells that divide six times as they mature. Then at a particular and predetermined point the granulocyte is released from the bone marrow into the bloodstream, where it stays only five or six hours; its whole life-span is less than forty-eight hours. The coming and going of blood cells is a well-ordered traffic flow of astronomical proportions, which it must be because they proliferate in incomprehensible numbers. Every day a normal body produces 210 billion red cells (for carrying oxygen to the body's tissues and bringing carbon dioxide to the lungs for exhalation), 105 billion white cells (for fighting infection), and 175 billion platelets (for clotting). A typical adult male has three trillion red cells in his blood, or about one billion in two or three drops. There is one white cell for about every 800 red cells, and one platelet for about every 20 red cells. While white cells die after forty-eight hours, red cells live for four months. But whatever the life-span of a blood cell, it is crucial that it live only as long as it is supposed to, in order to keep this intricate system in such fine balance.

Leukemic cells destroy that balance. For reasons not yet understood, they are not programmed to reach maturity and die. In a sense they are a new type of cell in a system that has no room for novelty. Instead of dividing a specific number of times, each division being another step on the road to maturation, leukemic cells stop maturing at a very early stage in their development but continue to divide over and over again, producing billions and billions of equally immature cells. Because these cells that should die in a day, or two at most, are able to continue dividing for months, they are, by white cell standards, immortal. So instead of the body maintaining a healthy balance of red cells, white cells, and platelets, it instead becomes flooded with immature, useless white cells. Thus a leukemia victim usually dies for one of three reasons: because he has no mature white cells that can defend against infection; because there are too few red cells to carry sufficient oxygen to keep him alive; or because there are so few platelets that he bleeds to death internally.

There are two main types of leukemia: myelocytic, in which the leukemia arises from the blood-forming cells of the body; and lymphocytic, in which it is derived from blood cells of the lymphatic system. The lymphatic system helps maintain the proper fluid balance in the body's tissues and blood, conserves protein, and removes bacteria and other particles from the tissue. Leukemia is also either acute, meaning that death generally occurs within months of its onset; or chronic, in which case there is a gradual onset of symptoms and death usually occurs after several years.

Most varieties of the disease affect a specific age group. Chronic myelogenous leukemia (CML) can occur in children, but most victims are middle-aged or elderly. Chronic lymphocytic leukemia (CLL) usually attacks people over fifty. Acute lymphocytic leukemia (ALL) is the most common childhood leukemia. Acute myelogenous leukemia (AML), Linda's disease, affects all ages equally.

Linda was unwilling to accept only the hematologist's word on her disease, and the first thing she did when she and Dan got home was call her thirty-one-year-old uncle, Dr. John David Mullins, a surgeon in Atlanta who is Jackie's brother. Because he and Linda were about the same age, they had a certain sibling rivalry while growing up in their close family. Jackie often bragged to her youngest brother about her oldest daughter. Both were academically oriented, and they talked a lot about ambition, school, and ways of life. When Linda was a teenager in California and John David was still in Georgia, he used to tease her about the fast and loose ways of the West. They compared notes on boyfriends and girl friends.

There was no panic in Linda's voice when she called her uncle. Rather, it was as if she had been given another challenge to face and she was looking for how best to meet it. What she wanted from John David was an assessment of her condition and a suggestion as to what course to follow.

Without telling Linda, John David had been suspicious about her health. The lowered red blood cells counts and fatigue she had told him about at their onset had set off a cautionary alarm in his head. Thus her news saddened him but did not catch him totally off guard. He quizzed her carefully as to what kind of leukemia she had, but Linda did not have much information at hand. She had put some notes on paper at the doctor's office, but they were incomplete, and she suggested that he call the doctor directly. John David tried to reassure Linda. He told her that he would check all alternatives thoroughly and that he would find the best possible place for her to go for treatment.

After talking with Linda and the doctor, John David went to Emory University and sat down at their medical computer. He dug out every article on AML in the hope of finding an innovative treatment Linda's doctor might not yet have known about.

He learned that less than 10 percent of people with the disease stay in remission after the first course of chemotherapy. But he also found a volume of articles on bone marrow transplantation showing that about 50 percent of patients in situations similar to Linda's who underwent transplants were free from leukemia and leading normal lives as long as six years later. In reading the articles, John David noticed that many were written by doctors working at the UCLA Medical Center on a team headed by Dr. Robert Peter Gale, who has an international reputation as a leukemia researcher and who is a pioneer of bone marrow transplantation technique. When Linda and Dan heard John David describe the procedure, their hopes soared. Maybe there was a way out of this horror after all, they thought.

"If there's a donor," Linda told Dan, "we may have this thing whipped."

"It sounds like a miracle," he said.

In many ways it is. A bone marrow transplant does not involve taking a bone from one person and putting it into another. It is, rather, as simple as it is dramatic. A liter of bone marrow, mixed with the blood that is passing through it, is withdrawn through a needle inserted into the upper hip of a donor.

Once withdrawn, the marrow is passed through two fine-wire meshes to catch any tiny pieces of bone and clumps of fat and is then given like a blood transfusion to the patient, whose own leukemia-producing marrow has been destroyed by massive doses of chemotherapy and radiation. Within a couple of weeks, the new marrow engrafts and begins to produce healthy blood cells. (A donor must be genetically matched with the patient in several immunologic ways, which can be easily tested. For this reason, bone marrow transplants can usually be performed only if the patient has a brother or a sister who is properly matched. Because a child inherits two sets of chromosomes from each parent, there is a 25 percent chance that any two siblings will match. It is believed, but not yet proved, that the probability of a genetic match between any two unrelated people is about 1 in 10,000. Doctors in England have been able to find some matches between unrelated people, and have performed a few successful transplants.)

If one of Linda's four brothers and sisters turned out to be a match, she and Dan thought, a transplant might be just the thing that would allow her a full life with their baby. Later, the UCLA doctors would explain the problems and difficulties that can follow transplants and warn them that, while a transplant offered hope, it wasn't as easy as it sounded.

Before all that, however, there were more immediate problems to confront. Linda had to tell the people at Petoseed about her disease, and she had to tell her parents. She wanted to be especially careful about whom she told and when she told them, because more than anything she wanted her life to appear as if it were still normal, even if only superficially. Normalcy indicated control, and control was something she always appeared to have over her life. Now that her life was threatened, the more normal she could keep things, she felt, the better the chance of beating the disease.

The first person to know at work was Audrey Andrianakis, the company's industrial relations manager, whose job includes helping employees with problems. Although she was twenty years older than Linda, the two had become good friends. Linda's office was near Audrey's, but she was careful about going to see her. Everyone in a company notices the movements of everyone else, and if Linda suddenly began spending time with Audrey, the women in her department would suspect something was wrong. So Linda saw her after work, for an hour or an hour and a half at a time, seven or eight times in the month after she was told she had leukemia.

From the time Linda came to Petoseed, she had got on well with Audrey. Each had an analytical mind and was capable at breaking down problems to find the best way of solving them. Also, their age difference, added to their natural liking of each other, made for something of a mother-daughter relationship. Audrey had children Linda's age, and she was about the same age as Jackie. In May, when Linda had told her that she had anemia, Audrey, like John David, had worried to herself that it could augur something more serious.

When Linda walked into Audrey's office to break the news of her leukemia, Audrey sensed immediately that something was wrong.

"Do you want to visit with me about something?" she asked carefully.

Linda nodded. "There are some things that have happened to me—I don't know why—and I want someone to talk to."

Audrey was impressed in all their talks by Linda's self-control. Occasionally Linda would cry softly, but she never broke down completely, never lost control. Her tears were of frustration over being in what she referred to as "this mess I don't know how to resolve." And so Audrey tried to help her sort that out. They made what Audrey calls a Ben Franklin sheet, something she does with most people who come to see her. They wrote down the problem from every angle they could think of, broke it into parts, weighed advantages and disadvantages. Linda's three concerns were how to tell her parents, what to do about the baby, and how to keep the appearance of normalcy while at the office. Linda abhorred the thought that people might feel sorry for her.

What Audrey didn't know but what she sensed more and more as they talked was how much Linda wanted to have this baby. It seemed to her that Linda had wanted to have a child longer than she had ever let on to anyone except perhaps Dan. Still, it was her opinion that Linda should have an abortion and begin treatment for the leukemia immediately. After she was well, she could try again. What mattered more than anything was that she protect herself. But Linda, who knew better than Audrey how devastating leukemia is, wanted to take the chance, wanted to have the baby while she knew she could have one.

"I have a choice," Linda told her one day after they had talked for a while. "I can leave something of me behind, or I can take the chance of leaving nothing."

At one point or another during most of their talks, Linda asked why this had happened to her, often more with a sense of curiosity than with grief. Linda was, after all, analytical by nature. Her mind naturally sorted out cause and effect. But hers was a case of effect without known cause, and that was why the frustration set in, why the tears came. Linda finally resolved it, at least well enough to be able to concentrate on the things she could do something about. She did it in typical fashion.

"I'm strong enough that I can go through this and be a better person," she told Dan and Audrey, "whereas someone else might not have the will or endurance to go through all this, and it would serve no purpose."

Linda was a much-loved daughter, and she knew it. It was not that her parents loved her more than their other children, but she was the child whose life had gone most smoothly. She had been an easy child to raise, she had a winning personality, and she had been successful academically and athletically; now she was successful in her career. She was a daughter any parent would cherish, and Linda knew her parents would take her news very hard. After some thought it became clear that the only way to tell them was in person.

A year or two earlier, John and Jackie had moved back near Atlanta, so Linda made arrangements with John David to meet her at the airport and made him promise not to say she was coming. Linda had wanted Dan to come, too, but they had just used their vacation time and most of their savings for a trip to Georgia.

The day after they realized that Linda would have to go alone, the president of Dan's company asked him how things were. He told him that Linda was going east to break the news to her parents.

"You're going, too, aren't you?" he asked in surprise. Dan told him that it was too expensive.

"You have the company Visa card," the president said. "Put the tickets on that."

They went a couple of days later. They had visited John and Jackie only two months earlier. It had been a relaxed and enjoyable time. Linda and Dan had even entered a raft race down the Chattahoochee River just before leaving, and they had returned to California feeling wonderful. This trip, however, was anything but that. When John David met them at the airport he noticed that Linda looked tired and was a bit ashen. She still had a great smile, but she didn't look as healthy as she had in May.

During the drive from the airport John David and Linda concocted a strategy for telling her parents. They decided that Linda would do most of the talking and that John David would back her up with medical information. More than anything they wanted to convey to John and Jackie that people can be cured of leukemia, and that she was determined to beat, or at least go after, the disease.

It was a half hour's drive from the airport to John and Jackie's house in Dunwoody, which was set on three acres of heavily wooded land. It was large and C-shaped with an enclosed swimming pool in the middle onto which several rooms opened. Many large plants thrived in the humid, almost tropical environment of the pool.

It was about 9:30 P.M. on a pleasant summer night when they arrived at the one-story wooden house. John and Jackie were out, so the three of them stood in front, John David and Linda still talking about how to start the conversation with her parents. John and Jackie soon returned and saw Linda and the others when the car's headlights shone on them. Jackie's first thought was that Linda had lost the baby. But she saw in a moment that she was still pregnant, so she wondered if Linda had somehow managed a free trip home. John, however, felt it was an ominous sign. Linda wouldn't come just for a surprise visit, he thought; it simply wasn't like her to come unannounced.

The five of them sat in the living room, and Linda told her parents about her leukemia, about trying to buy extra time for the baby before starting treatment, about her desire to have the baby at practically any cost. John sat quietly by the fire with his

27

head down. Jackie sat next to him, not believing what she was hearing. Later, she recalled "feeling every hair on my head standing up, like I was plugged into a light socket." Years earlier she had thought one of her sons had leukemia and worked herself into near hysteria; then the tests had come back and showed it was mononucleosis. This time she controlled herself, not wanting to make things worse for Linda, although it was Linda who was the calmest of everyone in the room. She didn't want her family to be more upset by seeing *her* upset.

Like Linda in the doctor's office, Jackie asked every question she could think of in an effort to comprehend what was happening. But it did her little good. It seemed unbelievable. There was her daughter who was never sick, who had had but one chicken pock, telling her she had leukemia. "You gnash your teeth and pull your hair and beat your head against the wall," she said later, but nothing helped. They all went that night to see *The Empire Strikes Back* just to do something, but afterward no one could recall anything about the film. Small talk was an effort and did little good, so everyone went to bed early. John and Jackie didn't sleep for a long time. They just lay there and cried.

The next day the four of them went to Lake Lanier, about thirty miles north of Atlanta, for a picnic. When they were there in May, Linda had thought of going waterskiing, a sport that had taken her ages to learn, but she had decided against it because of her pregnancy. This time there was no question about doing it; she was too tired. And the weather turned bad anyway. A summer storm with terrible lightning made them take shelter at the home of Jackie's other brother, who was there with his wife and their three children. Linda went reluctantly. She didn't want any other relatives or friends to know her situation yet, and she asked that they not tell anyone she had been in town.

* * *

One night soon after they returned to California, Linda and Dan lay quietly in bed. It was late, but as Dan was falling asleep he could tell Linda was thinking about something. He decided not to ask what was on her mind but rather to wait until she sorted out whatever it was and told him. Soon she turned and said, "I want to change the baby's name." In the early months of her pregnancy they had tentatively settled on a name for a boy and one for a girl. Dan, however, was still open to suggestions and asked her what she had in mind.

"Angela Hope," she said.

"That sounds fine," Dan said, "but why that?"

"She'll be my little angel of hope if I get through this," Linda said, simply assuming she was going to have a girl. In fact, from then on, she never considered that she would have a boy.

At the end of July, Linda's doctor ran more blood tests. They showed that her leukemia was advancing quickly and that the baby had therefore been given just about all the time it could have. The question was, could Linda both have the baby and receive proper treatment for the leukemia?

Linda's mood was cautiously optimistic when she checked into the UCLA Medical Center on August 4. Her room on the fourth floor was part of what is known as the J service, which specializes in the treatment of cancers. (All medical areas have letter codes that denote an intern-resident rotation; general medicine, for instance, comprises both the A and C service; H is cardiology.) The room was of the two-bed variety with a curtain that can be drawn between the patients, the type one sees in any medical television show or movie.

Dr. Gregory Sarna of the division of hematology and oncology gave Linda a standard admission physical examination. He found her blood pressure normal, her pulse a little elevated, her temperature normal, her eyes clear, her ears without problem, her teeth excellent. He did notice some small petechiae—

purplish dots caused by bleeding common to leukemics—on the right side of her palate but no other oral problems. Her neck was supple, her chest clear to both percussion and listening through a stethoscope. She had no visible or palpable nodes on her body. Her heart was normal, and the fetus's heartbeat was audible on the right side and beating a normal 120 times a minute. The edge of her liver and her spleen could not be felt. She appeared neurologically sound: She had recent and remote recall; her cranial nerves were intact; she was appropriately sensitive to pinpricks, light touch, and vibrations in all areas; her motor strength was fine, with normal bulk and tone in all major muscle groups. She walked normally and could touch the index finger of either hand to the tip of her nose. Her body showed no sign of edema—abnormal amounts of fluid in the tissue. Prior to her diagnosis of leukemia, she had had no fevers, chills, cough, sputum production, painful or difficult urination, or diarrhea. There had been no bleeding from her gums and no vaginal bleeding. She had had no known exposure to organic chemicals, pesticides, benzene, or ionizing radiation. She had broken her left elbow, right wrist, and several fingers in various falls from horses, but she had no deformities in her hands or feet. For someone with leukemia, the appearance of her skin was significant for its absence of petechiae or bruises. In short she was, as Dr. Sarna wrote in his report, "A pleasant, healthy-appearing, pregnant woman in no acute distress."

Unfortunately, appearances weren't all. Beneath that healthy-looking facade were both a system being overtaken by leukemia and a thirty-two-week-old fetus doing its best to gestate normally and arrive in the world on schedule six weeks hence. Each problem demanded immediate attention, but only one could be done at a time, and at the cost of increased difficulty in treating the other. The oncologists wanted to treat the leukemia right away, because the longer it went unchecked the greater Linda's risk. Yet there was the matter of the baby Linda was determined to have. Although antileukemia drugs could be given during the third trimester of pregnancy probably without deforming the baby, they would most likely interfere with its blood production and lessen the capability of its immune system to fight the bacteria it would be exposed to at birth.

"Usually a patient in Linda's position will worry about her own survival and so will abort the baby and get on with her own treatment," a doctor later explained. "But here was a case where the baby was just viable; after twenty-eight weeks we now have a pretty good survival rate."

Linda's case attracted the attention of several doctors, including the obstetrics chief of faculty. He assigned the case to Dr. Nelson Teng, twenty-nine, the senior resident, and briefed him on it. Teng has a degree in physics as well as training as an obstetrician and an oncological gynecologist. He is a tall, slim man whose conversation is dotted with literary and scientific allusions. He was scheduled to go on a short vacation in a few days, but it was expected that the case would be in hand by then.

"We have a real problem," the chief told Teng as they talked in a hospital corridor, something Teng realized as soon as he started asking him questions. Pregnant leukemics are not that uncommon, but Linda's circumstances were unusual because she was so close to term. A decision had to be made whether to keep her on the medical ward or transfer her to the obstetrics ward on the second floor. Teng went into Linda's room to meet her. Like everyone else, he found her cheerful and pleasant. She was also a bit frightened and, like any patient, was denying some of the gravity of her situation. She told him she was concerned whether the baby would live and whether it would be healthy.

It struck Teng that Linda had a mission to accomplish, which was to deliver a baby. It was an attitude he had seen before in mothers whose lives were imperiled: Even though their lives were endangered, they felt their job was to continue life by having their babies. He recalled one case in which a terminally ill woman was brought to the hospital in a helicopter and died on the table in the delivery room, but not before she had given birth to a healthy child.

Teng was impressed by Linda's determination and by her seeming understanding of most of the problems she faced. After he talked with her he attended the obstetrics division's weekly meeting to discuss high-risk cases (patients with severe diabetes, heart problems, and the like). All staff, residents, and nurses attend the meetings. Teng presented Linda as a difficult and challenging case, one of a premature baby counterbalanced by a fast-progressing leukemia. As would be expected, almost everyone present had an idea of what course to follow, and many possibilities were drawn from the experience of the staff. A large number were in favor of aborting the fetus and starting chemotherapy for the leukemia right away. But everyone understood that there was no one, right decision, and Teng knew that whatever he decided it would be one of the most difficult decisions of his residency. He also knew what everyone else knew: The doctor in charge of a case is the one to make the final decisions about its medical course. At the end of the conference he decided to transfer Linda to the obstetrics ward. Later, he told Dr. Charles Dubin, twenty-eight, that he would be taking over the case during his absence. A dark-haired man of medium height, Dubin has the sort of kindly face one might expect an obstetrician to have.

The oncologists conferred with the obstetricians, and a plan was devised to try for a premature delivery. By ultrasound and amniocentesis, they would determine the baby's position in the womb and whether its lungs were capable of sustaining breathing if premature birth were induced. The ultrasound showed that fortunately the fetus was in the proper head-first position, for only then does a child have a reasonable chance of surviving a premature vaginal delivery. A caesarean section, while a possibility, was hardly a good one. Because of the nature of her disease, Linda had a very low supply of platelets. (Platelets, the blood's clotting agents, course through the veins like subway riders looking for a strap to hang on to, which in their case is any rough-edged tear in a blood vessel wall. They adhere to that and to each other in clumps that stanch the flow of blood from the vein.) Combined with a leukemia-caused susceptibility to infection there was as high as a 90 percent probability that Linda would not survive a caesarean section; she could either bleed to death or be killed by infection caused by bacteria that the operation would introduce into the abdominal cavity, and that would be aggravated by a poorly healing incision caused by her body's lowered immunity. If the baby was to be born and Linda's life not overwhelmingly endangered, a vaginal delivery was the only chance. Dr. Teng explained this to her. Linda told him that, provided the tests showed the baby healthy, she wanted to do what would give it the best chance of survival, even if that meant risking a caesarean section.

However grim the situation might appear, it was not without hope. The possibilities of what *could* happen were terrible, but both Linda's and Dr. Teng's expectations were not. Teng believed that the baby could be born safely. Linda believed him and felt on her own that it could, too. It would be a difficult physical and mental challenge, but difficult physical and mental challenges were things Linda had met all her life. Thus, beside the phenomenon Teng had observed before of a mother's sense of mission in delivering her child at any cost, there was Linda's normal grit and self-confidence. She knew how serious her plight was, but she had neither the time nor the inclination to dwell on it. One did not conquer tough obstacles by sitting around and wringing one's hands over how hard it would all be. She knew from experience that action was the best antidote to fear, that self-confidence was the best replenisher of physical strength. So while her prospect was a difficult one, it was one she was ready to meet. And the way to do that was for her to summon up the weapons she had always used against a challenge: calm; determination; positive thinking; self-reliance.

On August 5, Linda had some bone marrow withdrawn from the pelvic bone beneath her lower back to confirm the diagnosis of AML and to check on its progress. It was AML, and it was moving quickly. Her white blood cell count, which at the end of March had been a normal 4,700 per cubic millimeter of blood, was now 56,000, up from 43,300 only six days before. Moreover, her hematocrit, the percentage of oxygen-carrying red cells in her total blood supply, was 27.8, about ten points below normal. And her platelet count was dangerously low —20,000 per cubic millimeter instead of a normal 250,000. All in all, she was a very ill woman.

An amniocentesis was scheduled for August 7. Before going ahead with the test, Dr. Dubin reviewed with Linda the risks the procedure presented. The two greatest were hemorrhaging and/or infection. Linda said she wanted to go ahead anyway. Because her platelet count had dropped even lower, to 18,500, she was given an infusion of fresh platelets prior to the test to help with clotting and thus, it was hoped, avoid any hemorrhaging. For the amniocentesis, a 20-gauge spinal needle (about four inches long and one-sixteenth of an inch wide) was inserted into the amniotic sac, and 20 ccs of clear fluid were removed. No complications ensued. The test results would be available in the morning.

What the doctors needed to learn was the fetus's L/S ratio, that is, the ratio of amniotic fluid lecithin to sphingomyelin, a protein of the nervous tissue. That in turn would tell them whether there was enough surfactant in the lungs. Surfactant works as a lubricator to decrease surface tension in the lung tissue and therefore allow for easy expansion in breathing. Too little surfactant and the lungs tend to collapse. If the ratio was 1.8 or above, it meant the baby would be able to breathe on its own. Children born with a ratio below that are plagued with respiratory disease syndrome (RDS) and often die. If the ratio was 1.6 or 1.7, the doctors would give Linda steroids for forty-eight hours to stimulate the fetus's lungs. Whether the steroids actually increase the ratio is not known, nor are doctors sure of the overall effect they have on the child. But they do decrease the possibilities of RDS.

Dr. Dubin was happily surprised when the results came in the next day. The L/S ratio was 2, which is considered the level of maturity. The chance of RDS was less than 5 percent, he told Linda, and added that she could expect a child with no pulmonary problems. He was so pleased that he followed his recording of the results in her medical chart with several exclamation points.

"We didn't expect an L/S ratio so high," Dr. Dubin said afterward. "Usually it takes a fetus thirty-five or thirty-six weeks to reach so high a level. What caused the baby to mature so quickly in this case was probably the chronic stress brought on by the mother's disease. It seems to be nature's way of protection."

With the health of the baby determined, plans were made to move Linda to the labor and delivery suite on the second floor on Saturday the tenth. She would be put in a labor room where she would be given the drug Pitocin intravenously for eight hours a day in an attempt to induce delivery. If all went as it should, the baby would come after three days of the drug. Then Linda would spend two more days in her isolation room before going back to the fourth floor to begin chemotherapy for the leukemia.

"Pitocin causes uterine contractions," Dr. Dubin explained one day. "We use it when there is an unfavorable cervix. How it works is not fully understood, but it makes the cervix susceptible to dilation, which in turn makes it contract and soften. In normal circumstances it is given for three days. The first day softens it a bit, during the second there is further activity, and on the third you go for broke. We start off on a low dose and slowly work it up to a proper level for the patient. You start at 0.4 units and work up to an arbitrary maximum of twenty. What you want to avoid is overstimulation of the uterus. If you give so much that contractions come, say, every minute, you could rupture the uterus."

In preparation for Linda's induction, Dr. Dubin ordered that a minimum of six pints of A positive blood (Linda's type) be available at a moment's notice, and that platelets also be available. He discussed with other doctors the pros and cons of administering antibiotics to guard against infection, even though at the time Linda showed no sign of any. Even so, induction and long labor make a body susceptible to infection, because the contractions draw in bacteria from the vagina. Dr. Dubin briefed the obstetrics chief of faculty on the case in the event he had to be brought in, and he made sure the pediatrics staff would be ready to care for the baby properly. He recommended that Linda have as much contact with the baby as possible for the first two days postpartum. He recognized there would be a risk of infection if Linda had the baby with her when she went back on the fourth floor for chemotherapy ("There are bacteria and bugs normally not encountered in the home and newborn nursery," he explained), so he arranged for a psychiatrist to be available to help her over what would undoubtedly be a difficult separation.

Dr. Dubin expected the baby to have an 85 to 90 percent chance of survival. He estimated that if it was born without RDS, it would have a hospital stay of two to three weeks, but one of three weeks or longer if it did have it. He told Linda that she could not breast-feed if she were on antibiotics. But he had rethought the problem of the baby being with Linda when she went through chemotherapy and recommended that the two be allowed to stay together if the infant was ready for discharge, if Linda had no infection, if her visitors were all healthy and did not handle the child, if the nursing staff and parents washed their hands prior to handling the baby, and if arrangements could be made to stock linens and diapers on the fourth floor.

On August 8, as all the preparations were being made, Linda rested comfortably. She knew, though, that she was about to begin a terribly hard and eventually painful ordeal. All mothers experience the pain of labor and delivery, of course, and Linda knew she would, too. Usually the onset of labor and its attendant pain is a natural event, something that comes spontaneously at the culmination of a normal cycle. In her case, though, the process was artificial. Her baby was not yet ready to be born of its own accord. Her labor would be forced, the pain starting any time after the Pitocin drip started. It could be hours or days, and thus, unlike in a normal birth, she would have the anticipation of pain hanging over her all the time. But she was determined to endure it without complaint. Linda and Jackie had talked from the time she was a little girl about birth and labor pains. Jackie had lived across the street from a hospital while growing up, and she had worked as a nurse's aide for years. Early in her life she had seen the difficulty of childbirth and heard mothers crying and screaming during delivery. It had made her resolve not to do so when she had children of her own, a resolution she kept and told her daughters about. By the time Linda was about to face the pain herself, it was axiomatic that she would stay calm, too.

That afternoon, the doctors decided to give her two antibiotics, Carbenicillin and Amikacin, prior to beginning induction. They were chosen because they have proved to be effective in leukemics with infections.

Dan came in the evening. Under the circumstances, they quite happily passed the hours before Linda went to sleep. They were both relieved that she was at a leading center for the treatment of leukemia and that she would have their baby there. It was, they felt, *the* place to be. And at last things were happening, which was just what Linda wanted. No more did they have to sit around thinking of what lay ahead. Now they could simply get on with it.

At noon on August 10, Linda moved to the second floor and at 4 P.M. was taken to a labor room and given eight hours of Pitocin drip. The room was a small, windowless, reasonably comfortable, and very functional place. Above the bed was a tachodynometer that sent out ultrasound (which works on the principle of sonar) to measure fetal heart rate. It and a device for measuring uterine activity were connected to a pressure belt that was strapped around Linda's belly. On the wall behind the bed were oxygen and suction lines. There was also a bathroom. On the wall to Linda's left was a clock. A color TV hung from the ceiling near the farthest corner from her head. There were only overhead lights, but there was a rheostat to adjust them to whatever brightness she wanted.

Linda was certain that the baby would come quickly, and she became excited with anticipation every time she felt a little twinge. When Dan came to see her after work she was anxious to have this all behind her. Soon after he arrived, a nurse came in to give Linda a crash course in breathing technique during labor. She and Dan had planned on going to Lamaze childbirth classes in late August or early September to learn that technique, but obviously things had changed. In half an hour, the nurse gave them a month's worth of instruction.

John and Jackie flew out from Georgia that day, too. On the way out each talked optimistically of Linda's being able to deliver the baby successfully. Because of Linda's size when she had visited them, Jackie was sure the baby wouldn't be too tiny.

Linda was affectionate but reserved when they arrived at the hospital. To John, she looked bored; her let's-get-on-with-this attitude was typical of her in tough situations, and so was what she said: "Well, here we are."

John and Jackie left after a short visit and checked into a Holiday Inn near the hospital. Dan stayed behind to coach Linda in breathing exercises.

Linda appreciated the support from her family, but she believed that the bulk of her support had to come from within. In her room, she was preparing herself for what lay ahead. In the way that she went out in the weeks before a 100-mile ride and rode for hours on end to get herself into shape, taking on the hardest terrain she could find to toughen both herself and her horse, she prepared herself mentally for the birth. It required her to withdraw some, to concentrate on herself at the expense of long conversations with those she loved. Dan and her parents knew why she did this. Even so, for Dan especially, this time it was particularly hard. He had readily supported her decision to try to have the baby, but he felt caught in a very uncomfortable dilemma. He wanted Linda to live and for nothing to jeopardize that. Yet he wanted to do all that could be done to save the baby. Had all this happened a few weeks earlier, there would have been no question of how to proceed. But, as he put it, "This is her crack at motherhood. She knows if she has a bone marrow transplant that in all likelihood she will be sterile from the radiation. This is something she has to do." Two lives were at stake, yet he could only watch and wait while Linda went on alone.

The oncologists could only watch and wait, too, and it worried them. Once again they stressed to the obstetricians the urgency of Linda's beginning chemotherapy within a few days or a week at most. But the obstetricians considered a caesarean section, which was the only way for an immediate delivery, an unacceptable risk. They would have to keep waiting.

Dr. Teng returned on the eleventh, which was opportune. Linda liked him, and the medical decision to comply with her wish to have the baby had been his. When he went in to see her in the evening he found her slightly discouraged. She had expected she would have delivered by now, and yet that event seemed no closer than it had two days before. It was a low point for her, and she wondered aloud why nothing seemed to go right. Teng remained optimistic and told her he felt it would all go well.

By the next morning, the twelfth, Linda's spirits had improved. She joked with the nurses when they came in with meals and to change her sheets.

"I don't know how I'm going to get used to cooking and cleaning house after being in the hospital," she said to one.

This was the day she was expected to give birth, but although an examination of her cervix showed it had softened somewhat, delivery was nowhere near. Because of the possibility of infection from her lowered immunity, she was started on Vancomyecin, another antibiotic.

Linda's daily blood work-ups topped off the day's disappointing news. Her white count was up to 58,600, her hematocrit was down to 28.6 percent. She was given a transfusion of red cells, and an order was written to keep her crit at 30 or greater, with more transfusions if necessary. The white count would be watched, and if it reached 100,000, the doctors would consider leukapheresis (a drawing off of some white cells) to reduce the count below that. It could be done prior to delivery as needed, they agreed.

After three days had passed without delivery, there was a great deal of pressure on Dr. Teng from doctors in all quarters to change his course. Some felt that it was time to force a delivery by rupturing the membrane, thus putting Linda into a labor pattern. Delivery usually follows within twelve hours. If not, an amniotic hook can be used to pull out the fetus. There were good reasons for the pressure. Linda's suppressed immunity could be transferred to the fetus, thus risking infection after birth. If that were the case, then the baby would have only a 40 percent chance of survival. It was better for it to have RDS than to be infected. Teng, however, believed the baby was not yet in that severe danger. It was an instance, he said later, when a doctor's intuition is valuable and where medicine is more an art than a science. From all he had seen so far, he felt Linda could eventually have a successful vaginal delivery.

His confidence passed over to Linda and her family. There was natural disappointment over the baby's not coming according to plan but, in all, they felt things would still work out well. Linda was sore from being hooked up to monitors and IVs and was bored from being cooped up in the small labor room, but she knew the only thing to do was to press on.

Even though there was no change on the next day, the thirteenth, there were two promising signs. One was the state of Linda's blood. Her hematocrit was in good shape at 33 percent, her platelets were holding at 42,000, and her white count had even dropped a bit, to 57,600. The other was how well Linda was tolerating her ordeal. She was glad to see Dan and her parents but not always for long periods. John and Jackie came at noon and left when Linda took a nap at two o'clock. Dr. Teng happened to be in the hall, and they talked for a while about the difficulties they were having. He could see that they had not been sleeping well, and when Jackie said that she felt all this was more of a strain on her than it was on Linda, he agreed.

"This is an emotional experience, a stressful situation for them," he said afterward. "Not only could they lose their grandchild, they could lose their daughter as well. I like her parents a lot. They're very concerned but providing the best support they can. I'm very impressed."

The Peters were in turn impressed with Dr. Teng. His calm and optimism in the face of concern by both oncologists and obstetricians was a great help to them.

They needed all the help they could get. Still nothing had

happened by the morning of the fourteenth, and a new problem had developed. Linda had had intravenous lines in her for a week, and the IV sites in her arms were getting irritated, a common occurrence. IV needles have to be moved every twenty-four to thirty-six hours because of trauma to the vein and irritation to the skin. As time goes by it becomes more and more difficult to find a good spot, and the probing is a source of pain for the patient. Moreover, prolonged intrusion into a vein by an IV needle can cause the vein to collapse. When that happens doctors are forced to make a cut down (an opening of the skin over a larger vessel), but that sacrifices a vein and is still another source of discomfort to the patient. Yet Linda needed prolonged IV care. Something more permanent had to be done.

The answer was to implant a Hickman catheter, something that Linda would need anyway if she had a bone marrow transplant. The device is a happy alternative to long-term IV needles, developed in the mid-1970s by a Seattle pharmacist named Robert Hickman. It is a flexible catheter approximately eighteen inches long and one-sixteenth inch thick, made of silastic (a combination of silicone and plastic) that can be implanted above the left breast and passed through the subclavian vein into the vena cava and then into the right atrium of the heart. The Hickman catheter can stay in the body indefinitely without irritation to the skin and vein, and the patient is spared constant jabbing. The line can also be used to withdraw blood samples, thus avoiding another painful exercise. In effect, it is a two-way line into and out of the patient's bloodstream. A needle is simply inserted into the end of the catheter, which hangs about two inches out of the patient's chest, to introduce medicines, saline solution, hyperalimentation—whatever—or to withdraw blood. Using only a local anesthetic, a surgeon can implant the catheter in about twenty minutes. Which is how long it took to put in Linda's. She was given no Pitocin that day, both because of the implant and because it was hoped a day off and a fresh start would help.

On the fifteenth the Pitocin was continued. Linda was as comfortable as she could be under the circumstances and had no complaints. But when the morning blood tests came in they showed that she had only 10,000 platelets, 41,000 fewer than the day before, an acute drop to a dangerously low level. A repeat test was immediately ordered to confirm this unusual decrease, and the doctor ordered that, if the count was correct, she be given a transfusion as soon as possible. The second test showed the level to be only 9,000, so she was quickly given ten units of platelets (the amount accumulated from ten pints of whole blood, or about 500 ccs). In case it became necessary, Dr. Teng asked Linda to sign a consent form for a caesarean section. He told her that she was not progressing normally, but he felt there was no better alternative to the course they were following. He said he would do all he could to avoid an operation and explained everything on the form. Linda signed it without saying much and without consulting her family.

Linda slept late on the sixteenth. Her platelet count was up to 53,000. She was tired but in good spirits, even though nothing was happening with the baby. The Pitocin drip continued. The oncologists became increasingly concerned about the continued delay in treating the leukemia.

Sunday the seventeenth was Linda's eighth day in the labor room. It was also Jackie's birthday, something she was in no mood to celebrate. Linda was hanging on emotionally, but she was tired and in pain. In many ways, however, she was in better shape than her mother, who was walking an emotional tightrope. Linda had the dubious satisfaction of at least being the person this was all happening to. She could bear down and concentrate on herself. But for her mother and father and husband, who could only watch and wait, the suspense was becoming intolerable. Jackie wanted nothing more that day than for the baby to be born, for Linda to be delivered from pain. She even wanted to do it for Linda, to take her place, to do anything to make things better. She and John took a drive in their rented car to get away from the hospital for a while and to try to calm down a bit, but it was no help to Jackie. Things just couldn't go on as they had, she thought. She was so distressed that she thought of jumping out of the car rather than have to suffer through any more of this.

Her frustration and despair were not without cause. The evidence of Linda's leukemia was abundantly clear that day, and her doctors' concerns rose. Her platelet count had dropped to 31,000; her white count was up to 68,000. Then she developed a fever that rose to 101 degrees at 5:00 P.M. Oxacillin was added to the antibiotics to try to bring the fever down. To make matters worse, two potentially deadly medical complications were discovered. Linda's lungs were congested, and, with the fever, it was feared she had developed pneumonia. A chest X ray was taken, and the problem appeared to be only fluid overload. She was given diuretics to draw off the water.

Of even more immediate concern, chorioamnionitis, an infection of the amniotic fluid, occurred, and contractions came every two to three minutes. Under normal circumstances prompt delivery—within four hours—must take place, because a longer delay means a high risk of infection in the baby. But in Linda's case the only means of prompt delivery was by caesarean section, and that would likely be fatal to her. Still, it would increase the baby's chances of survival. Some doctors counseled a caesarean, but Dr. Teng kept holding back. He watched the fetal monitor to see how the baby's heartbeat was. Tachycardia—an increased heartbeat—would be an indication of fetal infection. Fortunately, it was normal—a hopeful sign.

For Teng, Linda's case was immensely challenging. "It incorporated everything," he said later with some amazement. "Fetal disaster, chorioamnionitis, RDS, bleeding. *Everything.*"

The person who remained calmest through all this was Linda, but it was not easy for her. For the previous two days she had asked herself over and over, "Am I going to stay in control? Am I going to blow it?" Control was her shield against fear and doubt, and because it was something that she had practiced all her life, something that was, in fact, an integral part of her personality, she did stay in control; she didn't blow it. But as the days passed in the labor room her tolerance lessened for other women who lacked her will. Occasionally she heard the cries of someone who was in a nearby room for a few hours before being taken to the delivery room. She had listened to them without comment until this evening, when one let out a particularly loud scream.

"She sounds like she's being attacked with a knife," Linda said with some irritation. "What's going on?"

"A patient is having trouble," her nurse said, not very helpfully.

"Well, can't they give her anything?" Linda asked.

"She won't take it," the nurse said. "She's a Lamaze patient."

Linda rolled her eyes.

Linda's ability to hold herself together impressed Dr. Teng, who felt what he called her philosophical approach was a great help not only to her but to him. He knew how much she wanted to deliver the child and how willing she was to do so at any cost to herself.

In midevening, he went into her room to talk with her again. His straightforward, positive attitude from the beginning had been a help to Linda and her family, just as hers was to him, and it was one he had been careful to maintain. He knew patients can pick up on the slightest discouragement their doctor might feel, and he didn't want to discourage Linda in any way. He believed the medical track he was following was the best one, but now, as problems came from every side, a little doubt entered his mind. More than anything, he wanted to be sure Linda didn't notice it.

He dimmed the lights in the room and sat down beside her. Once again he recounted the risks she faced and how dangerous a caesarean could be. They talked about the drive it takes to live, and Linda, without self-pity, told him she hoped she had the strength to go through this. They talked about Teng's career, of the constant necessity of caring for acutely ill patients and the demands it put on him. Linda asked him how he could do it, how could he face dying patients all the time? With practice, he told her. He said that, as a medical student and then an intern and resident, he had shown a lot of emotion and compassion, but that as he gained experience he hoped he had also gained skills that could augment empathy with healing. By the end of their talk, both of them were feeling better.

The timing of their conversation could not have been better, for at 11 P.M. Linda's fever had abated, but vaginal spotting had begun. She lost about 50 ccs of blood over thirty minutes, and Dr. Teng observed a clot of about 100 ccs in her vagina. If the blood was Linda's, the problem was not so bad. She could stand the loss. But if it was fetal blood, the baby was in grave danger. Teng sent a sample to the lab to see whose it was and kept his eye on the fetal monitor, which registered a normal heartbeat. That, combined with the lab report showing the blood was Linda's, reassured him that he was doing the right thing.

At 1 A.M. on the eighteenth, the bleeding was 30 to 40 ccs an hour. Linda was given ten units of platelets and a bag of red cells, but they had no effect on the rate of bleeding. Between 2:20 A.M. and 3:20 A.M. she lost nearly 300 ccs. The Pitocin was shut off, and the Carbenicillin was discontinued because, while it is an effective antibiotic, it also has an antiplatelet effect. Bleeding was now more a problem than the risk of infection.

At 4:10 A.M., Dr. Gary Lazar, the hematologist-oncologist

on call, was notified of Linda's condition and agreed with the course of treatment, which was by then, said Teng, "just guts and watching."

All this time, Dan and John and Jackie were waiting as calmly as they could in the corridor not far from Linda's room. They knew something had to happen soon and didn't want to go even as far away as their hotel. As she had done many times during the past week, Jackie phoned John David, both to keep him apprised of Linda's progress and to hear his thoughts on what it all meant.

At 5:30 A.M., Dr. Teng estimated the last clot Linda had passed as being 150 ccs, which was worrisome, but he found there was no vaginal or cervical laceration, which was encouraging. He believed the bleeding was caused by cervical dilation, low platelets, and a combination of drugs. Linda's vital signs were stable, and she had no fever, but she was pale and, for the first time, overtly anxious. She had spent nearly nine days lying in bed with IV lines poked in her and a monitoring strap around her stomach, and now, she knew, if the bleeding went on much longer the doctors would have to do a caesarean and all this agonizing effort would probably end with her dying. She was at a point where she just wanted it all to end, one way or the other, when a nurse prepped her in the event a caesarean was necessary.

After talking with Linda, Dr. Teng went out to the corridor to see Linda's family, not to seek their permission for what would come next, but simply to give a status report. He was very candid with them.

"Our backs are against the wall. We have to do something in the next few hours," he told them. "It may be that we are forced to do a caesarean to save the child, because that is what Linda wants. But I must tell you that the operation will most likely be fatal for her. She has been prepped for a caesarean, so that if we have to do one, we will not lose any valuable time. For the moment, however, we can still avoid doing one. It has been my decision to proceed as we have. I've tried to follow Linda's wishes as best I can, and I've done all I can to give both of them every chance to live. There is no absolutely right decision, but I want you to know that after weighing everything, I've done what I feel is best."

Linda's family tried to grasp some hope from this bleak prognosis.

"Do you still think there is a chance they both can make it?" one of them asked.

Teng nodded. "Yes. The bleeding is the key. If that can be stabilized, there is a good chance. Perhaps if the baby moves around, it could seal it off."

"You mean you're giving her as much blood as you can and that it is coming out as fast as it's going in?" John asked.

Teng nodded again.

Perhaps the greatest solace to Linda's family at this time was Teng's manner. They felt that he had a personal interest in Linda and that, like Linda, he was analytical and very good in a crisis. They trusted him completely. He neither sugarcoated his answers to their questions nor talked over their heads. He just told them exactly what was happening and how things were. As he spoke with them, other doctors and residents kept coming and saying that a caesarean was the only alternative and that it had to be performed now. Teng discussed their concerns but each time said it was better still to wait and see what developed next. He refused to be pressured into action simply because the majority of physicians felt it the best course.

As all he was saying sank in, however, Dan began to cry. It seemed to him all too real a possibility that his wife or child or both might die. Jackie consoled him and told him all was not yet lost, although she wasn't sure if she believed that herself. He soon stopped. They all felt that they had to stay in control of their emotions. Linda was, and they must be, too. Each found a kernel of hope that it would work out well.

After Teng left, Jackie wondered to herself who had washed out the room where a caesarean would be done and if that person had done a thorough job. She half-seriously considered whether she should go in and do it herself, just to be sure the possibility of Linda's being infected was reduced as much as possible.

Linda's total transfusions for the night were three bags of red cells and 30 units of platelets, a large amount. But finally at 6 A.M. they began to have some effect. Her bleeding slowed to 20 ccs an hour. For now, at least, a caesarean wasn't necessary.

By 9:30 A.M. there was even more improvement. Linda remained anxious about the bleeding and was exhausted, but Teng was hopeful that there would be a delivery soon. Her cervix was 1.5 centimeters dilated, and she was 50 percent effaced. (Cervical effacement percentage is a relative figure, estimated by the doctor doing the examination. As the cervix dilates it shortens, and the percentage is useful as a measure of progress, especially if the same doctor makes the estimations.)

Even though things were looking better than they had for some time, Linda's family was told to be ready to give platelets if the bleeding became brisk or uncontrolled, because then there would be no alternative to a caesarean. But the good news continued. At 11:30 A.M. the bleeding was level at 50 ccs an hour, and her cervix was 80 to 90 percent effaced. At noon her platelet count was 76,000, the highest in days. It was possible the worst had passed.

At 2 P.M., Linda requested a painkiller, which gave her relief very quickly. Her family came in for a brief visit about two thirty. Linda was miserable and had very little to say. Now especially she wanted to be by herself as she prepared to have the baby, which she knew had to happen soon. After nine days of labor, though, she also asked herself, have I gone on this long, this hard, only to lose it in the end?

In many ways this time for Linda was like the last twenty-five miles of a twenty-four-hour trail ride. It was the time when mental stamina was even more important than physical stamina. The last thing she—any rider—ever wanted to do after the fourth and last hour break was to get back on the horse for the final leg. It was always dark, the body always ached from exhaustion, and, on the rides she entered, still to be crossed was a train trestle 150 feet above the American River, something most people wouldn't want to walk over sober in the middle of the day, let alone exhausted and on horseback at night. But she had done it because she loved the challenge and the satisfaction that came from meeting it.

Now in the hospital she faced the biggest challenge of her life. It was a time when one's character wills out. Some people go berserk when confronted with adversity. Linda thought it was a luxury to come unglued in those situations. By staying together, she could control her destiny. Medical science had done all it could to get her to this point. Now she had to do something. Her family, who had seen her overcome so many other tough obstacles, knew this was something she needed to do on her own.

At 3:30 P.M., Linda's cervix had dilated to between two and three centimeters, and she was 90 to 100 percent effaced. Even though delivery could now come at any moment, the bleeding had not worsened. The Pitocin drip was continued to try to push things along.

Dr. Teng came by at five thirty to see Linda before driving over the hill to his home in the San Fernando Valley for dinner. He told Linda that he would be called if anything changed. Linda asked for and was given another painkiller.

Linda's family went down to the hospital lobby, which had comfortable sofas and chairs, to rest for a while. Dan and John were stretched out on sofas for short naps when, at about 7:00 P.M., Jackie thought she'd go upstairs to see what was going on; she had an idea something was about to happen.

A mother's intuition is something to trust. Jackie asked Linda how she was.

"I feel like I have to go to the bathroom," she said.

"Well, that's a good sign," Jackie told her. The nurse in the room thought so, too, and went to get Dr. Dubin so he could check on Linda.

"She's fully dilated," he said with some excitement. "Let's get her to the delivery room." She was taken in at 7:40.

Dr. Teng was still at home when his beeper sounded, and the clerk at the hospital told him he was needed immediately, but not what had happened. As he drove on the freeway at 80 miles per hour, he was sure that either Linda or the baby was dying. Jackie, meanwhile, rushed downstairs to wake Dan so he could join Linda in the delivery room, which was equipped to handle either vaginal or caesarean births.

It was a light green showroom of modern medical devices. It had an anesthesia machine with vials of the anesthetics Halothane and Fleurothane, and cardiac and arterial monitors. The delivery table was in the middle of the room. Along one wall was a surgical cupboard filled with every sort of forcep wrapped in sterile white towels. Boxes of various types of sutures filled two shelves above them. There was a Kriselman unit for fetal resuscitation, if that was required, consisting of a small table for the baby, a canister of oxygen below it, racks of drugs an infant in trouble might need, even a heating element as a hood. There were, as well, two obstetricians (Dr. Dubin presiding), two pediatricians, two nurses, and two anesthesiologists (a second one is always present in case another possible caesarean is required on short notice in the next delivery room). Between the two rooms were a defibrillator in case of cardiac arrest, a stat line to the pediatrics unit, and a small refrigerator with A positive blood and platelets at the ready. All this could be seen from the observation room, which was jammed with doctors and nurses from the ward.

Dan stood by Linda's head telling her to push and coaching her in her breathing. As he watched the veins on top of her eyelids strain and turn purple, he thought they would pop. They didn't. Nor were the anesthesiologists needed. In fact, all the accouterments of modern medicine went unused as Dr. Dubin performed what he called in perfect medicalese, "A simple, straightforward delivery, with forceps to expedite it."

At 8:02 P.M. on August 18, a four-pound, twelve-ounce girl slid into the world. The doctors and nurses who had jammed the observation room acted, Linda said later, as if the Dodgers had won the World Series. No single event can bring a hospital to a stop, but this birth came close to halting an entire floor; word of it spread everywhere in minutes.

Dr. Teng made it to the delivery room just as the baby was born, and he and Dan embraced each other; the ordeal was over, and for the first time Teng could let his emotions show. His faith and intuition had paid off. He could scarcely have been more pleased if it were he who had just become a father. As for the father, Dan had never felt prouder, nor more relieved. As he watched Dr. Dubin put the child on Linda's chest he began to cry, because, he thought to himself, Who knew how much time they'd have together?

When a nurse asked Linda and Dan if they had a name yet for the baby, they smiled and said they thought they had an appropriate one: Angela Hope.

There is no greater euphoria than the relief that follows the happy resolution of an apparently hopeless crisis. After the birth, Linda, her family, Dan, even the doctors and nurses, were ecstatic. Having faced the increasingly probable death of both Linda and the child, everyone was astounded to find both alive. For the moment, at least, Linda's leukemia was forgotten.

John and Jackie and Dan went in to see Linda, who was very happy but was also exhausted. They left after a few minutes of kisses and hugs so she could sleep, and went to the neonatal intensive care unit to see Angela Hope, who had been taken there for a checkup. John suggested to Jackie and Dan that the three of them go out for a celebratory dinner with lots of champagne. But just as they were getting ready to leave, they were told that an X ray showed a film on Angela's lungs that could be pneumonia. It was like a cruel joke, as if they were attached to a demonic emotional yo-yo. They were given the unit's phone number and told to call later when the doctors would know for sure. The three of them were crushed. Linda had not been told yet, and they turned to go to her room to fill her in but then stopped. The baby was Linda's hope for the future, and they didn't want to dash it unless there truly was something wrong. Instead, they walked back to their hotel in despair, the thought of a celebration long behind them. But when they called the hospital later, they were told Angela was fine and there seemed no cause for worry. They ended the night euphoric once more, and, for the first time in days, everyone had a good sleep.

The day after Angela Hope was born was the best day Linda and her family had had in weeks. During Linda's labor, everyone had put aside all thoughts of the chemotherapy that would have to follow the birth; the leukemia had been put out of mind. But even the knowledge that a new battle was about to start couldn't dampen the happiness and optimism everyone felt. Linda—everyone—believed that nothing that followed could be worse than what she had just come through. Certainly Linda was apprehensive about the treatment she was about to undergo, but she viewed it as the first step to her cure.

Linda had had a little trouble breathing in the night because of all the fluid that had accumulated in her body during the induction of labor. But it had been a minor problem, at least by comparison, and the first thing Dan and her parents thought when they went in to see her in the morning was how quickly she had recovered. She looked rested and in quite good shape. Her only real complaint was that she wanted to get out of the labor room she had been in for nine days. She felt as if she had been stuffed in a closet and was delighted when, in the afternoon, she was moved up to the fourth floor, where she would have the chemotherapy.

TWO

On August 20, less than thirty-six hours after she had delivered Angela Hope, Linda began a common but rigorous course of chemotherapy known by the acronym TAD, for Thioguanine, Ara-C, and Daunorubicin, three antileukemia drugs. (Acronyms litter medical terminology and conversation, if only because doctors would otherwise have to spend most of their time saying what they were going to do instead of doing it.) The treatment is given for seven days, and its effect is to destroy not only the leukemia cells but also the normal bone marrow. Cancer cells have a growth advantage at first over normal cells, and in some cases that advantage is never closed, so a second and sometimes third course is required. In about 80 percent of AML cases, the disease can be put into remission at least once. In the 20 percent where it can't be, however, the patients die in a matter of months.

Because chemotherapy kills both diseased and healthy blood cells, patients are kept in the hospital while their marrow recovers. Normally this takes between three and four weeks. Over that time a patient is given up to 20 pints of whole blood, plus many other transfusions of platelets, red cells, and occasionally white cells to help the body repopulate the marrow and in the meantime keep it operating with at least minimum acceptability. But that is not easy. The low white blood cell count inevitably allows viruses or bacteria in the body a chance to thrive, so antibiotics are administered to fight the fever that ensues. While platelet and white blood cell transfusions have little overt physical effect on the patient, red blood cell transfusions do. Fresh red cells carry more oxygen through the body, and thus one feels invigorated after receiving them. Linda was no exception.

"Getting red cells," she said one day, "is like getting a new lease on life."

Linda would have enjoyed her new lease even more were it not that Angela couldn't live in with her after all; the nurses on the fourth floor were too divided on whether it could be done safely and without disturbing other patients. Jackie argued that she would be there with Linda and they wouldn't have to worry; the nurses argued that they weren't properly trained to take care of the baby if something went wrong. A compromise was worked out. The nursery found a basket for the baby and put together a bundle of diapers, bedclothes, and formula. Angela could stay with Linda during the day but not the night. But even the nurses who were totally against having the baby on the floor came around as time went by. Jackie did all she could to encourage it. Almost every day she went to a department store across the street from the hospital and bought clothes for Angela.

"I made her so appealing they couldn't turn her down," she said after her strategy worked. "They'd wait every day to see what she was wearing—a yellow bonnet, a rosebud dress. The nurses on our side would say, 'Let me see the baby.' The others would stand back. After a while they began to crane their necks to see how she looked, but they didn't want to appear too interested. But slowly they came around, too. I told them that this may be the most time Linda will have with this baby and that they couldn't deny her that." She laughed. "She had more new clothes than any baby you've run across." Jackie also began making a quilt with the letters of the alphabet for Angela, which she stitched away on while visiting Linda every day.

Linda suffered few side effects from the chemotherapy, and this time with Angela was wonderful for her. She could concentrate on and enjoy her child, whom she had fought so hard to have. She was also comforted that, regardless of the outcome of her treatment, she had accomplished what she set out to do: to leave something of herself behind.

On August 26, when Angela was eight days old, the doctors felt she was strong enough to go home. Even though she would come back with Jackie every day to visit, it was a terrible disappointment for Linda not to have her at night, and several of her doctors felt in part responsible.

"We had often said to her, 'When is the baby coming up?' " one said later. "The two of them had been able to spend some time together, but we had expected that when the baby was ready to be discharged it would work out for her to live with Linda in her room. But from a nursing point of view, there just wasn't any way for a baby to be on the floor twenty-four hours a day. It was a very unfortunate situation." The only consolation was that Angela could be brought in to visit as much and for as long (during the day) as Linda liked.

Still, that made for a lot of separation. Dan became a full-time father in a way he had never imagined even a month before. His parents lived nearby and helped out, and Linda's mother was there, too, but the fact was he didn't know anything about raising a child. Throughout Linda's pregnancy Dan had relied on her preparations. She was the one who read the baby books; Dan took it for granted that he'd learn as they went along together. Now, however, he had a lot to learn in a hurry. Jackie was a great boon. She not only helped with the baby, she always had a good hot dinner ready when he came home as well. The two of them became closer than they had in the years before. They consoled one another, and Dan appreciated how she took off some of the pressure at home for him.

Sometimes at night Dan would hold Angela and talk to her in his mind, telling her how much he hoped she would have a long life with her mother. On occasion he acknowledged the gravity of Linda's condition by adding that if Linda did have to die, at least they would have enough time together so Angela would know her.

It was a difficult period in many ways for Dan. With the exception of Saturday, when he would spend the night with Linda in her room, he made the 160-mile round trip to the hospital every evening. When he was with Linda they'd talk about little things Angela had done, or about people they knew at work, or about cards and calls that had come to Linda at the hospital. There was nothing to be gained by dwelling on Linda's health. All they could do was take things a day at a time and hope. Even so, Dan still felt helpless. In many ways, he was. There was really nothing he could do to make Linda better. The relief of having the baby born in good health was tempered by the stark fact of Linda's leukemia and of having to cope with it. He was in favor of anything that would make her well, yet he was apprehensive about her chances for long-term survival with only conventional treatment because he knew how bad the statistics were. The apprehension affected his work. Sometimes he would find himself in a daze from all the pressure and worry. Other times he threw himself into his job with such vigor that everything else was temporarily blotted out. It was the solitary drives to the hospital that were the hardest for him, because there was no escaping the reason he was making them.

* * *

When she began chemotherapy, Linda's goal was to be in remission and out of the hospital by her birthday on September 23, or at the latest by Dan's and her fifth wedding anniversary on the twenty-seventh. She was out on the seventeenth, the course of her treatment as unremarkable as her delivery was dramatic. One cycle of TAD had been enough to put her leukemia into remission. Moreover, she had tolerated the treatment well and had not fallen victim to the severe nausea that often accompanies the medication. The dustup with the nurses about Angela Hope staying with her in no way diminished the regard the staff had for her. The resident who had been in charge of her case for the last two weeks of her stay summed up the feelings of everyone who had come to know her when he wrote, as part of her discharge report, "The patient has been a pleasure to take care of despite her unfortunate circumstances."

The first month Linda was home was a pleasant time for the three of them. Linda mothered Angela Hope, and she and Dan would sometimes drive her twenty minutes to the beach near Ventura. It was a favorite spot of Linda's. Apart from the beach she liked so much, the access ramp there, which leads from one freeway to another, brings a car up at a steep angle, and at one point all that is visible ahead is the ocean. Linda loved flying with her father, and this bit of road gave her the sensation of taking off in a small plane over the sea. They bought a sun hat for Angela, and she lay on the beach with them while they worked on their tans. They did all they could to keep their life as normal as possible. They talked some about whether Linda should have a bone marrow transplant, but for the most part Linda kept her own counsel.

While she said very little, she was sorting out her dilemma in her mind. As she had asked Audrey and Dan soon after the diagnosis, she continued to ask herself why it was she who had leukemia. There were periods when she was sure she had done something terrible to deserve what had happened to her. For a while she searched for what could possibly have caused her disease, but she knew there was no answer, and after a while she accepted her doctor's advice not to dwell on something she couldn't resolve. In her talks with Dan about how best to treat her illness she was without self-pity because she believed that action rather than pity was all that could help her. Her stubbornness and self-reliance were not only a help, they were a shield as well. By being strong in the face of adversity she could feel as if she could overcome it. Only once did she show any great distress. One evening Dan, who was in the living room, heard Linda crying in the bedroom, and he ran in to see what was wrong. Linda was afraid, she said as Dan held her, that if she died Angela wouldn't know her. As he comforted her, Dan told her that she would make it, that after all they had gone through the tide had finally turned. He reassured her as best he could but also promised her that if the worst did happen, Angela would know all about her mother.

Even though she seldom showed her concern, Linda knew that no matter what she did, there was a good chance that she would not live to see her baby grow up. If that was to be the case, she wanted to be sure that Angela was properly taken care of, so, knowing her odds, she hedged her bets a bit in looking after Angela. She never said anything about it to anyone, but she made sure that John and Jackie had an important part in Angela's life. She was aware that as Jackie had been raised for some years by her father's mother, so might Angela's grandmother play an important part in her life. It had been Jackie who took Angela home from the hospital, and it was Jackie who looked after her the most during her first six weeks. Linda was forming a bond with her daughter, but she wanted to be sure that, just in case, Jackie did, too. No matter what happened to her in the future, Linda had succeeded in creating something of herself that would live on, and that fact gave her great comfort.

Never was all this clearer than at Angela's christening. As soon as the baby had been baptized, Linda handed Angela to Jackie. Jackie was a little surprised, but, without having to ask or say anything, she knew why Linda had done it.

Within a few weeks after her chemotherapy, Linda felt strong and wanted to go back to work. The early fall is the busiest time of the year in the accounting department at Petoseed, because that is when the yearly audit takes place. Linda had a strong sense of obligation to the company anyway, but as she was about to be appointed the company's assistant controller, she especially wanted to pull her weight. Petoseed had carried her at full salary during her hospital stay and offered to keep doing it indefinitely while she recuperated. Linda wanted nothing of that. She wanted to work. Slowly her co-workers understood that by burying herself in her work she could hold on to an apparently normal life. The people she worked with tolerated that to a point but would literally throw her out of her office after six hours or so, just as they had done when she was pregnant and leukemic. Everyone of course knew about all that Linda had gone through, but she was determined that no one would feel sorry for her. Just as she had also done when she was pregnant.

"When I was first pregnant," she said one day, "I was sick every morning, but I didn't want to tell the people at work about the pregnancy until it showed. I didn't want people coming in every day and asking, 'How do you feel? Are you sick?' Never once did I get sick. But," she added with a slightly self-satisfied smile, "I did on weekends."

During this time Linda and Dan grew closer in many ways. Most important in the talks they had was their desire to put what had happened to the best use they could. They acknowledged the mistakes they had made in the early years of their marriage and resolved to do everything they could not to commit them again in the future. They had to grow together, not apart.

Linda had looked increasingly anemic and ill in the month before Angela was born, but now she looked better every day. Being in remission, she was technically disease-free. But a first remission from AML ensures perhaps a year of healthy life; almost everyone relapses, sometimes in only a few months. A second remission is difficult to achieve and is almost always of a shorter duration. Chances for a third remission are almost nil. The optimal time for a bone marrow transplant is during first remission, and it was an alternative that Dan and Linda kept coming back to when they talked about the future, which, because of the baby and their strengthened marriage, was important beyond simply Linda's survival.

Leukemia was not recognized as a specific disease until 1845. And for the first hundred or so years after its description, so little was known about the production, makeup, and function of human blood, that scientists could only speculate as to the nature and cause of the disease.

The French physician Alfred Velpeau is credited with the first description of leukemia in 1827. His patient was a sixty-three-year-old florist and lemonade vendor who, wrote Velpeau, "had abandoned himself to the abuse of spiritous liquor and of women, without, however, becoming syphilitic." He died soon after being admitted to the hospital with pronounced swelling of the abdomen, fever and weakness, and symptoms caused by urinary stones. An autopsy revealed an enormous spleen and liver—the liver weighed ten pounds—and thick blood, "like gruel . . . resembling in consistency and color the yeast of red wine. . . . One might have asked if it were not rather laudable pus, mixed with brackish coloring matter, than blood." It was this peculiar character of the blood that piqued the interest of other doctors, and in 1839 Alfred Donne was the first doctor to look at the blood of a living leukemia patient. More than half the blood appeared to be "mucous globules," he wrote. The white cells appeared so colorless that he first thought they were pus.

Exactly who was the first to recognize leukemia as a specific disease is debatable. In 1845 a Scottish doctor, John Henry Bennett, and a German doctor, Rudolf Virchow, published independent cases within a month of each other. Bennett would later become a leading physiologist and Virchow the founder of cellular pathology, but at the time they each spent considerable effort to be accorded the dubious honor of identifying this terrible disease. Virchow's name for it is the one that has stuck, however. As the relationship between the red and colorless corpuscles (white cells and their importance were not yet understood) was the reverse of what it normally was, he called it *Weisses Blut*, or White Blood (because of the large number of leukocytes).

Within the next twelve years the two chief varieties of chronic leukemia as well as the acute form were described and the pathologic features tabulated. But because of the crude hematologic methods then available, it was possible to make only a superficial examination of the white cells. A realization that they divided and matured was seventy years away. (It was not until 1913 that all the forms of leukemia were identified.) All that could be understood was that the changes in the blood came not from pus but from a proliferation of the white cells.

Even with the evidence and description of the disease, there were doctors who denied the existence of leukemia. At a conference in Paris in 1855, one physician exclaimed, "Leukemia has no special causes, special symptoms, particular anatomic lesions, or specific treatment, and I thus conclude that it does not exist as a distinct malady." Said another, clearly more wishful

63

thinker than scientist, "There are enough diseases without inventing any new ones."

The first attempt to manipulate the human blood system was made about a hundred years ago by the French physician Charles-Edouard Brown-Séquard (a surname known to every medical student, if to no one else, for its denotation of a lesion in the spinal cord that on one side causes a loss of sensation and on the other a loss of motor power). His theory was that patients suffering from chlorosis, an anemia that causes the skin to turn green, would benefit from an oral dose of calf's marrow. In fact, many did benefit, and Brown-Séquard pronounced the treatment a success, although it would later be learned that what caused the improvement was the iron in the marrow and not the marrow itself.

Very little else was attempted over the next sixty years. The bridge between early investigation and what could be termed the modern era of investigation in bone marrow manipulation was an experiment carried out in 1938 by Dr. Edwin E. Osgood and a team of doctors in Portland, Oregon. They tried to save a fatally ill nineteen-year-old girl with aplastic anemia, a failure of the bone marrow to produce new blood cells, with intravenous doses of human, though genetically unmatched, marrow. The experiment failed.

It was not until the end of World War II that doctors took a serious interest in bone marrow transplantation. One of the horrifying side effects of nuclear warfare came to light when people at Hiroshima and Nagasaki who had not been killed instantly by the nuclear blasts died within a month from aplastic anemia. Investigators turned their attention to the effects of radiation on the blood system.

Experiments in 1950 and 1951 showed that if the spleens of laboratory mice were protected by lead boxes when they were irradiated, the mice lived. Just why they did took some time to figure out but was of great significance: The spleen contains stem cells, the progenitors of blood cells—a concept no one had even considered. This discovery radically altered scientists' understanding of the human blood-producing system. Before then, no one had thought about hematopoietic (blood-producing) cells; they had instead thought vaguely of factors in the spleen and of spontaneous generation of blood cells. Once researchers understood how blood was produced, they could examine how bone marrow related to other diseases of the blood, such as leukemia.

One of the great contributions to medical research was the development of inbred strains of mice, first accomplished by George Snell in the early 1950s. (This led to discoveries that earned him a Nobel Prize in 1980.) A consistent strain of mouse meant that experiments could be conducted on genetically identical animals time after time; different results from the same procedure done on virtually the same mouse could be noted and compared.

A scientist working at the National Institutes of Health in Washington, D.C., using Snell's strain of mice, transplanted bone marrow into some who had been irradiated and had thus had their own bone marrow destroyed. Normal procedure was to destroy the mice after one month. But a cageful of mice was misplaced after the transplants, and when they were found, they were still alive but ill in a way doctors had not seen before. Their hair was falling out, they had a rash on their palms, and they were afflicted with terrible diarrhea. At first this was thought to be a delayed reaction to the transplant, in which some delayed immunological factor had come into play, or a late reaction to the radiation. What it turned out to be was graft-versus-host disease (GVHD).

GVHD is the reverse of what often complicates other transplant operations, such as those of a heart or kidney. In those cases the patient's immune system attacks the new organ because it recognizes it to be foreign, or nonself. But in the case of

65

a bone marrow transplant the body's own immune system has been destroyed by radiation, and the immunologically mature cells present in the transplanted marrow can perceive the body to be an enemy. As the name implies, the graft fights the host—so fiercely that it may kill it.

The accidental discovery of GVHD led to a seminal breakthrough in understanding the body's immune system. But to understand that, it is first necessary to understand how cells behave.

Cells relate to each other much as fraternity brothers from different chapters. Fraternity brothers have characteristic handshakes; cells have characteristic shapes and structures, which are identifiable on surface contact. The surface of a cell looks like a piece of coral. It is more or less round, but the surface has many different shapes on it. Each shape is a protein or carbohydrate called an antigen. The more antigens cells have in common, the more compatible they are. Certain cells in the body's immune system (T cells, B cells, and macrophages) are programmed to recognize other cells as friendly or foreign, as self or nonself, by examining their cell surface antigens. In a way not yet fully understood, T cells, B cells, and macrophages also communicate with each other to determine whether another cell is alien or friendly, and, if it is alien, to destroy it. It is known that individual B cells, and believed also that individual T cells, are programmed to recognize only one alien antigen. Often a cell will go through its life and never run into another cell bearing the alien antigen it is designed to recognize. In a sense it dies of boredom. But if it finds the antigen it is looking for, it begins making active cells to attack the intruder.

Macrophages are like bouncers at a nightclub. They engulf and devour bacteria and debris such as dead red blood cells, but in some cases they latch onto a foreign cell and drag it to a T or B cell that will recognize the alien antigen and is equipped to deal with it; the macrophage's job is, anthropomorphically, to say, "Hey, boss, what are you going to do about this guy?" In this way, too, the body maintains a system of checks and balances that prevents it from accidentally attacking itself.

A person becomes diseased because the cells of the immune system that are designed to destroy an enemy cell never run into the intruder or because they run into the intruder too late; they are already outnumbered. Most scientists believe this also is the case with leukemia, which can spring from just one damaged or altered cell (from, say, excessive radiation). It is known that T cells are capable of killing leukemic cells in mice, and some researchers believe they can in man. But it is also thought that leukemic cells break through immune surveillance. Then they divide so quickly that it comes down to a deadly race between T cells and leukemia cells as to which can gain advantage over the other first.

Because the immune system is so finely balanced, any transplant has to be compatible, or appear to be compatible, with the various cellular guardians. That was the initial problem with bone marrow transplants. While in theory they looked as though they ought to work, doctors repeatedly failed to find a way for long-term success. A key piece of the puzzle was still missing.

It was found in the late 1960s. The work that George Snell and co-workers did on mice produced evidence that the more antigens in common, the greater the chance of a successful transplant. Furthermore, they found that the formation of most important antigens is controlled by a specific group of genes on a specific set of chromosomes, the major histocompatibility complex. Humans inherit twenty-three chromosomes from each parent, which in turn pair up and determine their genetic makeup. The gene determining the major histocompatibility antigens is always on the sixth pair. For the record, in mice it is on the seventeenth.

One of the two scientists who shared the Nobel Prize with

Snell is the French researcher Jean Dausset. Dausset compared the white blood cells (leukocytes) of blood donors and their recipients and identified the antigens on their surfaces. He called them human leukocyte antigens (HLA) because they were first found in white cells. In fact, they are on almost all tissues except red blood cells. So far, four sets of antigens have been discovered: A, B, C, and D, with variations in each set. There are more than 100 known antigens. All are primarily concerned with recognizing and rejecting foreign tissue—hence their importance in transplants of any kind. DNA in the HLA-D region may also code for genes that determine the level of immune response that the body mobilizes to fight viruses and bacteria—everything from the flu to tooth decay.

To determine whether it is possible to perform a transplant, the HLAs of the patient and the potential donor are compared by mixing a tiny drop of white cells with an equally small amount of antiserum from which HLA-A, -B, -C, and -D antibodies have been removed. Under a microscope it is simple to see what the reaction is: The cells are or are not killed. About sixty different mixtures with specific antisera are examined.

HLA-D matches cannot be detected through antibody reactions alone, so a potential donor with a match in the other sets has a sample of blood tested in a mixed-lymphocyte culture (MLC). White cells from the patient and potential donor are mixed in a culture dish with a radioactive substance. If the lymphocytes attack each other they become radioactive in proportion to the severity of the reaction; the presence of high levels of radioactivity in the cells indicates incompatibility in the HLA-D locus.

Different transplants require differing degrees of compatibility. A kidney transplant, for instance, can successfully be done under some circumstances even if there is no agreement between HLA sets. But for a bone marrow transplant there must generally be a complete match of all HLA antigens.

Dausset's discovery showed why bone marrow transplants had always failed: Patients were not receiving marrow that sufficiently matched their own cells. After nearly a generation of concerted effort to determine whether bone marrow transplantation was indeed a useful treatment, doctors had at least part of the answer. The first successful bone marrow transplants were performed in the late 1960s by teams headed by Drs. George Mathé and E. Donnall Thomas.

In early October, about three weeks after being discharged from the hospital, Linda and Dan went to the UCLA Medical Center to meet with Dr. Robert Gale, the head of the bone marrow transplant team. Everything they had heard from John David made them think it was a relatively simple procedure. Dr. Gale's talk with them significantly changed their thinking.

A bone marrow transplant, he told them, was a double-edged sword. On the one hand about 50 percent of the patients who had undergone one were alive and doing well and were free of their leukemia. On the other hand, where a transplant offered a chance for a normal life-span, it also posed an immediate risk.

The first month post-transplant is filled with life-threatening problems, the most common being graft-versus-host disease. Half of all patients get it, and half of those die from it. Even though the new marrow is genetically matched as closely as possible under present technology and understanding, there are still minor variations between the new marrow and the patient's body, and thus it is still a foreign element in the body. (GVHD never occurs if donor and patient are twins, because they are genetically identical, not just genetically matched.)

Then there are the problems that come from viruses or bacteria that have entered the body and lain dormant for months before the transplant. Because a patient lives for two or three weeks after transplantation with no immune system at all and has a considerably weakened one for about a year, viruses and bacteria that could not establish themselves before suddenly find that they can thrive without being attacked. Patients are particularly susceptible to pneumonias, which are often fatal. Also, irreversible organ damage can be caused by the chemotherapy, radiation, and support drugs a transplant patient needs; the liver and kidneys are especially endangered.

It is somewhat encouraging that, if a patient has problems in only one of those areas, she or he will more than likely pull through. But if one builds on another, it is usually more than a body that has been so damaged can handle. Leukemia, it must be remembered, is an overwhelming, pernicious disease. Defeating it requires treatment that sometimes must be as aggressive as the disease itself.

Because the cure can be as deadly as the disease, doctors waited several years before attempting bone marrow transplants on patients who were in remission and therefore technically well. Thus, between 1973, when the first transplant at UCLA was done, and 1978, only people whose leukemia was active and resistant to other therapies qualified for transplants. Ten percent of those patients survived. This may not seem like much of a success rate, but since the patients treated were assuredly going to die from their leukemia—were, in many cases, very close to death when the transplant was done—the survival rate was significant, and better than that which could be achieved with any other treatment. Based on those successes and other medical evidence, doctors began performing bone marrow transplants on patients in remission, achieving a 40 to 60 percent survival rate. The rationale for this approach was to perform the transplant at a time when the patient had a relatively small number of leukemic cells, and before the leukemia became resistant to treatment.

As of mid-1983, doctors in forty medical centers around the world had performed transplants on 3,000 patients. A bone marrow transplant costs between $60,000 and $100,000. As expensive as that might seem, it is less costly than repeated hospitalizations for maintenance chemotherapy for leukemia. Also, a successful transplant works out to only a few thousand dollars per year of added life, a figure that compares favorably against other modern therapies. A coronary bypass operation is more expensive and on average adds only a few years to a patient's life; kidney dialysis costs $12,000–$15,000 a year.

Linda and Dan listened to Dr. Gale recount the statistics, enumerate the potential problems, and detail the course of treatment, as he tried to apprise them fairly of the risk and of the hope a transplant offered. Only ten weeks earlier Linda had been leading her life as a generally happy, slightly anemic, increasingly pregnant young woman who was building a family and a career. But the moment she was told she had leukemia, her life was unalterably changed, and changed in a way that only someone in her position could fully appreciate. We all live under sentence of death, but the young person being told she has a disease that is almost surely and almost immediately fatal loses what every healthy person takes for granted: the future. And the future was something Linda had a huge stake in. She had just endured as difficult a birth as can be imagined, and she wanted nothing more than a life with her child. Not only was her future involved, her daughter's was as well. Linda was faced with a terrible choice. She had risked her life to have her child. Now she had to consider whether to risk the immediate future with her so that she might afterward have a life free of leukemia or to take a chance on being one of the 10 percent of leukemia victims who stay in remission. Few of us who lead normal lives can comprehend the emotional implications in making such a decision.

Dr. Gale showed them the consent form Linda would have to sign if she decided on the transplant. Medical ethics and malpractice are serious matters. As it unavoidably must, the form recounted everything that might happen to Linda as a result of the procedure: viruses, bacteria, radiation poisoning, organ damage, drug reactions, graft-versus-host disease. It was a catalog of infirmity, infection, and fatality that went on for three single-spaced typewritten pages. At the very end it allowed that a bone marrow transplant might also eradicate her leukemia.

Then he said to her, "If you definitely want to be here a year from now, don't have a bone marrow transplant. But if you're willing to risk not being here in a few months for a chance to be here several years from now, you should consider it."

What Dan and Linda had thought of as a great savior had turned out to be something of a monster. Gale was friendly enough, but what he was saying seemed rather impersonal. It was all so black and white: These are the statistics, this is what happens. Gale was speaking as he ought to, pointing out the chances and drawbacks of the operation and appealing to reason rather than emotion. But to Dan it seemed a case of being damned if you do and damned if you don't, and that was not an alternative he and Linda had been expecting to find. Yet, as he considered what Gale was saying, he also realized there wasn't much of a choice. One either had a transplant while in remission or not at all. The choice, he realized, was either to do it then and hope Linda was around twenty years hence or to use chemotherapy alone, knowing the chance of being alive a year later was slim. It was a choice that would prove itself right or wrong only after it was too late to choose the alternative. If it worked out, it was a great choice; if it didn't, it was a bad one.

Linda, too, realized for the first time how serious the gamble was. They talked in the car about how Gale's description was so much starker than they had expected, and for the first time Linda voiced some apprehension about undergoing a transplant. Even so, by the time they had left Gale's office, she was almost certain of her choice. They both knew there was very little Dan could say. It was Linda's life, and the decision on what to do with it was Linda's alone. Dan could only support her in whichever choice she made.

"What would you do if you had leukemia?" she asked him.

Dan thought a moment and said, "Have the transplant."

"I gave it a lot of thought," Linda explained later. "I knew that there was a small chance that I could stay in remission indefinitely. I would have been willing to bet a couple of dollars on that, but not my life. I knew, too, that I could probably put off having the transplant for several months and still be in remission, but I couldn't face the idea of waking up every day and saying, 'Is this the day I relapse?' Even though I could die within a month of the transplant, the risk of waiting a long time didn't seem worth it to me."

Linda's brothers and sisters had blood samples drawn to see if any of them was a genetic match with her, but Jennifer, five years Linda's junior, was sure the others were wasting their time. She was in many ways Linda's opposite, but in this she was sure they were the same.

Their personalities had made for both a special bond and a lot of arguments while they were growing up. By the time Jennifer was thirteen, she and Linda wore the same dress size. Like many younger sisters, Jennifer borrowed Linda's clothes without asking. When Jackie saw her in a dress of Linda's, she would tell her her sister was going to kill her, and Jennifer would tell her not to worry, she'd take good care of it. But almost invariably she would return it with a stain no cleaner could get out. And there was the problem of Linda's shoes. Jennifer's feet were half a size bigger, but she would cram them into a nice pair of Linda's shoes, only to stretch them out of shape.

Yet for all that, they got on. Jennifer looked up to Linda, and Linda showed general forbearance with her sister. Linda even let Jennifer ride Dagger, the ultimate possession to lend, in a trail ride once. Jennifer was in the junior division and Linda in the adult. They rode side by side, and Linda kept Jennifer going over the rough terrain when she was tired and her spirit was flagging. "Come on, Jenny, come on. We can do it," she said over and over, and they did. Jennifer finished second.

Jennifer had her blood sample taken just a few days before she and her husband and their two-year-old twin boys were due to leave for Samoa, where he was going to work for the next six months. The results weren't in before they left, but the outcome was no mystery to her. She was certain that she was the match her sister needed. She told Linda so and assured her that she could come back whenever she wanted her.

Jennifer was right. When Linda called her with the news she was not surprised, only relieved. Linda asked her to come back in early November, three weeks away. She was going to have the transplant then so that she could spend Christmas, her favorite holiday, with her family in Georgia.

THREE

R obert Peter Gale—he uses all three names—was born in 1945. He is five feet, nine inches tall and weighs a very trim 125 pounds, the result of several miles of running every day. He has intense dark eyes and a square jaw, and clearly looks intelligent. His black hair is flecked with gray and is kept neatly trimmed. He has an Aristotelian manner about him in that his statements are often preceded with questions. An associate professor of medicine at UCLA (he took his M.D. at the State University of New York at Buffalo and a Ph.D. in microbiology and immunology at UCLA), he is an excellent lecturer who lightens his presentations with humor. In informal conversation and in discussion with his researchers he is witty and relaxed. On the ward he appears more reserved, although his comments to the nurses and other doctors during morning rounds contain nuggets of humor that aren't always noticed. He is sometimes criticized by the nurses for being aloof and emotionless, a criticism more perceptual than actual. Because he spends much of his time in the lab or in designing new protocols from research results, he has been accused of considering his patients more as numbers in a research sample than as individuals. His wife, Tamar, discounts both notions.

"He knows the name of every patient who dies," she says. "They may not see it at the hospital, but every one of those patients is carried in his mind. I see it every night." Gale's critics immediately seize on that as proof of his hardheartedness, but in fact the reverse is true. The names of the people who go home well are not so much on his mind because with them he did what he set out to do.

"We don't feel a particular elation or sense of satisfaction when we send a patient home successfully transplanted," he said one day, setting up a no-win situation for his emotions. "We did the procedure, after all, because there was an expectation that it could work, that it was the most appropriate treatment. So when it works, it was expected. On the other hand, when a patient dies we tend to feel responsible for contributing to the death. But the fact is, they had a disease that would surely have killed them. It is easier for a doctor to do nothing in such a case, to simply say, 'You have leukemia. Go home and die.' But there is no reason why young people should be dying of leukemia. It's better to do something about that if you can. It's a great privilege to have the confidence of these people. It's extremely hard, but it's a great privilege."

Tamar Gale is an Israeli whom Bob met when he was traveling there in 1975. She is a strong-featured, very handsome woman with shoulder-length curly brown hair and an unfettered laugh. Like all Israeli citizens, she spent two years in the army. She was just out of the service and helping a friend administer a medical conference when she was pressed into duty as a tour guide for Bob, who found he had an extra day in Jerusalem and wanted to see the city. The rest of the story is simple enough. They were married in 1976.

The Gales live in Bel Air, three miles up into the hills behind UCLA, in a house with a pool and a spectacular view of the Los

Angeles basin. They have two young daughters who speak Hebrew as fluently as they do English. Music ranging from Rachmaninoff to the Rolling Stones (with a concentration on the classical) is usually on the stereo. They subscribe to no U.S. newspapers, although Tamar receives one or two Israeli papers. Magazines are limited to *The New Yorker*, *Time*, and medical journals. Until very recently there was no television, because Bob and Tamar felt that there are better things to do with time. They bought one because Gale's parents, who visit often from their home in New York City, finally convinced them that the girls should not be deprived of such learning tools as *Sesame Street*.

Gale is a well-organized man, if only by necessity. He rises usually before dawn and sets immediately to work on his current research paper (he has authored or co-authored about 150, and he has an English teacher's grasp of grammar and vocabulary) or a grant application; or he makes calls to Washington, D.C., on matters connected with his grants from the National Institutes of Health and to other bureaucratic and scientific people on the East Coast or in Europe. He arrives at the hospital by 8:00 A.M. and during the next ten or eleven hours will not only deal with patients on 10 West or in the cancer clinic but will also coordinate the work of the fifteen researchers on his staff, screen prospective transplant patients (about one in ten are acceptable), give a lecture to a group of medical students, confer with lawyers on issues of medical ethics and consent forms, work with statisticians on the design of clinical trials for new protocols, eat a bran muffin or two and some fruit for lunch, and either at midday or about 5:00 P.M. run six or eight miles around the periphery of the campus, in part for exercise and in part to be free, if only for a while, of the relentless pressure of his work. At the end of the day he drives home to an affectionate welcome from his wife and children, and that should be that. But several evenings a week (and often on an hour's notice to Tamar) the Gales entertain visiting doctors or scientists. For all that, they are a remarkably close-knit family.

A *New Yorker* cartoon by Roz Chast is taped to the wall outside Bob's office at UCLA. It is of two slightly overlapping circles. One is labeled "Fun," the other "Boring." The small area enclosed by their intersection says "Bob." He put it there. In a way it neatly describes his life. He has no hobbies, nothing he does, besides running, to take him away from his work because, he says simply, "I like my work." Yet for all the deliberate style and organization of his life and work, he came to bone marrow transplantation quite by accident. The story is a good example of the serendipity of science.

In 1972 he finished his internship and residency at UCLA and was supposed to go into the Navy for two years. But at the last minute the Navy deferred his entry for four years; they had enough doctors at the moment. So, as he explained one day by his pool, "Suddenly on May the first I found I had to find something to do by July the first, which wasn't easy because most positions are filled a year in advance. So I stayed at UCLA to study immunology, which was the up and coming thing then. I began a Ph.D. program with one of the doctors here, working for two years in his lab. It was not my intention, but it seemed an excellent opportunity. The NIH had given him a huge cell separator with which we planned to take cells off cancer patients with the idea of giving them transfer factor, a type of immunotherapy. The separator was out in a hall because it was too big to fit into a room. Another physician I was working with was supposed to be in charge of setting it up, but he wouldn't do it, so I literally uncrated the machine and set it up. With the help of a nurse we learned how to run it but thought I ought to go and see one in operation before we used it on a patient. The U.S. Public Health Hospital in Seattle was the closest place that had a cell separator in operation, so I went up to see what I could learn. But when I arrived the physician I saw told me they'd decided to stop using theirs temporarily. 'That's unfortunate,' I said. 'What type of research are you using it for?' 'Bone marrow transplants,' he said. 'That's interesting,' I said, but I'd never heard of a bone marrow transplant. Having spent the time and money, however, I didn't want to come for nothing, so I went on clinical rounds and to the operating room and read all the articles there were. Their hospital was like Dresden after the war—it was a small public health hospital, and they were clearly working under less than optimal conditions. We had this huge university with hundreds of hematologists and immunologists and the major HLA-typing lab in the world. Since Seattle was one of only a few places doing bone marrow transplants, I figured we could do them, too. A week after I got back to UCLA, a twelve-year-old boy with aplastic anemia was admitted. He had an HLA identical sister, so we decided to try a transplant since there was no other potentially effective treatment. Like many things, the first time you do it, it works. The twelve-year-old is now a college student. When you start with that kind of success . . ." He paused and shrugged. "It's all serendipity—the machine, finding something to do."

The something-to-do has developed into what is in many ways a $5-million-a-year corporation with Gale as its head. It presents a problem that is increasing in medical research: The doctor must not only be a good physician and scientist (itself a hard double), he must also know how to get and administer grants, how to deal with personnel, and how to read and navigate the sociopolitical currents that influence the course of his work. Although federal funding agencies such as the National Institutes of Health would deny it, and in fact do all they can to keep politics to a minimum, whom a doctor knows and how he maneuvers can be important. The same is true within any university, where faculty politics are notoriously Byzantine.

Gale has a reputation for both helping and hindering himself in his relationships with various circles of power. He has shown himself to be very adept at working through the federal and national medical establishments. He has had somewhat less success at UCLA, because for all his political sensibility he has little patience with bureaucratic procedure when he believes it interferes with the best interests or care of his patients. Not surprisingly, some people find him arrogant, an accusation he agrees is sometimes warranted. Because of this, and even more so because bone marrow transplantation is still considered experimental medicine, he is the lightning rod for the unit. And, because of the unconventional medicine and the life-and-death nature of his unit's work, there have been periods of severe lightning. Gale has grounded the bolts remarkably well—something he has to do.

"Ten West patients are as sick as or sicker than the patients in the Intensive Care Unit [ICU] and Respiratory Care Unit [RCU]," he said in explaining some of the problems his unit faces. "What they don't have in common is that Ten West is primarily a clinical research unit. You get yourself into the ICU because you got hit by a train; it's not an elective admission. No one would argue that we need to have an ICU. But you can argue whether a bone marrow transplant unit is really necessary. That's why Ten West is more identifiable."

Ten West consists of seven rooms in the 800-bed UCLA Center for the Health Sciences (as the medical center is officially known), which fills thirty-five acres of the university campus, itself some of the nicest real estate in Los Angeles. Set just below the hills of lavish homes in Bel Air, with Beverly Hills to the east and the Pacific Ocean not far away to the west, UCLA is a huge educational estate. There are gracious old Romanesque brick buildings, lawns, playing fields, and eucalyptus-lined roads. Alongside one of those roads, the medical center overlooks the village of Westwood, one of the few places in Los Angeles where one can easily walk around.

When the center was built in 1954, it was designed to combine treatment with teaching and research, a triple role that was unique at the time. Laboratories and classrooms integrated with inpatient wards on the same floor was unprecedented. Because the emphasis was on academics, patients were selected on a value-for-teaching basis. That is still somewhat true today, although there is greater emphasis on community health needs than in the past.

It began modestly enough: a $23-million, six-story, 600,000-square-foot building. In twenty-five years, however, it has quadrupled in size. Now it is a $110-million, ten-story, 2,400,000-square-foot conglomerate of modern medicine. The Pentagon supposedly has slightly more available space, but with about twenty miles of corridors—no one seems to know exactly how many—the medical center is larger. In addition to the original hospital, medicine and nursing schools, and laboratories, there are now a complete emergency medical center, extensive outpatient clinics, the Marian Davies Children's Clinic, the Jules Stein Eye Institute, schools of dentistry and public health, a neuropsychiatric institute, the Charles E. Reed Neurological Research Center, a brain research institute, the Jerry Lewis Neuromuscular Research Center, the Jonsson Cancer Center, and a biomedical cyclotron. In 1980 the center admitted more than 26,000 patients, treated almost 56,000 emergency cases, and had operating costs of $130 million on gross revenues of $132 million. About 1,800,000 clinical laboratory procedures were performed, more than 11,000 operations were done, and nearly 12,500 babies were delivered. And the scientific enterprise of the center's doctors and researchers was underwritten by grants of more than $130 million. Only three universities received more. Modern medicine is big business.

The medical center is a far more pleasant-looking place than most hospitals, although there is no mistaking what it is. The second through eighth floors all have rooms containing two beds (the first floor is for administration) and wide linoleum-covered corridors in which there is brisk traffic consisting of visitors, gurneys, wheelchairs, doctors, and nurses, who must constantly shuttle between the four or five patients they care for at a time.

The ninth and tenth floors, however, are what the Beverly Hills Hotel is to a roadside inn. The rooms are all private, the halls carpeted and quiet. The floors even have their own kitchens that offer patients a choice of lobster tails, steak, or lamb chops for dinner, plus assorted specials and freshly squeezed orange juice. The other floors have food brought up from the central kitchen two levels below the main entrance to the hospital. No lobster tails grace the menu, no steak, no lamb chops; no specials; canned juice.

At the west end of the tenth and top floor of the hospital is the bone marrow transplantation unit. It is both spatially and medically separate, a tiny recess in the uppermost corner of that gargantuan place. The rooms on one side look out over Westwood and past Santa Monica to the Pacific. With the exception of a few (but now ever-increasing) office buildings and condominiums of twenty or so stories along Wilshire Boulevard, the view is of the low-building sprawl that is typical of Los Angeles. The view from the rooms on the other side is of the UCLA campus, green, wooded, tranquil, and the Bel Air homes in the hills across Sunset Boulevard. The rooms are comfortably furnished, which is a help since a transplant patient can expect a stay of at least a month. An easy chair and a small refrigerator stand along one wall; a large TV rests on a platform for easy viewing from the bed. The kitchen for all the patients on the floor is on 10 West, and at mealtimes carts of freshly cooked food are pushed down the hall and delivered still hot. The irony is that a transplant patient seldom feels like eating.

The seven rooms that make up 10 West are worlds unto themselves, the doctors and nurses moons that orbit them. Seldom are two patients in need of the same treatment or at the same point in the transplant process, and thus every one requires an adjustment by the staff. Every patient is treated as much in line with his personality as possible, too. The nurses' philosophy is that even though the patients are in a life-threatening situation, they cannot be treated as though they are sick. Thus a Vietnam vet who had had a transplant a few months earlier but had returned because of a herpes infection (which can be fatal to an immune-suppressed person) that covered the area around his buttocks was greeted one morning by his nurse with, "All right, turkey, drop your pants."

Every morning the doctors make their rounds (generally Dr. Gale or one of his two co-directors, Dr. Richard Champlin and Dr. Winston Ho, and one or two fellows in hematology and oncology who are assigned to the unit for a month at a time). At about 10:00 A.M. they meet with the nurses in the nurses' station to discuss in detail each patient's condition and course of treatment. The ups and downs of vital signs are noted, the lab reports on blood and other tests mentioned, treatments suggested and agreed upon. Moods, appetite, pain are all discussed.

The report room is the hub of the six-room nurses' station. There are off-white walled offices for the head nurse and the attending physician, a reception area, and a room each for supplies and medications, but the ten-foot by ten-foot wheat-brown report room is where everything happens. On one wall is a blackboard with the name and room number of each patient. Every pertinent detail is listed below: age, sex, disease, days pre- or post-transplant, medications to be given, transfusions to have. A glass-fronted bookcase with appropriate medical reference books as well as games and books for patients hangs above half the counter that runs along another wall. A third wall is half glass, looking into the reception area and hallway. On the fourth is a large bulletin board, for the most part filled with a collage of hundreds of pictures of patients, nurses, doctors, and staff parties that have been trimmed to cut out everything except the people in them. Beneath it is a table with three chairs for making notes on charts, which nurses must do throughout the day to record a patient's course. It is too small a room for all that goes on in it. During morning report it is especially crowded. With doctors and nurses and other staff who may be in attendance, there are usually more than a dozen people crammed in, some sitting on the counter, others standing, squeezed like coatracks against the walls.

Because the needs of each patient are different, because there is a continuous cycle of patients representing all stages in the course of treatment, and because patients' conditions can change quickly, there is no predicting what any day will be like on the ward. The only regularly scheduled events are bone marrow transplants on Wednesday (because that is the day they have regular operating-room time) and chemotherapy treatments the weekend before transplantation. There are periods of a few days when no one needs much of anything and others when almost all of the patients need intensive care.

Ten West is a young person's ward. The nurses and doctors are mostly in their twenties and thirties. The average age of a transplant patient is twenty-one. It is common for family members—usually spouses or parents—to sleep in the rooms with the patients, particularly when they are quite ill (there are times when everyone who enters the room must wear a surgical mask to limit the spread of germs, although the main source of infection to an immunologically weakened patient comes from within his own body). The staff in the kitchen will prepare an extra meal for visitors, and coffee, tea, and assorted juices are always available across the hall from the nurses' station in a small room with a sink and refrigerator and a plaque on the door that proclaims it to be a "nourishment center." Members of the different families get to know each other, but seldom are any lasting friendships formed. The weeks and months pass in

84

limbo and anxiety. All sense of normal life vanishes when a parent or spouse moves in. At 6 A.M. one day I met the father of a patient as he came out of his son's room. He and his wife had been there for several weeks. Their son's condition was poor and getting worse (he did, however, eventually recover). The father was a tall, muscular man who usually ran ten miles a day. In the hall of 10 West, however, he looked gaunt and vulnerable.

"I haven't rested well since this began," he said. "In this place, sleep leaves you."

For all its superficial tranquillity, there is no such thing as easing one's way into a place like 10 West. The diseases being fought are almost sure killers, and the stakes are both high and simple: The patient will either live or die as a result of what happens on the ward. It is important to keep sight of the improved chances the ward offers, but the problem of talking about chances is that they are gross statistics, and 10 West is a very personalized place. A patient does not really have a 50–50 chance of living because he had a bone marrow transplant, even though that is the case overall. Individually, a patient will either live or he will die. His chances are 100 percent or zero.

My first day on the ward was lesson enough. I arrived with Dr. Gale just before morning rounds. We were met by Dr. Gary Lazar, a fellow in hematology and oncology doing that month's rotation. Lazar was the hematologist/oncologist on call when Linda was bleeding so badly prior to Angela's birth. Dark-haired, with a neatly trimmed beard, and in his late twenties, Lazar had a sad, what-are-you-going-to-do? smile. He had just left the room of a twenty-year-old with aplastic anemia who had declined badly during the night. The young man, who was from Mexico and spoke no English, did not have an HLA match and so had been treated with antithymocyte globulin (ATG), a drug introduced in the 1970s whose effectiveness against aplastic anemia has been recently proved by the

85

10 West doctors. (ATG and bone marrow transplants have about the same degree of success in aplastic anemia, but there are differences in their effects. A bone marrow transplant virtually cures the patient, because he is given a new blood-producing system. On the other hand, there are the complications that can accompany a transplant. ATG avoids those problems, but the marrow is not returned completely to normal, nor is the drug always immediately effective; it can take up to six months to work. The 10 West data shows that, if there is a donor, a patient fares better with a transplant if he is under twenty. If he is over thirty-five, however, ATG is preferred. People in between those ages do equally well with either treatment.)

The young man had been treated during the summer and, only temporarily, it turned out, cured. He was sent home to Mexico, where he was fine for two months before the disease took over again. When he returned to UCLA there was little the doctors there could do. He had recently developed breathing problems and had been placed on a respirator. Then he developed subcutaneous emphysema—the force of the air necessary to keep him alive had caused air to leak from his lungs and gather in his tissue; he had become a human balloon. His eyes were swollen shut. His scrotum had inflated to the size of a softball. He was scarcely conscious and would die before the day was out. His condition more than graphically demonstrated the hideousness of the diseases the doctors and nurses—and patients—of 10 West are up against.

Happily, the news of the other patients was better. They were generally holding up well, and one, who had had AML and was transplanted three weeks earlier, was going home the next day. As they almost always did, the doctors and nurses discussed the patients with scarcely any benefit of notes, although they keep comprehensive ones. The history of the patient and the course of the disease were on some sort of memory tape. Latest vital signs, results of blood tests, X rays, and various cultures, and other pertinent data were at tongue-tip.

Although there were few medical problems, there were other considerations for the staff. One of the patients had, at first appearance, an air of bravado about him. A doctor who had been treating him added that he found him "nice, but a little weird." A nurse told him that on several occasions after she and others had talked with the patient the bravado had given way to fear.

"He cries often," she said, "and he is afraid, afraid most of pain." All they could do, the staff agreed, was comfort him as much as possible.

Family members are encouraged to stay with 10 West patients because they can provide emotional support unavailable from anyone else. But on occasion a family member can add to a patient's problems. A case in point was the sister-in-law of a patient (her husband was his donor) who was doing fine medically but who was very concerned about what *could* go wrong. The woman was studying to be a nurse, it turned out, and she proved that a little knowledge can be dangerous. She knew enough to augment his fears but not to relieve them. After some discussion it was decided that the best and least threatening way to curb her would be for one of the nurses to take her aside and talk to her on a nurse-to-nurse basis. If that didn't work, then a doctor would intervene.

A different kind of family problem requiring the staff's intervention was the case of the father of a twenty-one-year-old American-Chinese who had a cot in his son's room. He had been staying in the hospital for days at a time, no matter how much doing so tired him out. Only when one of the nurses would, in effect, give him permission to leave would he go home where he could properly relax and rest. His behavior was typical of many family members who feel guilty if they leave the ward while their child or spouse is so ill. So the doctors were asked by the nurses to make sure that from time to time one of them suggest he go home for a while.

The dying young Mexican man was the last patient discussed. The main concern was over what to do when he had a cardiac arrest, which was likely to happen at any time. A nurse said to me under her breath, "Do you know what will happen if we try to resuscitate him?" The answer required little imagination: It would be like applying pressure to a tautly inflated balloon. It was quietly agreed that heroic measures would be useless.

After the discussion of the patients, the doctors toured each room *en masse.* The first stop was the man who would be discharged the next day. He had set a record for the shortest recovery following his transplant, which had quickly engrafted and set to producing healthy blood. He sat on his bed with his knees drawn up to his chin, his arms around his legs. He was tall and bald (from the chemotherapy and radiation) and thin and happy. Asked by one of the doctors what he would do the next day, the man, who for most of the last several weeks had been fed intravenously, replied with a big smile, "Eat a chili dog."

About noon the mother of the grievously ill young Mexican man arrived. Because she, too, spoke no English, she was accompanied by a Spanish-speaking psychiatrist who had tried to prepare her as best he could for what she was about to see: a son with tubes in his nose, another tube in his chest, bottles putting some things into him and others catching what came out— blood from his stomach, for instance; his body was simply breaking down. The force of the respirator pushing air into his lungs caused his body to jerk wildly. The mother was shaking as she walked into the room, one hand over her face.

She did not stay long and was not there when, a couple of hours later, the nurse came out of his room and down to the nurses' station to say in a quiet voice to the other nurses that the young man had died. The psychiatrist was called and asked to tell the mother. He was also given the unpleasant task of asking permission for an autopsy, as the findings would be helpful in research aimed at sparing others what her son had had to endure.

Late in the afternoon Gary Lazar sat briefly at the nurses' station. He had been on call most of the preceding forty-eight hours and had spent much of that time, which included several middle-of-the-night telephone consultations, on the patient who had died. The next day would be the end of his month's tour on the ward; he was certainly leaving with a flourish. He looked exhausted, and I asked him what he was going to do that night.

"Get drunk," he said.

Things were better all around the next morning. The patients continued to progress well; the one who was going home was nearly packed. In honor of doctors Lazar and Ian Drew, the two fellows for the month, the nurses brought in a platter of bagels and lox and other delicacies as a farewell breakfast for them. They had been the most popular doctors in some time, and they would be missed. After the food, and when rounds had been completed, doctors Gale, Lazar, and Drew went from 10 West down to the chief pathologist's office on the A level, the first of the hospital's two basements.

It was Halloween, and the people in the medical center had a look unlike that on any other day. A parade of odd costumes coursed through the halls: patients dressed as doctors; a man and woman silver-laméd from head to toe; interns draped like patients. In front of one lab on the A level a mannequin sat in a chair, a Son of Frankenstein-type mask over its head, a cigarette in its mouth, and a beaker in one hand with dry ice in a little water spewing fog.

All was normal in the chief pathologist's office, two small rooms lined with books in the middle of the bowels of the building. On a table in one of the rooms was a Zeiss microscope with two sets of eyepieces, so that two people can look simultaneously at a piece of tissue or a culture on a slide and know what the other is talking about.

The three doctors had gone down to examine a bit of lung tissue taken from a twelve-year-old boy who had recently died. He had had a bone marrow transplant in an attempt to overcome his leukemia. The marrow had engrafted, but later the boy had developed graft-versus-host disease. Just what he had died of, however, was not really known. His parents had balked at giving permission for an autopsy but had permitted the piece of lung to be withdrawn via a long needle. The hope was that the biopsy would provide some clues. The specific question the doctors hoped to answer was whether there was any evidence of pneumocystis, a disease that shows up on a slide as little black dots. It is a curious disease in that it cannot be grown in the lab and no one is sure where it grows in nature. For some reason, it is prevalent in neonatal wards in Europe but not in America, where it occurs mainly in patients with suppressed immune systems.

The doctors took turns looking at the slide but could not agree on whether the disease was present. Lazar went over to one of the bookshelves and pulled down a text on microbiology. After a minute of thumbing through the index, he asked, "How do you spell pneumocystis?"

"P-n-e-u- . . . ," the others chorused.

"It's not in this book," he said in disbelief.

Dr. Gale, who was looking through the microscope, said, "It's a protozoa. You need a book on protozoology." Everyone laughed, including Lazar, who kept on looking.

"I swear to God, it's not in this book," he marveled. Turning to the front, he asked, "When was this book published?"

"1910," Gale said without skipping a beat, still looking through the microscope. More laughter.

At last a picture was discovered, and Lazar looked at it and then at the slide.

"You mean all this is pneumocystis? I sure wish it was in focus."

Someone mentioned that the microscope sells for around $10,000. Lazar was impressed.

"I'd sure like to have one of these in my office," he said, peering into it. He paused and then added, "I'd sure like to have an office."

"You could buy a car with this," a nurse said of the microscope.

"Not much of one," Gale said. "Wouldn't buy a Porsche, even a 924."

After a few more looks on everyone's part, the consensus was that pneumocystis was indeed evident, and the three doctors trooped off to check in on the autopsy of the young man who had died the day before. It was supposed to have started over an hour earlier but had not; the doctors were not particularly surprised. Pathologists, it seems, are often the butt of hematologists' jokes. As they passed the mannequin with the boiling beaker, one of the doctors compared it favorably with a pathologist.

"Their idea of an examination," another said, "is to take a slide, hold it at arm's length, look at it with a naked eye, and say, 'There's nothing there.' " They all chuckled, and Gale told a supposedly true story about a 10 West patient who was sent down for an autopsy, only to have the report come back saying, "No obvious pathology." The doctors on the ward were furious, Gale said, and sent a memo back: "Since there is nothing wrong with the patient, would you please sew him up and send him back so we can continue treatment?"

Linda checked onto 10 West in the afternoon of November 5. The day before, she and Dan had packed her things but kept the conversation to everyday topics. It was Election Day, and they had voted, then taken it easy during the evening. They were living on the hope that this hospitalization would allow Linda to go home and lead a normal life.

Dan drove her to the hospital. When Linda saw the freeway exit sign that reads "UCLA," she took a deep breath.

"Well, this is it," she said softly.

Neither of them said much more. There wasn't much to say. Dan helped Linda get settled in her room. In spite of the optimism each felt, Linda was a bit nervous about what lay ahead. Dan tried to make her as comfortable as he could and to reassure her that it would all work out well. He couldn't stay long, though. He had to go home and take care of Angela, and he left the hospital before the rush-hour traffic jammed the freeway and doubled the ninety-minute drive.

Nurse Patti DeLone, twenty-eight and the mother of a six-year-old boy and seven-year-old girl, helped Linda with the last of her unpacking and made sure she was told how everything worked in the room and on the ward. It is standard practice for at least one nurse to spend a little time with new patients to get a sense of their personalities and of their understanding of what they're getting themselves into. She asked Linda how long she had had leukemia and how it was diagnosed, checked to see whether she had any bruises, which would be a sign of a low platelet count, and asked what her reaction to chemotherapy had been. Patti explained the routines of the ward: Nurses change shift at 7 A.M. and 7 P.M., doctors make rounds between 9 and 10 A.M. Linda told Patti about the plan she and Dan had drawn up for his visits, that he would come around dinnertime and eat with her. Patti showed her the guest menu, how to turn on the nurses' call light and the TV from her bed, and the two chatted about Angela Hope and the long labor Linda had had.

When Patti returned to the report room she sat down beside me and said, "I've got your patient. She's nice, bright, articulate, and very strong." Patti, who has shoulder-length straight brown hair and an arm that can throw a Frisbee a mile, was impressed by Linda. "I can't imagine going through what she's gone through," she said, shaking her head. "She's really something."

After telling Linda what I was doing on the ward and asking if she would like to meet me, Patti took me to Linda's room. Linda was sitting in the easy chair, dressed in a dark skirt and light blouse. She looked like a rosy-cheeked, clear brown-eyed, smiling young mother who had scarcely a care in the world. She was thoughtful and intelligent and spoke with utter calm about what lay ahead. She had risked her life to have her baby, and she was willing to risk it again to have the chance for a full life with her. She showed me a picture of Angela and another she had brought of a Halloween party at work. She was in a western outfit with a bandanna and cowboy hat. She was surrounded by friends, and she had a big smile. Now, a week after the picture had been taken, she flashed the same smile again. It was clear in talking with her that she was well aware of the risks and difficulty that lay ahead, but it was equally clear that dwelling on them was of no value to her. As in the past and as I would see as I got to know her, there was a challenge ahead and she was eager to meet it and get on with her life. She knew that her baby was well taken care of and that she wouldn't see as much of her in the next four or five weeks as she would like. The sense she gave was that that was the price she had to pay; she was having the bone marrow transplant for the future, and that meant giving up her baby for the present.

The only sign that she wasn't the healthy young mother she appeared to be came when she took off her short brown curly wig and immediately tied a bandanna around her head; her hair was thinned by half from the chemotherapy that had put her leukemia into remission.

"From time to time the seriousness of this disease sets in," she said in an even voice, straightening the bandanna. "This sounds silly, but it bothers me when I see a patient walking down the hall without hair on her head. You'll never see me not wear a bandanna or a wig. I don't want the world looking at me and saying, 'Oh, you poor thing, you've been through hell.' "

The next two days would be easy ones for Linda, only some tests and talk with doctors about what was coming up. Her sister Jennifer, her donor, was due to arrive from Samoa on Friday or Saturday; an airline strike had made the once-a-week service from Samoa even more difficult. The first day of chemotherapy in preparation for the transplant would be Saturday, providing Jennifer had arrived; because of the toxicity of the drugs, the doctors would not start treatment until she was safely in Los Angeles.

In order to transplant bone marrow effectively, the patient's own marrow has to be destroyed, because it manufactures diseased blood cells. This is done by administering a cell-destroying chemotherapy medication called Cytoxan (a clever if grim combination of *cyto*, from the Greek for "cell," and *toxicum*, Latin for "poison"), followed by a dose of radiation that is strong enough to destroy the remaining bone marrow without excessively damaging the body's vital organs, although it usually causes sterility. Cytoxan is used against a variety of cancers, but a person having a bone marrow transplant is given a dose ten to twenty times stronger than normal. It is administered intravenously on two successive days.

"I hope Jennifer gets out all right," Linda said. "The strike has made it hard to get a reservation out. But the doctors sent a telegram saying this was a medical emergency, and that should do it."

She picked up the menu and looked it over to see what she would have for dinner, settling finally on lamb chops. No one had to tell her what she already knew: Once the chemotherapy and radiation began, it would be a long while before she had any interest in food again.

The 10 West nurses are impressively competent and specialized, and in some ways they know more about the specifics of bone marrow transplantation than do the hematology and oncology fellows who rotate through the ward monthly assisting doctors Gale, Champlin, and Ho. No one knows more about the patients' lives and conditions than the nurses; they spend hour after hour, day after day, with the patients, and take care of only two at a time. In fact, new doctors are told by the nurses not to leave the floor after writing an order on a patient without checking it with them first to ensure it is written according to protocol. It is not uncommon for a nurse to question a doctor's decision on a medication, because they know how each patient responds to all the drugs they are given and how others responded before them. The future of bone marrow transplantation may be with the doctors and in the labs, but its history is with the nurses on the ward.

If the doctors don't know this when they first arrive, they know it by the time they leave. "Medicine is like an orchestra," Dr. Robert Figlin, thirty-one, said after his second tour on 10 West. He and the nurses had often been at odds his first time around. During the second, he developed a different attitude after two of the nurses took him aside and kindly but pointedly told him how difficult he had been to work with. "The nurses are the violins, the body of this program. The violins are always playing. As I think about this analogy, only the rare doctor is in the orchestra. Doctors are the orchestrators. We set up. We lead. But only as people who begin the movement. It takes a lot of thought to get a piece of music to the orchestra, but only the orchestra can carry it out."

In all, there are twelve full-time and four per diem nurses in the 10 West orchestra. Head nurse Janice Campiformio, thirty-

95

six, is the concert master. She has been on the ward since 1975. Cheri Shilala, twenty-eight, is second in tenure; she has worked on the unit all six years of her nursing career. Of the sixteen, one is a man, Peter Belauskas, thirty-four, a former Peace Corps health worker who did two stints in Africa and who runs the night shift. The average age of the nurses is about twenty-eight. They work twelve-hour shifts, four days a week, but what with reports, rounds, meetings, and a lecture or two a week by various doctors about specific medical issues, they put in more like fourteen hours a day. For this they are paid barely adequately in relation to their expertise—around $20,000 a year. Most would like to work the day shift, but with only three or four on duty at a time, that is impossible; permanent day-shift assignments come with tenure. So, many work days one month, nights the next, building up seniority and waiting for a day spot to open. It is usually a long time coming. The average tenure of a 10 West nurse is two or three times that of a nurse on a regular oncology ward.

No one can explain exactly why this is so, although each nurse has a theory. Part of it must be because the work is challenging and requires a good deal of self-motivation. All the nurses have strong personalities, and most of them have a mordant sense of humor, which helps break the tension of each day. Despite the superficial tranquillity and comfort on 10 West, the staff is fighting a ferocious disease with ferocious treatment. Timid, unambitious people don't last long in such an environment. In fact, nurses who come to the ward realize fairly quickly whether or not the work suits them. They also realize that the intensity of the work is something that no one can endure forever. They all go through periods of burnout. There is a weekly meeting with a hospital psychiatrist (who is also available to the patients) to help the nurses cope with the frustration and pain of dealing with their patients.

"Every time you're about to leave the job, you get closer to the place," Jeanette Leslie, thirty, a five-year veteran of the transplant team said one day, trying to explain the longevity of the 10 West staff. "The place is physically and situationally intimate. Everyone knows the details of everyone else's life. It has all the advantages and disadvantages of a family."

The 10 West nurses sometimes feel excluded by the other nurses at the hospital. In the beginning, when only patients in the terminal stages of the disease were receiving transplants, 90 percent of them died. By the time patients were moved to the intensive care units they were terribly ill and almost never recovered, and the other hospital staff members built up an attitude of: What horrible things are they doing to those patients up on 10 West?

That attitude is no longer so pervasive, but it lingers. Bone marrow transplantation is still experimental (although increasingly less so), and the recipients are in many ways research patients. At times there is tension between doctors and nurses about that, which is as it should be; checks and balances make for better care. Head Nurse Campiformio views working on the unit "as a chance to make sure these patients are treated with dignity."

Janice's attitude and influence are evident in the tone and manner in which the ward is run. She is a chronological contemporary of Gale, and her concerns and personality neatly counterbalance and augment his. Gale's personal emphasis is the science of bone marrow transplantation; Janice's is the humanity of the procedure, but he of course knows the personal side and she the medical as well. She is a dark, curly-haired woman with brown eyes and gypsy looks and a high laugh. She often escapes the rigors of the ward by going to the northern California woods where she owns property and where her sister lives. She is a combination of 1960s fierce humanist and 1980s scientific specialist, although the science never overrides the personal; Janice is the patient's greatest advocate. When the op-

97

portunity came in 1975 to set up the bone marrow transplantation unit, she jumped at it.

"I had the chance to put into practice things that could counter everything that had frustrated me since nursing school," she said one afternoon. "Nurses couldn't take initiative, they couldn't be creative, they couldn't contribute much to the patient's care. Here was a case where we could take care of the whole patient and where doctors and nurses could contribute equally, where care was all interrelated. We would be part of a team, not separate. Most nurses have to work under conditions that are not all that desirable—a strict schedule, inflexible circumstances. I grasped the opportunity to put together something different than that. UCLA was very supportive of what it would take to make the unit work. It is a *clinical* research center."

She feels that the dual role of caring for patients and finding new ways of treating them, which is the essence of a clinical research center, is split along pretty clear lines. "The goals of the nurses and the goals of the researchers are different," she said flatly. "No one can match the *feeling* we have for our patients. It is a research center, but we have a feeling for the patients as human beings and their need to be recognized as human beings, because doctors so often view them as research subjects. I set up this unit so we could honor those needs, and I think it's worked. We hardly ever have a family come by and say they wouldn't go through it again, regardless of the outcome. The nurses have helped that. We've helped patients and families maintain a certain amount of control over their destinies."

Janice had worked on 10 West five and a half years at the time I met her, even though the average oncology nurse spends only about a year on a ward. I asked what accounted for her longevity, and that of the other nurses. She thought for a few seconds and then said, "What does it for me is to help someone go through a procedure they've chosen and to make it a bit easier for them, to help them maintain their dignity as they're being researched upon. They've made the choice to go through it; we can help them to go through it with the least loss of personal integrity." She stopped and then added, "That's what did it initially. I don't know what does it now. I said that in the beginning it was the ideal nursing situation. Now maybe it's seeing the fruits of my labor." She looked away and then continued, "I've thought often of my own death and whether I'm in this because I'm afraid of dying or because I'm not afraid of dying. I don't know which. I know one thing—I'm really happy with my life this far, and I make every single moment of it count. If a doctor came to me tomorrow and said, 'You have leukemia,' I'd know that I have lived my life to the fullest. It's something I learned to do early in my nursing career. Something else I learned early on was to take a trip when I burned out. I had a great time in my twenties; that's what kept me in nursing. Some people, their priority is making money. Mine is enjoying life. It's important to help someone else. What could be more important than giving yourself to another human being? You're never going to meet a group more needy than this type of patient. I think what keeps nurses on this ward is that they can give to someone."

The average transplant patient stays on 10 West for four to six weeks, and for much of that time there is no one in the hospital who is sicker than he. The nurses are not only the orchestra, they are the front-line troops, too. The doctors who pore over the patients' problems on the ward and in the lab admit that their research and their dealing with aggregates and percentages serves to insulate them from emotional involvement but not to avoid it. They also see patients in the clinic after they have been discharged from the ward, which the nurses seldom do, and so have the benefit of seeing patients who have returned to a normal life. One of the reasons nurses so seldom see former patients is revealing of the intensity of the procedure for the patients.

"I grew close to many nurses, but it is hard for me to go back and see them," a man who had recovered said one day during a brief visit to the hospital. "They go ape when I go up to see them, but I can only bring myself to do it every couple of years. Just the smell of the hospital brings it all back. I went to 10 West once, and the nurses were all in a short meeting. I stood in the hallway for five minutes waiting for it to end, and emotion washed over me in waves. I had to leave before they came out. I just couldn't stay on the ward."

"I don't know how the nurses do it," Gale once said. "We at least have lab experiments and scientific papers to divert us. They, by contrast, are totally committed to patient care. What do they have?"

Patti DeLone tried to answer that one afternoon a couple of weeks after Linda checked in. "Professionalism helps maintain a certain detachment from many patients," she said, "but there are some you inevitably grow attached to. Working twelve-hour shifts is good because it gives you an extra day off, and that helps distance you. What's gratifying is to send someone home. But I'm always ambivalent about getting involved with patients. When you are involved and one of them dies, you build up a wall and say, 'I'm not getting involved again.' Then someone like Linda comes in. She's someone you could really grow close to. I'm team leader today and can choose whichever patients I want. And who do I choose? Linda."

Patti works days only, but on those days she seldom sees her children awake. She has to get up at 5:30 A.M. to be at the hospital by 7:00 A.M., works until 7:00 P.M., reports on the status of patients to the night shift, and doesn't get home until 8:30 or 9:00.

"When I get home," she continued, "my kids are usually

asleep. But I always go in and hold their hands and just sit on the bed for a minute, glad they're all right."

For all the difficulty and conflict that the work engenders, what seems to keep the nurses going is not only all that Janice said but also, in a sense, ambition.

"It's fulfilling to take care of patients who have a terminal disease," explained one nurse, who echoed many others. "This is the mainstream of modern medicine. I know there will be a cure, and I want to be there. The questions are, when, and how many people must die in the process? There's a rare opportunity to be a pioneer if you're willing to take on the responsibility. It's an area of nursing that's not well taught or represented. In my four years of training I had three hours on the art of cancer nursing.

"The focus on this unit is on a cure, on living," she went on. "It's difficult when a patient dies, especially when, as is usually the case, they have been taken down to the respiratory care unit. There's something lost in not having a patient with you when he dies. Our job is helping them live, and helping them to die if it comes to that. It's a real thorough kind of care. We make an all-out effort with every patient, even though the prognosis is known and a lot will die. We have to cloud that over and make believe we're going to cure all these patients. Everyone shares in the spirit that there will be a cure. And of course many do well. But the ones who die are the ones you remember."

On Thursday morning Linda heard that Jennifer had left Samoa and would arrive in Los Angeles that night. Everyone was relieved, no one more than Jennifer. She and Linda had talked weekly on the phone after she went to Samoa, but they had almost never discussed the leukemia or the transplant. Instead it was sister talk about whatever came up. Jennifer thought that in those conversations they sounded like two birds in spring. Coming to Los Angeles to help her sister was something she excitedly looked forward to. Like almost every donor, she worried that her marrow might not be good enough, and like every donor she wanted hers to be the best there was. In Samoa she watched her diet and exercised and did all she could to be in good health. Samoa was, she felt, a purification for her; she could imagine no better environment to make herself ready. She felt in the weeks before the transplant as if she had been looking at a pot of gold at the end of the rainbow; now, going to UCLA, she would be able to reach it.

Later in the morning a radiologist came in to explain the total body irradiation Linda would have the following Tuesday and to have her sign the consent form for it. The realization of the amount of radiation she would receive set in and, although it was disquieting to think of being given a dose big enough to kill off her bone marrow, she had no second thoughts about going ahead with the transplant. She talked with another patient who had had his transplant. He told her that he got through it by asking for enough Valium to keep him knocked out during the procedure. It set her to wondering just how difficult this was going to be.

The condition of the other patients that day was mixed. Suzana Raymond, a twenty-year-old from Long Beach, was in the best shape. During rounds her doctor reported that her donor's bone marrow was growing fine; they had taken a sample the day before by pushing a long needle through the upper part of her buttock into the pelvic bone—which sounds more painful than it is, although it is not a comfortable procedure. One way the doctors could tell she was doing well was that her blood type was changing. She had had type O before the chemotherapy and radiation killed off her own marrow. Her brother, who was her donor, had type A, and that was now being produced. In time (when all the blood already in her system was replaced according to the body's normal schedule, which would be about

120 days, the life of a red cell) she would have only type A. She would also have some male chromosomes in her blood as well as her liver and spleen, but her own sexual makeup would not be altered.

The patient whose sister-in-law was such a problem was continuing to do well, but his brother, who was his donor, was not. He was feeling terribly worried about what would happen if his brother died, a not uncommon concern among donors. They tend to feel that it is wonderful if their marrow saves the patient, but that they have failed if the patient dies. The sister-in-law was having problems, too. Although one of the nurses had taken her aside a few days before, they still felt that she was taking on more of the nursing load than she knew how to handle. The nurse who had spoken with her suggested that a doctor speak with her also and remind her that she needn't lay out the worst scenario for everyone, especially since the patient was doing so well.

Dr. Robert Figlin, one of the two fellows who had started their rotation at the beginning of the month, joined in the discussion after a few minutes.

"Maybe she has long-stemmed things going on and they're just manifested in a concern for the donor," he suggested.

Dr. Deane Wolcott, the psychiatrist who works with the staff of 10 West, concurred, as did several others.

"They may have been pathologic long before they met us," Figlin continued with a smile. The others smiled, too. Case closed.

Two unrelated patients on the ward had the same surname. One was doing quite well, the other was not and was getting worse. Dr. Richard Champlin, a co-director of the unit, held the chart of the well one while talking about the ill one. He said two or three words, then stopped, puzzled. Nurse Cheri Shilala handed him the proper chart.

"How about this?" she asked. Champlin smiled.

"Well, I was close," he said. "The last name was right."

"Close," Cheri answered, "but no banana."

But the patient's condition was no laughing matter. He had been transplanted three months earlier and released in good health. Now it looked as though he might be developing pneumonia, which could be fatal. Head Nurse Campiformio told the staff that the patient's mother had been having a tough time accepting her son's condition, which was why she hadn't been on the ward in days. The young man's father had told him that his mother was absent because she had the flu. Dr. Wolcott, whose responsibility is in dealing with staff problems, deals with patients and their families only when asked by them. Because the father had said nothing to him, he felt he could not intervene. Moreover, the whole family was upset over the death of a patient they had come to know during the boy's first stay on the ward. They did not hear of the death until he was readmitted. The patient they had liked died in room 1048, the largest room on the ward and one they would have liked. It was also where the young Mexican man had died a few days earlier, however, and under the circumstances by which it had twice become available, it made no sense to offer a room that would, for the family, have ghosts.

In the afternoon, Dan brought Angela Hope by the hospital to visit Linda. She would stay there with her while Dan went to the airport to meet Jennifer and her two boys, who were due to arrive in the early evening. The baby had had a bit of a cold the day before, so this was her first visit to the ward. The nurses could scarcely wait to meet her. When she arrived, it was to many oohs and ahhs. It was easy to see that because of her personality, her age (the same as almost all the nurses), and the baby, Linda would be an emotional hat trick for the staff.

"There is so much peer identification here," one nurse said. "We were all about twenty-two when we started, but we've grown older, so that helps. And for some reason, usually it is young men here." She shook her head. "Linda is two weeks away from me in age."

Linda saw Angela almost every day during the first two weeks she was on 10 West. Jackie usually brought her in during the afternoon, often with Jennifer, and Linda would lie with her while Jackie worked away on the alphabet quilt she had started during Linda's chemotherapy. Jackie usually left with the baby before Dan arrived in the evening after work. As the baby grew older, pacifying her was sometimes a problem while Jackie was driving. One day nothing she did seemed to help, so she pulled over to the side of the road to try to calm her down. But even holding her didn't work, and Jackie, willing to try anything, noticed a McDonald's restaurant ahead. A bottle hadn't worked and a pacifier hadn't worked, but for some reason she thought a french fry might. She bought an order and gave one to Angela, who loved it and settled down almost immediately.

But as Linda's stay progressed she saw less and less of her baby. She knew when she decided to have the transplant that it would entail separations, so she was prepared not to see her all the time, although not as seldom as it turned out. Angela had an off-and-on cold, and whenever she had it she couldn't come to the hospital for fear of infecting Linda. On other occasions it was too difficult for Linda to deal with her. The inevitable nausea that is a by-product of a transplant made it painful for Linda to hold Angela or put her on her stomach and play with her. And as the baby grew she became more active. When Linda was feeling poorly, she said Angela's fussing made her nervous. Linda missed seeing her but was content that Jackie was taking care of her. She would just have to try to make up for the time she had lost with Angela after she was home.

For much of the ten-hour flight to Los Angeles, Jennifer wondered how Linda was and what she was thinking about. She was anxious to see her and glad that Dan was going to take her directly to the hospital from the airport. But her plane was delayed, and because it was late in the evening by the time they got to the hospital, they decided she should wait until morning to see Linda, who was already asleep. When Dan came out of the hospital with Angela Hope, Jennifer saw them through the car window and thought to herself how beautiful and how tiny her niece was.

Jennifer's twin boys took an immediate liking to their new cousin and fought to see who would sit next to her. As everyone was hungry and it was nearly an hour and a half's drive home, Dan pulled in at Tommy's, a hamburger palace in the San Fernando Valley that was a favorite of Linda's and his. It was a strange drive home for Jennifer, who in Samoa could travel no faster than twenty-five miles per hour. As Dan zipped along the freeway, she kept putting her foot to the floor, as if she had a brake.

When Jennifer walked into Linda's room the next morning, the first thing she thought was how real this all was now. Her immediate sense was of seeing but not believing. There was her older sister, desperately ill, and only she could save her. They gave each other a big hug and kiss and began talking almost nonstop.

They had not seen each other since before Linda's chemotherapy. Still, Linda looked physically all right except for her loss of hair; she took off her wig to show Jennifer how she really looked. Over the years her hair had varied from short to shoulder-length brunette. Now it was wispy brown.

Linda was animated and full of cheer as she tried to assure Jennifer that everything was fine. But Jennifer was not convinced. She was terribly sad as she looked at Linda; her stomach felt as thought it had been suddenly emptied by a suction drain. She didn't argue with Linda's cheer, however. She tried instead to see things the way Linda wanted her to see them, because she had total faith in her. Linda had never steered her wrong before, she thought, and she remembered that it was Linda who had held the family together after her leukemia had been discovered. Her matter-of-fact manner, her nothing-has-changed air, was typical of her behavior in difficult times. She marveled that Linda had been able to make even leukemia sound somewhat positive by the determination she showed in talking about how she was going to go after it. She also knew that this was no false bravado on her part. It was how Linda coped and how she overcame obstacles.

They talked very little about the transplant. Rather, Linda told Jennifer all about Angela Hope, and Jennifer recounted her adventures in Samoa. It was an easy conversation between two friendly sisters. In the afternoon, Jennifer had a chest X ray and her blood pressure was checked in preparation for the operation the following Wednesday to extract some of her marrow for Linda's transplant.

Richard Champlin is the middleman of the 10 West co-directors. Bob Gale looks after the bulk of the administrative duties. Winston Ho runs the pheresis unit, where blood cells are gathered from donors. Champlin spends the most time on the ward. He is a tall, erect man with thick, sandy-colored hair and a reserved manner that can be misleading. He has a good sense of humor that is even dryer than Gale's. Comparisons to Gale are appropriate, because Gale, four years Champlin's senior, has been his mentor over the past several years. Now, however, he is coming into his own.

He was graduated from Purdue University in 1971 with a degree in engineering, although he knew by then that engineering was not for him. He had become disillusioned with large corporations—the usual place for an engineer to work—after he spent his summers working for a manufacturing company.

He found himself in a room with fifty other engineers who watched the clock with one eye while working on little projects that offered no flexibility and no influence on one's career. He thought medicine would be more fulfilling and so entered the University of Chicago medical school, where he was graduated with honors in 1975. He attributes his high marks to the very few distractions there are in South Chicago. "You can't do much but study or be mugged," he said one day. When an opportunity to do his internship in California arose, he took it. Like Gale, he is an avid runner—the two of them run together most days—and the notion of "being able to run outside in January and not worry about penile frostbite" appealed to him.

His interest in hematology and blood diseases began in medical school. Bone marrow transplantation was a new field then, and both it and its pioneering quality interested him. In 1978, after a year's residency at UCLA that included a month on 10 West, he applied to be a fellow in hematology and oncology at both UCLA and the Fred Hutchinson Cancer Research Center in Seattle. Seattle does more transplants than any other center by far, and after he weighed going there and working with twenty other doctors against staying at UCLA to work with only Gale and Ho, he chose UCLA. It has turned out to be a happy choice. Gale and Champlin complement each other and have co-authored papers on many of their research projects. Along the way, Champlin married, and he and his wife have two children. He is also an assistant professor of medicine at UCLA.

It was Champlin who went into Linda's room after Jennifer returned from her X ray and tests to review with Jennifer what was going to happen in the transplant.

"We'll give your sister high doses of radiation and drugs," he told Jennifer. "If we did not give her a bone marrow transplant after that she would die, but your fresh marrow cells will restore her system. For you it involves being in the hospital three days. On Tuesday we'll take some X rays and blood tests to make sure everything is okay. On Wednesday we'll do the operation. Taking one bone marrow sample is no problem. We do it all the time. But we're going to take a hundred from each side of the two small punctures we'll make over your hips, and that's a little much to ask without a general anesthetic. We'll take out close to a liter, which amounts to 10 percent of your bone marrow. The operation will last about two hours and will not disfigure you. There will be a tube in your trachea for air during the operation. You'll be up and around in the evening and discharged the next day. You'll have a charley horse-like pain for a few days or a week. No donor has had a serious reaction as yet.

"There are risks, however," he continued. "Anytime someone is given a general anesthetic there can be an idiosyncratic reaction to the gases. It could be fatal, but we've never lost a donor. Nothing is free in life. We go over everyone very carefully before we operate, but you need to be aware of what you're getting into. Okay?"

"Okay," Jennifer said easily.

She and Linda had lunch in Linda's room and chatted until dinnertime, when Jennifer went home to tend to her boys.

Now that Jennifer was safely in Los Angeles, the two doses of chemotherapy in preparation for the transplant would be given the next day, Saturday, and on Sunday. Monday would be a day of rest, and on Tuesday night Linda would receive the massive dose of radiation that would wipe out her marrow. The transplant would take place a few hours after the marrow was extracted from Jennifer on Wednesday morning. Jennifer would check into the hospital before the radiation began, a standard procedure. No one wants to risk having a donor accidentally run down by a bus when she is the only person who can save a patient's life.

On November 8, Linda was given her first dose of Cytoxan. A

nurse stays with the patient for the hour or so it takes for the drug to be given, and Linda's nurse that day was Jeanette Leslie. Linda had met many of the nurses on the ward over the past days, but there had never been time for an extended conversation.

"I look forward to this time as a chance to get to know the patients a little," Jeanette said in the hall before going into Linda's room. She is a tall, slender woman with long, curly black hair and a huge smile.

It was a sunny day, and Linda was in a sunny mood, or at least as sunny a mood as one could be in when facing the several hours of discomfort and nausea that almost invariably follow a Cytoxan treatment.

"I'm going to check your vital signs every fifteen minutes, because this can cause a sudden reaction," Jeanette told Linda as she connected the bottle of Cytoxan to the Hickman and a liter bag of saline solution to a catheter in her urethra. "Your face may get a little tingly, and you could get nauseated right away, although that doesn't usually happen for several hours."

"Can this cause fluid to collect in the lungs?" Linda asked as Jeanette opened the tube and the fluid began to flow into her.

"It can."

About thirty seconds passed. "Okay, I'm not sick yet," Linda said with a laugh.

The saline solution was set to pass through the bladder at a rate of one liter per hour. Cytoxan passes through the bloodstream at full strength but needs to be diluted when it reaches the bladder to prevent cystitis, a severe bladder inflammation. Jeanette asked Linda if the catheter in her urethra was causing any discomfort. The line from it was hooked over the bed rail to assure that a little fluid was always in the bladder. Linda said she felt fine.

"There's a wide range of reaction to catheters," Jeanette told her. "Men find it harder and have more trouble than women, in part because men have longer urethras and the trigone muscle sometimes has spasms from the trauma of insertion. Also, some men are embarrassed to talk about it. I kept checking with one patient to see if he was comfortable. He kept saying yes. Finally he said with some shyness that he felt like he needed to urinate. It turned out that very little had been flowing out over the bed rail and that about a liter was in his bladder."

Linda smiled and told Jeanette about her nine days in labor and her sense of constant discomfort. "I kept asking myself, Am I going to stay in control? Am I going to blow it? I never did." She recounted the story of the screaming woman who would take nothing to ease her discomfort because she was a Lamaze patient, and they both laughed.

"Do you have any questions about what will happen in the next few days?" Jeanette asked.

"Any sickness I have will be pretty much over by the time I go down for total body irradiation on Tuesday, I think," Linda said. "I wasn't afraid at all until the doctor came up and talked to me about it. It sounds like a real bizarre thing."

"It's not really that bizarre," Jeanette told her. "You can even take a tape deck with you to help pass the time. It's just a big room with a machine. You lie on a table, and they turn you a couple of times during the experience."

"Experience!" Linda exclaimed.

"Treatment, what have you," Jeanette replied quickly.

"The doctor said I could have a Valium," Linda said. "I said, 'You mean I have to be sedated?' He said, 'Some people do it to relieve the boredom or anxiety of lying still for two and a half hours.' I said, 'Hey, I was strapped into a bed for nine days.' Then he said that three out of ten don't have nausea."

"I think it's less troublesome than Cytoxan," Jeanette said. "What happens is that bone marrow cells, white cells, and the hair follicles on your head divide the fastest. During that stage of division is when they're traumatized by the radiation. Also, the cells in your GI tract are damaged, and they respond by making you feel nauseous. On top of that, anxiety creates more nausea."

"Is that why the marijuana works?" Linda asked. (In 1979, UCLA and several other hospitals began participation in a government-sponsored experiment on the effects of marijuana in reducing nausea in chemotherapy patients. Prior to that, 10 West doctors and nurses turned the other way when they encountered patients smoking it for relief.)

"No one seems to know yet. It can help you over your nausea without making you feel sleepy, but it also makes you high, and some people don't like being high."

Just then, Linda's lunch was wheeled in, to the surprise of both of them. It was a steak sandwich with tomatoes and avocado on the side. Jeanette shook her head and said, "I can't believe they brought this in."

Linda looked at the plate and said, "I know I shouldn't eat, but the tomatoes and avocado are just calling me." She took a couple of small bites.

"I can't believe they brought lunch," Jeanette repeated. "We'll talk about nausea later."

The lunch was put aside, the treatment continued smoothly, and after more small talk Linda said to Jeanette, "I could never help somebody through this. I could never be a nurse here."

Jeanette said nothing as Linda looked out the window for a moment, then continued. "I really wish this hadn't happened. It didn't fit into my life plan. I thought I'd go on living forever." She turned to Jeanette. "I think I'd get really sick of being around sick people."

"Look at you," Jeanette said. "I'm getting to know you and you aren't always sick."

Linda brightened. "Couldn't we just have had lunch?" They both laughed, then were quiet for a moment. Jeanette picked up the conversation. "We just go through this together here to help you through a decision you've made. We have to be sensitive. We can't joke with some people as much as we have with you. But we have to treat everyone as though he or she were a normal person."

Linda raised her eyes to the ceiling and then quickly looked at Jeanette. "A normal person. You don't know how important those three words are. After I found I had leukemia I really faced—I could see it—re-al-i-ty. This is it. Before, it was wash the clothes and clean the bathroom and you don't have to deal with it. Then you drive up here and see UCLA Medical Center, and you walk through the door—it's like I had the weight of the world on my shoulders when I walked in, like somebody put a lead coat on me. I can stand it for now because I feel it will get better. I couldn't stand it for twenty years, but I can for now. Still, you feel cheated. Then you hear about a bone marrow transplant and you think, 'A miracle!' "

"For fifty percent it is."

Linda was pleasantly skeptical. "I thought it was sixty percent?"

"Eighty percent go home."

Linda continued along the same pleasantly skeptical line. "If I knew it was only fifty percent . . ."

They both laughed, then she went on. "There are worse ways to go. An uncle of mine was in a terrible motorcycle accident and was in a coma for months before he died." She paused a moment. "I don't want to live on life-support systems. I'd rather die." A minute or two passed. "When I walked through the doors of the hospital, a cloud just moved over me. Death."

Jeanette talked a bit about Elisabeth Kübler-Ross and her study of death, of it being part of life, and of the five stages she identified that patients go through—denial, anger, bargaining, depression, and acceptance. Linda said she was familiar with the book.

"The ones who are left behind are the ones who really suf-

Eric Lax

fer," she said. "The thing that hurts me the most is the baby. This will be decided for me pretty quickly. If I go, she'll never know who I was. She'll hear about me but never know how I felt about her. That's what hurts the most. As for my husband, he's known me, and he'll remember. And you know what's really strange? I can accept the idea of another woman being with my husband but not of another woman being with my baby—because *I* want to be there."

"You mean you tried a long time?" Jeanette asked.

"No," she chuckled. "Just once. I just said, 'This is the day.' "

When the infusion of Cytoxan was nearly completed, Jeanette went over some of the things Linda could and couldn't do for a while. "You won't be able to brush your teeth," she explained, "because when your platelets get low, clotting is diminished, and we don't want you cutting your gums. So we have some Toothettes, which are little sponges on lollipop sticks, and you can use hydrogen peroxide and water. But you have to clean your mouth four times a day. We'll really bug you about that. There is bacteria in the mouth that we don't want to get in the blood. As for things you want, because we're each responsible for only two patients, you'll find we can cater to many of your whims."

Linda grinned. "This is really uptown," she said.

After the treatment was finished, Jeanette stood in the hall and said of Linda's showing open concern for the first time, "That was on the border of what I can handle. That was a therapy session, and I'm not a therapist. I only know what I know, and sometimes it's hard to know what to say. My hands were sweating."

Later that afternoon, Linda lay in bed. It had been over an hour since the Cytoxan treatment, and she had shown no side effects.

"You know," she said, "before this happened and before I had the baby I thought my career was the most important thing in the world. It was the first thing to go out the door. I've already achieved all I wanted. I don't know that I want to go higher up the corporate ladder. It's not worth the price to advance at the expense of my family. I don't feel so driven by career motives as I used to. My obstetrician—he's older, with white hair and all—said, when you get to a certain age and look back on your life and ask what's important, it's your family. Not the money, which is spent, or the Mercedes, that's rusted away. I remember saying to my husband when he called to say we had to go to the doctor [who had just discovered her leukemia], 'I can't go to the doctor now, I'm in the middle of a project.' " She smiled a bit. "There was a very dramatic turnaround that day I found out about the leukemia. Years of one goal, one motive, one ambition, just gone. Originally I wanted to be the assistant controller. Now I'm supposed to be the next controller. Six months ago I would have said, 'Yeah! yeah! yeah!' Now I don't know if I'm willing to make that commitment. And money. Now it seems so unimportant. I make $10,000 more a year than a bookkeeper. But take off taxes and the nice clothes you have to wear—shoot. What do I get out of it? Five thousand maybe, for all the commitment and time it requires. When you get to be management, you live and breathe the job continually. After this, I'll do the job and do it well. But I'm not going to be a twenty-four-hour employee anymore. The job is not the whole thing."

She looked out the window again at the clear, balmy California day. "I really don't think I'm going to die," she said. "If it comes down to that, I'm going to be surprised. I know it's a possibility, but I'm different." She laughed. "It's not going to happen to me. But there is just the fear that maybe I will, maybe I'm not so special. Yet there are just so many things that have happened that maybe I believe that things go the way they're supposed to go—fate, or what have you. I could have died in the labor room. I could never have had the baby. That's why we named her Angela Hope. I just can't believe that I've come this far to lose it over a bone marrow transplant." She smiled and said, "I just hope my sister is more compatible with me than she seems."

Every patient who comes to 10 West comes there in hope, and it is hope that sustains them during the ordeal of a transplant. For the doctors, one of the best sources of hope is the slides of a patient's bone marrow aspirate that they study. Much of the technique of bone marrow transplantation is the result of pure science, but the doctor's daily life requires them to temper science with art, because science alone isn't enough. Looking at cells on a slide through a microscope gives major clues to the health of a patient, but more is required.

For instance, one day Gale and two hematology-oncology fellows were gathered around a microscope looking at the aspirate from a woman one of them had just seen in the clinic. Something was clearly wrong with her blood, but just what remained a mystery for them to solve. Gale looked first, speaking to the fellows as he did and naming the blood cells he saw.

"Here's a myeloblast [an immature white cell]," he told them. "That's the first I've seen in her marrow. Also a lot of megakaryocytes [platelet-forming cells]. A *lot* of megakaryocytes." He moved the slide to a microscope with two sets of eyepieces, and one of the fellows peered in the other side.

"Maybe all she'll be left with is agranulocytosis [a loss of granulocytes]," he said. "Most are erythroblasts [red blood cell precursors], like in a textbook. Unfortunately, I don't think they're a sign of recovery."

Gale spoke again. "See all those red cells? Look down at those two huge immature red cells. One is dead in the middle of the slide. It should have lost its nucleus and be one third that size. It's a pretty extreme example. Her cell maturation is bizarre. It's not malignant; more like marrow injury by a drug or toxin.

Maybe she's a little better, or it could be a sampling error." He looked some more. "I see some granulocytes for the first time. That's encouraging."

When they finished, Gale and I went back to his office. Sometimes a slide is obvious, he said, putting one in the microscope by his desk and having me look at it. It had cells of several shapes and sizes. Normal blood. He replaced it with another.

"See how monotonous this is?" he asked. "All the cells are the same, not varied like in the other one. The normal heterogeneity of bone marrow has been replaced by a rather monotonous placement of cells. I'm not saying every one is the same, but 90 percent are of one type." Leukemia.

The point he was leading to is that there are occasions when a diagnosis is clear but many others when one isn't, even if it looks as though it could be. He put in a third slide, which looked normal.

"Some of this is a matter of feeling," he went on. "I would like to say that it is a matter of science and that everyone who looked at it would say that the patient is in remission, but a lot of deciding whether that is true is having a feeling about the gestalt of it. I sometimes spend an hour or two looking at a slide. For instance, a patient I've just seen. A doctor who saw only this slide thought he was in remission. But I knew the patient and thought he was in relapse—a life-and-death difference. If I had just taken the report of the other doctor I would have walked into the patient's room and said, 'Good news!' But because of my suspicions I ran a test, and it showed he was in relapse."

Occasionally that mortal difference in what is or isn't on a slide affects Gale as emotionally as it does the patient. Such a case had just happened with a thirty-one-year-old father of two, whose leukemia had been treated at UCLA and with whom Gale became close friends. Hope was the one thing the patient had at the moment.

"He came to UCLA five months ago for remission induction therapy," Gale said. "He's an intelligent guy who knows a bone marrow transplant is the only reasonable hope. But after remission was induced we couldn't transplant him because his liver functions were abnormal. So we sent him home to recover. But he got there and he went bonkers. All he had on his mind was that he might relapse. Yet we couldn't go ahead because of his liver. Finally it got back to normal. He came back here planning to spend a couple of weeks seeing L.A. and doing things with his wife before entering the hospital, because he knew he could die as a result of the transplant. One of the first things he did was come to our house for dinner and say how glad he was to be here. But, unknown to him, five minutes earlier his wife had told me that his doctor at home thought he had found some blasts [myeloblasts, young white cells, an abnormal abundance of which could be a sign of leukemia] in his peripheral blood but had not told him. Well, if that's true, he's a dead duck—and here he is, all he's living for is a bone marrow transplant. It turns out that he was okay, but that was one of the worst moments of my life, I would say."

On Monday, November 10, there were mixed reports on the various patients. The Vietnam vet with the herpes infection had improved and would be released the next day or the day after. Another patient who had survived a bout with congestive heart failure a week before continued to progress. The fever he had had for several days was gone, and the question was what was really wrong with him. There were indications that GVH might be starting. Pseudomonas (a bacterium) was growing in his urine, but nothing else showed a positive culture. There was some sign that something was tickling his colon; even though it was not a classic indication, graft-versus-host disease was suspected. His Hickman catheter was also loose, and a culture would be made of the flesh around it to see what was up. GVH was also suspected to be the cause of the skin irritation another patient had developed.

A brief discussion was held about a new patient who would arrive Wednesday morning. Her name was Nellie Tapia, an eighteen-year-old from a small Arizona town. She had recently achieved a second remission from ALL, and the doctors wanted to be sure she was still in it, so she would have a bone marrow sample drawn as soon as she arrived.

Dr. Robert Figlin, the fellow whose patient she would be, said, "I'll say, 'Hello, turn over, I'll talk to you later.' "

The most serious problem was the twenty-one-year-old American-Chinese man who had had a transplant during the summer and gone home, only to return ten days before with what was now interstitial pneumonia. He had been in the respiratory care unit for the last three days, and the prognosis was not good. The air he was getting from the respirator was 70 percent oxygen, but the level in his blood was only 50 percent, a very poor sign (80 percent is normal). If he had been taken off the respirator in that condition he would not have been able to breathe for himself. He had recently been intubated—had a tube inserted through his trachea to assist his breathing. Janice Campiformio and Patti DeLone were particularly close to him, and each had visited him once or twice a day when they were on their shifts.

"He's still bright and alert and strong," Janice told the group. ("Most people who are intubated just lie there," she told me later.) "He's very frightened. He's not upset about the care, but he's very pissed off about what's happened to him."

Patti added, "A couple of days ago he said, 'People think we Orientals are very passive. *I'm* not.' "

As for Linda, she became nauseous about six hours after her Cytoxan on Saturday and then vomited about every five minutes for ten hours. She was asked by a nurse if she would like to smoke marijuana to see if that would help. Linda had never smoked it before and said she would think about it; she had always believed smoking pot was wrong. But after her second dose of Cytoxan on Sunday she understood medical applications are different from social usage and decided to try some.

The urethral catheter that is inserted for the irrigation of the bladder during Cytoxan doses remains in for twenty-four hours after the final dose to ensure that all the drug is flushed through the body without a chance to gather dangerously in the bladder. Thus Linda was still hooked up when I went in to see her at 11:15 A.M., after the doctors had completed their rounds. She was awake but drowsy from a recent marijuana cigarette. I mentioned that the reports of her every-five-minute nausea on Saturday sounded horrible, and she said with a small smile, "Yeah, but I felt great in between. The marijuana makes a lot of difference. I was sick only a couple of times last night." She looked up at the clock on the wall. "I can't wait for it to roll around to three," she said. "That's when they'll take the catheter out."

After I left Linda, two or three nurses were in the report room at the nurses' station, talking and working on the charts of their patients. Cheri Shilala, who is blond and pretty and has the most caustic sense of humor of all the nurses, was one of them. She was talking about a patient who had been in isolation for three weeks and who insisted on keeping the blinds drawn day and night, thereby shutting himself off from the real world and from real time.

" 'What are you going to do about the three guys in my room?' he asked me." Of course, there were none. " 'And the guy installing the refrigerator is making my right foot warm,' he complained. It turned out the sole of his right foot was against his left calf. It's called isolation psychosis," she explained. "It happens to someone like that who keeps the room dark and doesn't talk very much and has been in isolation for several weeks. In the ICU [intensive care unit], for instance, so much is going on that is meaningless that the patient can't even keep track of day and night. All the stuff is not understandable, and so he tunes it out. What makes a patient crazy, in descending order of severity, is perceptual deprivation, where there is a lack of meaning; sensory deprivation; and sensory monotony, like the Chinese water torture. A drop of water is no trouble. But the constant patter, that's something else. It also happens to some patients who can't stand the daily routine of isolation. There are permanent effects to the personality if the effects are extreme enough. With others, just a walk around the hall will snap them out of it. Usually within twenty-four or forty-eight hours after leaving the ICU a patient is back to normal."

One of the patients had been asking for a lot of pain medication recently. The nurses were careful to be sure that they were asked for it because of pain and not because it was a convenient, even blissful, way to avoid the boredom of recuperation.

"A lot of patients want to veg out," Cheri said. "I can understand that. I don't think I'd want this done to me. But the drugs are liver toxic. There are a lot of hazards to being drugged all the time. For instance, you don't use your lung capacity, and so you get a lot of gunk collected down there and catch pneumonia. Also, narcotics stop motility. The venous system can embolize and get all sludged out from not being kept sped up; good circulation is important. We're already doing things so toxic to the liver that taking more drugs adds risk of damaging it further."

To some, Cheri's easy argot might belie her technical and medical understanding. The fact is, she and Head Nurse Campiformio know as much about bone marrow transplants and treatments as anyone, most doctors included. Because of their experience and the amount of time they spend with patients, often it is the nurses who observe subtle changes in a patient's condition and alert the doctors.

"I was born and raised on the transplant unit," Cheri went

on. "No one really knew what they were doing at first. The nurses were the stable thing and still are. We knew from working and going through all the protocols [the various regimens tried on patients to find the most suitable for transplant]. There was a period a few years ago, just after we started, when we were changing protocols every five minutes."

Janice returned from another visit with the young man in the respiratory care unit. When she leaned over to talk with him, she said, he hung onto her.

"People don't realize how ostracized we were at first," Cheri said. "Even the other half of this floor [which is general private patients]. They kept talking about 'those terrible things you're doing to people'—but the people asked for a transplant. For a long time we were training those doctors who rotated through here because we were the only ones who knew what was going on. But you can't be a nurse at bedside and a policeman telling doctors their order is wrong and a patient's advocate and a comfort to the family all at once. When we tell people not to write an order and then leave the floor without checking it with us first, it's not being bossy. It's just, if a doctor is new here and he fills out the form wrong, the pharmacy won't send it and the patient won't get it."

In the beginning, the only people who were transplanted were people for whom there was no hope; all conventional treatments had failed, and the early transplants were what are called phase one studies, which determine toxicity rather than curability. The first question was whether the transplant would kill the patient, not necessarily whether it would cure him. That led to some horribly ill people being treated on 10 West, and few other people in the hospital truly understood how and why those patients were there. Years later, there are still indelible memories of the first transplant patients. One of the harshest was of a woman with a huge melanoma in her leg.

"I looked under her sheet and saw something move like earthworms," Cheri said. "There was a terrible stench, too. She had maggots in her leg. The problem was, I had to be very careful in my reaction, because the things dive if they're scared too much; they look for a vein so they can get oxygen from the blood instead of the air. They do that, and they go all over the body. Maggots are sometimes used for granulating tissue [making temporary tissue replacement in a wound], but her leg wasn't going to regenerate. That's what happens when you get into phase one toxicity studies," she concluded with a shrug. "We got end-of-the-line patients up here."

The talk shifted back to current patients on the ward, who were doing much better. One who was doing particularly well, however, was perceived by the nurses as wanting to do little to help himself, such as breathing exercises to keep his lungs clear.

"I've never seen such a wimpy guy about a bone marrow," Cheri said. "He's bored, but he won't do anything."

"He hides in the shower when he hears us coming," a second nurse added.

A third neatly ended the discussion: "He wants to be lobotomized." Everyone laughed and got back to work.

A few minutes later Dr. Richard Champlin went down to the fourth floor to see the young American-Chinese with pneumonia. After spending a few minutes with him he stood in the hall outside his room with the young man's father. The father held his wife's coat and purse while she stayed in the room with their son. The man had a fixed, friendly look on his face; he obviously trusted Champlin a greal deal.

"We're giving him all the oxygen we can and doing everything possible for him, but I have to tell you his chances are not good," Champlin said softly. "I know he appreciates your being here. He's very alert and doing well except for the lung trouble" (which is the curse of transplants; they can work, yet still a complication arises). The father said something about prayers.

"He'll have all our prayers," Champlin said. He shook the

man's hand and walked to the elevator to return to 10 West. He was plainly grieved.

"It doesn't look at all good," he said. "But others are doing very well, though," he added, naming three patients, perhaps reminding himself of the bright side.

The stress of working on 10 West becomes palpable after a nurse has worked three or four days straight, or, say, seven out of ten. After what might seem only a little time, they have often gone through immense professional and emotional turmoil, especially if it is during one of those periods when almost every patient is in great need and many are doing poorly. As for the attending physician (the doctors with overall responsibility for the month—usually Gale, Champlin, or Ho), by the end of the month he has begun to look ragged, too; for even though he is not there every minute of the working day as the nurses are, he is there much of the time and on call twenty-four hours a day. Occasionally, because of scheduling problems, someone will be the attending physician for two consecutive months. Such was the case with Gale, who at the end of one such stint appeared particularly worn out. The stress of two straight months is far greater than just twice the stress of one month.

Responsibility for the ward officially changes at 8:00 A.M. on the first of every month. I happened to have dinner with the Gales the night before such a change at the end of a nightmarish period in which several patients had died and the staff had been pushed to its limits. Before sitting at the table Bob and Tamar kissed each other as they do before each meal. Then he turned to his daughters, Tal, four, and Shir, three, and apologized for his many absences during the past two months. (I had been on 10 West for seven months by then, and Bob was more affected by his work than I had ever seen him. Two more beds had recently been added to the unit, making nine in all.)

"Even when he was here, he wasn't here," Tamar said. Bob

nodded. In part, she was right still. A patient, whom I will call Mr. Jenkins, had been Bob's responsibility for the course of his transplant. He had been close to death for some time, and the end seemed at hand. Gale was waiting for the phone to ring as he ate. It didn't, but by 9:00 P.M. he was scarcely able to keep his eyes open. He also could scarcely wait until 8:00 A.M. the next morning, when the burden could be transferred.

At noon the next day, a Saturday, he and the family were out by the pool, the girls drawing, Bob getting a little sun, Tamar showing him some clothes she had found for herself at a garage sale down the street. He appeared still a little dazed but also more relaxed than the night before, even relieved.

"The last two months were difficult, consuming," he said. "It's always this way. Attending is a twenty-four-hour-a-day responsibility at a level most physicians don't encounter in a lifetime—nine people, any of whom could die in the next twenty-four hours. It hit me at six-fifteen this morning. That's when Mr. Jenkins died. The final, official detail. When I acquired him he had just been transplanted. At the end of the first month he was within a day or two of being ready to go home. Then he developed a GI problem. I distinctly remember telling him, 'You and I are leaving together.' It turned out to be prophetic, but not as I envisioned it.

"We're locked into courses of action or direction," he went on. "Leukemia is a disease with a ninety percent mortality rate; aplastic anemia, with the ATG cure, has a fifty percent rate. Transplants in leukemia are fifty percent effective. It means that half your patients will die. If you knew which half they were at the outset, you could be at some sort of peace with yourself; it would be determined before they came to UCLA. Often doctors expect people with cancer to die. They don't maximize their effort. But with these nine, you go flat out. Physicians *try* to get them here. There's better care, I suppose—but also, at times the physician is correctly stating, 'I don't want to go

through this. I've done all I can, I'm turning him over to you.'
It's often masked by the notion that these people ought to go to a
specialized center. But the worst thing a doctor can do is be
afraid of a patient—or of death.

"We had a case recently," he continued, "where a doctor in
New York had alienated everybody at his hospital's blood bank
trying to support a patient of his we had transplanted and then
sent back to him; he had them working all the time, had everyone giving blood to keep the patient alive, and eventually he
had to have an out. In a way, we had to take the patient back
for him. And that was just one patient. Imagine *nine*. They
could eat you alive. It's different for me or Dick or Winston
than for someone passing through Ten West for a month. Although a fellow has a great personal stake as the physician responsible for the patient, he has no intellectual stake in the design of the protocols. In this regard, the loss of a patient is for
him a personal but not an intellectual defeat."

The second of the two months had been the most difficult, for
Gale and for the nurses and fellows. There were so many problems with so many patients that everyone was terribly taxed.
The nurses had complained often of burning out; their humor
had become grimmer (but more savingly funny). Professionally, the 10 West staff performed all their tasks properly and
well, but the team of nurses, fellows, and attending physician
had split into three camps. The nurses were mad at the fellows,
feeling they were not on the ward enough, and they were not
particularly impressed by the schedule Gale had been keeping.
He tried to put it into context, and to explain his role, while Tal
and Shir went to put on their bathing suits.

"It was a quiet first month, but that makes sense," he explained. "Deaths usually occur between days thirty and ninety
post-transplant. With one month as attending, you may have
patients die on you the whole time, but they weren't yours
initially—you didn't sit down with them and talk with them

and their families and explain all they would go through. On the other side, you could go through the month and leave with them all alive. It's in the second month that things can go wrong. That's why there's a breaking point. You can't have anyone attending on Ten West for too many months straight.

"So much of this is your expectations. You envision yourself as the composer and the orchestra leader in one. If you're out to cure people and you want full credit, you have to take the full impact. The nurses and even the fellows don't have to deal with that issue. They play a critical role in the orchestra, one without which nothing would work, and they take it as a personal defeat when someone dies. No one on that ward dies from poor nursing care. Still, someone has to write the music, and if it is a hit, great, we all share the praise. But if it's a failure, it was yours alone."

He summed up his position succinctly: "If you want to get the glory, you have to risk the defeat. If you try to get the big grants and succeed, you risk losing them." He shifted to the interrelation of nurses, fellows, and attendings, and his job as head of them all.

"The nurses are on one rhythm, the fellows on another. One of the fellows is on an upswing. The other day he came to me and said, 'I don't know where I was for eight months.' His understanding of transplants had entered a new phase. People are always on the way up or down. If the nurses sense an insecurity in a fellow and it's a difficult time on the ward, they may vent their frustrations on him. They demand one hundred percent of the fellows. They sometimes forget that the fellows come from a social environment, too; they may have marital problems, or a child who is sick. Alternatively, if a fellow makes an error or feels he may have, he may blame it on the nurses. Last night, one fellow the nurses complained about because he was not on the floor enough this week was involved in running a cardiac resuscitation all night. I sent him home. He was about to lose his mind. A lot depends on a fellow's point of view. If he sees himself as only another cog, he might just walk off the floor after rounds. It's not his baby in either victory or defeat.

"How different are everyone's perceptions of everyone else?" he asked rhetorically. "I could tell the nurses I'm totally drained. They could say, 'You're not there all the time more than a few months a year, but we're there *every day*.' But I see Jenkins go down the tube for sixty straight days. I lie at home sort of waiting for the telephone to ring. Or I walk off the ward to my office and face a continual barrage of calls from Washington, or other hospitals, or have to deal with fiscal or personnel problems. My first month was almost a luxury. I could avoid many of those calls and other concerns by saying rounds are sacred."

He came back to Jenkins, who was the last of several deaths in the past few weeks. Even one death upsets the 10 West team. A rash of them, which occasionally happens for no reason other than the way fate and statistics combine when there is a fifty percent mortality rate of all patients treated, sends them to and even up the wall.

"You take it as a personal defeat," he said again. "Actually, we went through the worst two days ago when we and his family decided not to intubate him." Then he shifted back to the nurses and his relationship with them. "This body-wrapping thing struck me," he said. (A nurse must wrap a dead patient's body before it is removed from the room.) "One of the nurses said, 'I wrapped two bodies last week. I notice you're here only two or three months, and we're here all the time.' You might think that wrapping the body was a relief, in a psychological sense," he mused. "The difficult part is over—the hope, the disappointment, the dying. All that's left is a final closing act. It made me feel that some of them don't really understand what Dick and Winston and I do. Some do understand how research is done, why a biopsy may prove to be of no help for the patient at hand but could help the next. But on the other hand, I don't know how the nurses take it, working twelve hours a day three or four days a week with these patients.

"Our system is built that way, though. Nurses take doctors' orders. They also don't get credit, unfortunately. When I wanted to reward the nurses by making them co-authors of articles, it turned out it wasn't a valued thing to them. There's no peer recognition for publications as there is with doctors. Nursing isn't built on those kinds of principles. I think that's a reflection on society, not unique to nursing. You have to view them in the context of what they are, not what they *could* be. Doctors live by a different set of standards. But these nurses are special. Typically a nurse is involved in direct patient care, not in making medical decisions. These nurses on Ten West are closer to interns. I would put our nurses up against the house staff of many hospitals. I'm sure they could do as well in a technical sense."

Tal and Shir came out in their bathing suits, and Tamar came over to sit down. She looked glad to have her husband home in mind and body again.

"It's very important to be thrown as an academic physician into all that has happened the past couple of months," he continued. "I have enough work to do in my office and lab without ever having to attend on the ward. You can do it like they do in Europe. They have chief's rounds once a week. It's a big deal. Or you can be there all the time for a concentrated period. But not both. Physicians in practice do it all the time, but not with this type of critically ill patient. You have to make the maximum commitment. What impresses me is the danger of trying to be a researcher without being a clinician, because then you don't know the quality of the clinical data you're getting from the ward. For example, recently there was a case of a guy with a rash. It looked like GVH, but we had treated the T cells of the marrow he received with monoclonal antibodies that in theory should have prevented GVH. If I had not been there the physicians would have considered the rash as evidence of the failure of the experiment, because it clearly looked like GVH. But the timing wasn't right. I had been there all month. I had seen the patient every day. So I did a skin biopsy. It turned out the rash was a reaction to penicillin. So we went from failure to success. But no one can be there twelve months a year."

He stopped for a minute and then talked about how as a clinician and a researcher and an executive he tries to balance the time he gives to the ward, to research, to nurses and families, and to himself. It is, he said, especially beguiling to spend a great deal of time with patients' families, particularly when the patient is in danger. "It's easy," he said, "to spend six hours a day talking with a mother who believes God wants her to take her son back to Pittsburgh. You have to become selfish at a certain point. You have to say to yourself, 'I'm going to go running.' Otherwise life goes by and you end up saying, 'What am I doing here?'

"How many world-class clinical investigators are there?" he asked, meaning physicians who are also researchers. "A few hundred. It's a rare bird, not fully appreciated. There's no Nobel Prize for it. I feel that it's as hard or harder to be an excellent clinical investigator than it is to be an excellent scientist. There are few harder things to do than a prospective, randomized, double-blind trial, where you give drug A or drug B to a hundred patients without knowing who's getting the drug and who the placebo. It takes five years of orchestrating a unit and keeping people from going crazy and trying to break the code. It's very demanding and achieved at a tremendous cost. You have to do it with your own two hands to really know how or whether it worked. At the same time, how do you do aggressive medicine without appearing uncaring? We have a human-subject protection committee; new protocols have to be approved by them. The committee has a lot of value, but then I go before them, a group of seventeen, many of whom are not physicians, talking about what is right and wrong to do to patients, and when I'm statted back to the floor I leave a conference on ethics to make life-and-death decisions that require immediate action.

"You have to balance your time in the lab with time on the ward," he concluded, mentioning one of his colleagues who had recently become aware of that. "He is spending so much time in the lab that he's losing his clinical sense. He knows he wants to recover his clinical skills. He doesn't want to give up on them." As for Gale, his clinical abilities had been tested every day for two months, and he was aware of the value of that. "When you're apart from patients you build a protective system, and it's useful to tear that away every six months, say, but not every day. Right today there's nothing that could walk into the emergency room that I would be afraid of. But in a week my defenses will be built up."

I asked him what he would do if he found that he had leukemia. Would he try for a remission and then go sailing or some such thing until he probably relapsed and died, or would he have a transplant, assuming he had a donor?

"Would I go off and have a good time or have a BMT?" he asked with a sardonic smile and a glint of humor in his eyes. "I'd have the BMT, because I don't enjoy having a good time, or I wouldn't be doing what I am now."

Tal, who had been listening to her father, asked him, "Are you happy or sad?"

"Happy," he said, with some surprise.

"But you have a sad face," she told him. Tamar nodded.

"He has nightmares," she said.

Once again he looked surprised at his family's observations. "Nightmares?" he asked her.

"He goes to sleep and wakes up an hour later."

"Waiting for the phone to ring," he said quickly. "If you're going to lie there waiting for the phone to ring you might as well go to the hospital and see for yourself. I don't have frequent dreams about patients. I do have scenarios of what we do every day, and I play those out."

Tamar mentioned a young woman who had died a couple of years earlier to whom Bob and Tamar and several nurses had grown close. "He went to her funeral," she said. "He stood at the back. It was one of the few he's gone to. It's so unfair," she added, shaking her head. "She was very pretty. Very nice."

"You get close to all of them, actually, even the un-nice ones," he said. "There are not many really bad people, and they're suffering so much. You have to respect these people. You can't envision yourself going through all that they do. You see them suffering, you feel sympathy for them, you see the strength and courage they have to go through this."

I left the Gales by the pool. When I looked back to wave good-bye, Tal, a frozen yogurt push-up in one hand, the other on her father's neck, was kissing him.

FOUR

In the afternoon of Tuesday, November 11, Jennifer checked into the hospital. She was put in a double room on the second floor with a twenty-year-old named Lisa, the mother of a six-month-old child. Lisa was to be the donor for her fourteen-year-old brother, who would also have a transplant the next day (although not by the 10 West staff. Children, whose leukemias differ from adults', are treated on the third floor by the pediatrics staff). The two were an incongruity in the hospital, for they certainly looked too healthy to be patients.

"The only thing that could stop us from going ahead with the transplant," Dick Champlin said, "is if she has suddenly developed leukemia."

At 4:30 P.M., Linda was wheeled in her bed down to the second basement level, where she would receive the radiation to kill off her bone marrow. All patients are moved by hospital escorts, who for one reason or another seldom arrive when they are expected. Linda's escort, however, arrived exactly on time. His promptness was in vain. The Catch-22 of escorts is that since they are usually late, no one expects the patients to arrive at their scheduled time for treatment. So the radiologists were surprised when Linda showed up right on time.

"Escorts are always forty-five minutes late," a doctor explained, adding that Linda would have to wait for a while. She was wheeled over against a wall, where she could wait more or less out of the way.

The radiation area consists of a half-dozen rooms off an L-shaped corridor in the middle of the medical center. There are no windows, and the walls are barren and institutional, although by the desks, which are in a corner near the treatment rooms, there are placid pictures and posters: one of dolphins; another of a sunset over a Japanese pagoda; a third of a forest glen with sunshine streaming through and onto a little pond. The wall of one room is papered floor to ceiling with a fall forest scene. Cutout letters are pasted above the doorways: WELCOME TO THE SIMULATOR ROOM, one sign reads. On another, arching over a porthole-like window that is blackened and bolted into a thick wall, are cutout letters that read THE COBALT ROOM. Linda was waiting to go into the cobalt room.

Dan had come down from the room with Linda and was waiting with her and with Janice Campiformio, who accompanies every transplant patient with whom she has a particular involvement for his or her total body irradiation. A doctor came over and asked if the bra Linda was wearing had any metal on it; bras are worn to keep the breasts over the lungs and thus give them a little protection. She thought it didn't, but on a second check it turned out there was some, so Dan went up to the room to get one Linda was sure had none.

"It needs to be without metal supports because the electrons will bounce off it and burn the skin," Janice explained. "The ribs are notorious for harboring leukemic cells. They, like everything else, will get a solid dose of radiation."

A few minutes later Dan returned with the bra, a smile on his face. Linda had smoked a marijuana cigarette shortly before coming down, to help control the nausea she had felt since the Cytoxan treatments.

"I walked into your room, and it smelled like Santa Barbara on a Saturday night," said Dan, who went to many rock concerts there in the 1960s and early '70s, as he handed her the bra.

"So *that's* what you were doing Saturday," she said back.

Janice suggested to Linda that perhaps she might want to use part of this waiting time to go to the toilet before the hours of radiation began. While she was gone, Janice went away for a few minutes. Dan stood around quietly for a moment and then echoed the fear of most family members of patients undergoing a transplant.

"It isn't the graft-versus-host disease that worries me so much," he said, thinking of what could lie ahead. "I don't think she'll get that. It's the viral pneumonia."

Linda returned, and so did Janice, with a bundle of linen.

"As long as you're going to be waiting, you might as well do it in clean sheets," she said. The bed was stripped, and a yellow tag on the powder-blue mattress proclaimed that the standard UCLA Medical Center bed was no ordinary one. This was, instead, a "Matiflex 9000 Hospital Mattress System. Featuring: Continuous Hinge Interspring, Anti-Static, Anti-Bacterial Cover, Resilon Foam, Permaroll Border, Safloc Handles, Coreflex Quilt Insulation System." Once the bottom sheet was tightly on, Janice spread another sheet, about the size of a baby's, across its middle.

"Certain traditions stay on," she said, pulling the draw sheet and tucking it snugly under. "It came into use when there was only one set of sheets a day for a patient. If the draw sheet was soiled, the large bottom sheet was still pretty clean. But now there are as many sheets as a patient needs, and it's really only a tradition to put it on."

When Janice finished making the bed, Linda climbed back in it. Dan leaned over her, talking softly with her, kissing her several times and stroking her head. She was understandably nervous about lying in a room and being bombarded with radiation and about what the long-term effects of that might be. Dan, who gets nervous when he has a chest X ray, was scared to death himself but tried to reassure her that everything would be all right.

The radiologists were finally ready for Linda. She was wheeled into the cobalt room and transferred from her bed onto a table along the wall. The room was bare and white. It had a high ceiling, and in the center of the room was the cobalt machine. It measured about eight feet by eight feet and resembled a giant sewing machine tilted on its side. The only other fixture in the room was a wooden cabinet for linens. Atop it was a huge pink and white stuffed dog that could have been won at a country fair. For children, someone explained.

The two radiologists taped a dozen or so inch-by-half-inch plastic sensors to various parts of Linda's body—behind the knees, on the wrists—to measure the radiation that passed through her. She was then put in a half-fetal position on her side, her back to the wall. Two meter-length sticks along the wall provided an accurate measurement of what the field of the radiation would be, which was indicated by a light from the machine, like that from a projector. Linda was positioned equidistant from either end of it. One of the radiologists asked her if she would like to be covered by a sheet.

"Yes," she said. "I get insecure if I'm not covered. I used to think when I was a kid that if my foot stuck out under the sheet, the boogeyman would get it." I noticed a bit of foot was still showing and pulled the sheet down over it.

Cobalt gives off high-level gamma rays, and the best protection against them is mass and thickness. The walls of the cobalt room are thus three-and-one-half-feet-thick cement. (Lead is best for blocking low-level radiation such as X rays because its atomic number makes it ideal against such electrically generated radiation. Gamma rays are thrown off naturally from cobalt and are released when the covering shield in the machine is opened.) Linda was to receive 1,000 rads—about the amount that, say, a person standing a few miles from the epicenter of a Hiroshima-like atomic explosion would receive. It is not enough to cause immediate death but is enough to cause bone marrow failure and subsequent death from aplastic anemia within two or three weeks.

A TV monitor by the controls outside the room showed Linda on the table. There was also a two-way microphone so she and the doctors could talk and so any sound she made could be heard. Because total body irradiation is simply a massive, lethal dose of gamma rays, administering it is not very interesting to radiologists.

"You just sit here and watch the screen," the resident who was overseeing the cobalt machine said. "The learning is done on the wards."

For the next several minutes Dan watched Linda on the screen without looking up. She was lying perfectly still in the position the doctors had bent her into, as she had been told to do. All Dan could think about was how totally isolated Linda was and how irrevocable her decision to have a transplant now was. He wished he knew what she was thinking as he said quietly, "I bet it's lonely in there."

Radiation poisons the human body because, during exposure to it, the body's quickest dividing cells are killed during mitosis. The cells that divide the fastest, and are therefore dividing during exposure, are those of the hair follicles, the bone marrow, and those within the gastrointestinal tract. Thus a person's hair falls out when he is exposed to large amounts of radiation, his bone marrow is damaged or destroyed, and nausea is caused by injury to the GI tract. To help mitigate the inevitable nausea that results, Linda was given 100 mgs of cortisone before being brought down from her room. The exact benefit of steroids is not wholly known, but it is thought that they produce an antistress reaction, one that the body cannot make sufficiently on its own, to deal with the physical trauma of radiation. She was also given 10 mgs of Valium orally. Additional doses of each were given through her Hickman during the three-hour procedure. (Medications given intravenously act faster than tablets, but they also pass through the system more quickly. Intravenous Valium, for instance, is gone within an hour.)

The radiation was administered in two periods of fifteen minutes, then two of an hour—front and back in each case. Linda began to feel nauseous by the end of the second fifteen-minute dose, but she managed to control it for a long time.

"I keep telling myself, 'Only five minutes more, only five minutes more, just hold on,' " she said at the end of the first dose.

While Linda was being irradiated, Jennifer was waiting rather impatiently in her room to have an electrocardiogram that was supposed to have been done hours before. Because donors are not allowed to eat for the twenty-four hours preceding the operation, both she and Lisa were hungry and bored with being in bed when they didn't have to be. A little while earlier an orderly had shaved the areas around their lower spines in preparation for the bone marrow withdrawal, and they were both laughing about it, mainly to relieve their anxiety.

"The lady who shaved me had hair under her arms and on her legs," Jennifer said. "She seemed to enjoy it and was very casual about it. I kept telling Lisa, 'Just wait until you get this.' "

"You know, they used to shave both back *and* front," Lisa said, and they both groaned.

Lisa talked a great deal about her baby, a six-month-old named Amanda. "Amanda Red Head is what I call her," she said.

Just then the phone rang. It was Jackie, who was home with her three grandchildren while her daughters were in the hospital.

While they talked, Lisa kept yelling for Jackie to bring Jennifer's kids to the hospital the next day. "Or if you can't bring the kids, bring in a wallet full of pictures." Jennifer finally had a quiet moment with her mother and Lisa said, "I just love little babies."

Soon Winston Ho came in to go over with Jennifer all that would happen the next morning. What he said was no different from what Dick Champlin had told her a few days earlier and what she had read on the form sent out by the hospital explaining what a donor must go through. He explained the procedure and the risks, and asked if she had any questions. Jennifer didn't, and signed the consent form for the operation, thinking to herself how comforting Ho's manner was.

At 9:15, Linda finished her radiation. The first couple of hours had gone smoothly, but all patients eventually become ill, and the radiation is interrupted to allow them to recover a bit from the nausea and diarrhea that are unfortunate by-products of the procedure. The last fifteen minutes of Linda's dose took nearly forty-five to administer, and during that time she had injections of 10 and 7.5 mgs of Valium through her Hickman. When it was all over she was put back in her bed and wheeled to her room. It was 9:30 by then, five hours after she had left, and the drugs and the ordeal had rendered her barely conscious. Dan stayed with her awhile. I left the hospital and went immediately to a friend's apartment nearby. I had been in the hospital for fourteen hours, and, looking at the lovely, clear night, I realized it was the first time I had paid attention to the weather that day. Even so, it wasn't much of a consideration.

"I need a drink," I announced when my friend opened the door. "I've just watched someone have a neutron bomb dropped on her."

* * *

When I walked into Linda's room the next morning she was sitting up in bed and feeling somewhat recovered, but she could not get the experience out of her mind.

"I was awake for most of the treatment," she said. "I don't think I fell asleep until the last little while. Things got real fuzzy then. The radiation bothered me more than the chemotherapy, lying there and listening to the machine going *rrrrrrrrrrr* and knowing that it's killing your bone marrow. It bothered me more than having the Cytoxan. Putting chemicals in you—even though I know it's not like penicillin—just doesn't seem as lethal as the radiation."

The irreversibility of what she had gone through dominated her thinking.

"Here I am going through this hellish decision in a valiant effort to save my life, so I will be here later on," she said with a trace of sarcasm. "But I worry, what will it do to me later? Will I die a horrible death twenty years from now? But this will be worth it. In terms of the baby, I think it will be. Nobody likes to think of some horrible death to face. There's nothing specific that I fear—like my bones will fall apart; just the fear of the unknown, that I'll have to pay some sort of price. Then I think of people who have cancers that are really painful, that eat them up."

She was silent for a moment. "Once I visited a terminal ward," she went on. "People were moaning, and they were sedated. They were just like animals. But animals are in a better situation. If your old dog has cancer, you don't sit around and let him waste away, you give him euthanasia and get it over with. I think everybody ought to have that choice. My situation is bad, but it has hope. There really wasn't much choice about having a bone marrow transplant. I don't like anything about it—being sick, being weak, being stoned out of my mind to make it through the day. But if it pays off it will be worth it."

She paused again. "Well, it's already worth it. Fifty years ago, I wouldn't have made it through obstetrics. I would have died in childbirth. I wouldn't have known I had leukemia."

As Linda spoke, Jennifer was being taken into pre-op. She had not slept well the night before, and shortly after she finally did nod off a technician had come in while it was still dark to draw blood and take her blood pressure. In part she slept poorly because she was away from home and in a strange place. But also, the reality of all she and Linda were going through was unavoidable. In the quiet of the night she stared out the window, waiting. As her mind wandered she could visualize her marrow uniting with Linda's body. It was, to her, as if their cells were at a party, clenching hands and hugging each other in happiness.

In the middle of the night she took a walk up and down the corridor, trying to relax. When the nurse woke her in the morning, however, all she wanted to do was sleep. As orderlies wheeled her on a cart to pre-op she wished she had been allowed to walk, or at least sit in a wheelchair. Lying on her back made her feel helpless, which was wrong; she was there to help.

In about an hour the operation on Jennifer would begin. In about four hours Linda would begin to receive her sister's bone marrow. For the time being, however, her body was on a direct course with death: Her own marrow was no longer producing blood cells. As she lay in her bed in that medical twilight zone she said, "From here on in it's the brink of death for three months. I'm pretty assured of living these three days of treatment, barring a heart attack. But after that it's borrowed time for three months. Things that seemed so important to me before, now I think, 'You could be worried about that?' "

Her thoughts returned to the radiation of the night before. "It was bizarre lying there in the room, but not that hard," she said. "The unknown is always the most fearful. If someone said, 'Okay, you're going to get graft-versus-host disease in two months and die two weeks later,' that would be better, just to know. It's just the weirdness of the thing, being locked in a room like that, the door clanks shut. Now there's no marrow in my bones. An empty shell. Mine will never be back." She looked out the window. "Radiation is also scary because I'm committed now and could be dead in a month. With conventional therapy I could have had much longer, at least for now. I feel cheated by this disease. But if I die tomorrow I couldn't say I didn't have a full life. They say you appreciate life more after something like this, but I think I've always had an appreciation of life. I used to drive a hundred miles to school, and during the drive I would look at the mountains and think they were something that man could never make. The light on them, the oak tree outside my house—they're all so beautiful."

She became less wistful and more matter-of-fact. "I am often curious to know what caused this. I once felt that the petro-chemical plant on the way to the Ojai valley did it. There's a feeling of death and doom to it. There was an explosion last year, and we were downwind of it. But I don't think that did it now. Then there are all the pesticides Dan has worked with. He'd come back with clothes reeking of the stuff. I'd wash my jeans from horseback riding with his. All that exposure. I wonder if that did it? We used to live in the country where you couldn't see another house. There was a two-hundred-fifty-acre field in the back and a stable. We had a huge garden, and I used to have some pesticides there. I wonder if *they* did it? Who knows from all those chemicals? But I'll never know, so it doesn't distress me as it used to. I think the doctors are right. The best thing is to find a prevention for it rather than a cure." She paused and smiled a bit and said, "I'd have been a whole lot better off without leukemia."

Linda's lunch arrived. A little soup was all she felt like having. I left the room and stopped by the nurses' station before going down to the operating room to watch the aspiration of

Jennifer's marrow. On the blackboard that lists each patient by room and details his or her status and treatment for the day, and where notices for staff meetings and other important events are noted, someone had written "Dave Scott Died 11/12 at 0100." Dave Scott (not his real name) had been a patient on the ward a year earlier. A nurse who had not worked there at the time saw it and remarked, "That's a terrible sign. I wish it said, 'Dave became the father of a baby boy.' "

In the operating room Dick Champlin and a second physician went through the final preparations for Jennifer's operation. ("Procurement" is the term the 10 West doctors use.) Jennifer was wheeled in by an attendant. She was conscious and calm. The anesthesiologist gave her an injection of sodium pentathol, which knocked her out in a matter of seconds; the last thing she thought of was how quickly she was going under. She was then given Halothane, which would keep her anesthetized, through a mask strapped around her head. Once that was done two attendants turned her onto her stomach. The top of her buttocks and the lower portion of her back were scrubbed with an iodine soap solution, then a piece of sterile, clear plastic was spread over the area to protect the skin from infection; it stuck to her like tape. The rest of her body was draped with sterile sheets.

The equipment needed for a bone marrow procurement is minimal, and it was laid out behind the doctors—eight heavy-duty needles, about five inches long (around the size of a ten-penny nail); eight syringes; a liter beaker with a small amount of tissue culture medium mixed with heparin to keep the marrow and blood properly suspended and unclotted; a 250-ml beaker with the same mixture for flushing out the needles after each aspiration; and two fine wire screens for filtering out any bone chips or clumps of fat from what is collected.

The doctors made a tiny puncture with a scalpel above each buttock to allow easy access for the long, wide-gauge needles.

143

Going through the same hole in the skin each time, they made about 100 separate punctures into the upper iliac crest on each side of Jennifer's pelvis. Each time they pulled out about a teaspoon of marrow and peripheral blood and emptied it into a liter glass on a table by Jennifer's feet. (They took so little each time because that is about all the marrow there is in one place; any more that was collected would be only blood passing through the marrow.) Two nurses assisted by flushing the needles and syringes after each puncture. Throughout the operation the doctors and nurses engaged in small talk: Where to get the best Chicago-style pizza in both Chicago and Los Angeles engendered a lively discussion. The nurses, however, were not very pleased about assisting in a bone marrow aspiration. They liked operations with more action and would have preferred a good kidney transplant. This was too tame. The conversation shifted to stories about surgeons (and underlying the nurses' talk there was the sense that doctors from the bone marrow transplantation team aren't really surgeons, who as a class are much more macho, at least judging by the stories). There was one about a surgeon who sliced his hand on a scalpel during an open-heart operation, bandaged it up, put on a fresh glove, and continued. Another recounted how two surgeons, in the middle of an operation, had an argument about the best way to proceed and ended up in a fistfight, the patient etherized upon the table between them.

It took forty minutes to gather 900 mls of marrow from Jennifer, about the normal time and amount. (It was about 10 percent of all her marrow. Her body would replace it in two to three weeks.) The entire procedure, in fact, was without incident. Midway through, the anesthesiologist had looked at the various dials and gauges he had to monitor, then shrugged and said, "Too healthy." While he turned down the flow of Halothane in preparation for waking her up, the doctors removed the surgical plastic from Jennifer's lower back and taped a pressure bandage over a six-by-nine-inch area of her lower back and buttocks. The tube that had been placed in Jennifer's throat to ensure clear breathing while she was under the anesthetic was removed, and within a few moments she was slightly conscious. Attendants then rolled her onto a cart on her back and wheeled her to the recovery room. Her first sensation upon waking was how cold she felt. She had very little pain.

Meanwhile, Dr. Champlin passed the marrow through a 200- and then a 100-micron wire screen to filter it, then poured the blood and marrow mix into two 500-ml bags for transfusing into Linda. The whole procedure took a little under two hours from scrubbing to dressing in street clothes.

Champlin brought the two bags of marrow up to 10 West, and Nurse Ellen Cummings took them into Linda's room. Nurses on the ward usually wear green cotton scrub dresses, but that day Ellen, twenty-six, who had come to the unit that summer, wore a white uniform. As she walked into the room Linda said to her, "Ah, my knight in shining armor has come to rescue me."

Ellen, who has curly dark blond hair and knockout blue eyes, explained the possible side effects as she hung the first bag on the pole beside the bed. "You could get a rash, or chills and fever, or shortness of breath, because this is a large volume of a foreign substance going into your system in a short period," she told her. "I'll monitor your vital signs every few minutes."

Linda gave me a look of mock horror. "My knight in shining armor has now scared me to death," she cried.

"Regardless of the side effects, you'll get the bone marrow, no matter what," Ellen went on.

"At least I won't die from lack of bone marrow. You know, you should bring it in here on a silver platter and on a white horse."

"At least I'm wearing a white dress," Ellen said with a smile.

Under normal circumstances it takes about two hours to complete a bone marrow transplant. It usually goes smoothly. Ellen gave Linda 50 mgs of Benadryl, an antihistamine, to help prevent hives and chills that might come as a reaction to the transplant, and 650 mgs of Tylenol. "You can sleep if you want," she said as she shot a couple of drops of marrow from the line to ensure all air was out of it before connecting the needle to Linda's Hickman catheter.

"Let's not waste too much of that," Linda said.

The transplant began at 3:15. At first Linda had no reaction, but after twenty minutes she started to cough and became tachycardic (her heartbeat quickened) and flushed. Her breathing remained unimpaired, but her blood pressure dropped from 120/70 to 100/50. Her pulse rose from 80 to 160. Her temperature rose slightly. The transfusion was stopped for five minutes, after which time her blood pressure had gone up to 120/50 and her pulse had lessened to 140. The transfusion was started again, but at a very slow flow. At 4:00 the flow was speeded up a bit, and Linda had trouble again. Champlin was called in.

"There is some fat in the bone marrow, and that sometimes causes trouble," he explained to Linda. He told Ellen to give her steroids if there was a further reaction but in the meantime nothing else. "It's possible there are minor differences between your blood and your sister's," he said, turning to Linda again. "If worse comes to worst, we can take out the red blood cells."

At 4:10 the transfusion was started again. At 4:20 her blood pressure was holding steady at 110/70. At 5:00 it was 120/70. Her pulse had dropped from 120 to 100. Her temperature was still a little above normal.

"You know that commercial of army boots tramping through the mud?" Linda asked Ellen. "My mouth feels like that. It's not the freshest mouth in town."

At 5:30 her blood pressure was 110/60. Because of her reaction and the resulting need for taking things slowly, the transplant was only half completed instead of being finished. Champlin checked in to see if there had been any additional problems and, satisfied with the proceedings, went down to the RCU to check on the young American-Chinese, whose condition had worsened. A tube was now in his nose for oxygen. He was bare-chested and surrounded by puffing respiratory equipment; the room echoed their muffled cacophony. The attending physician on the unit had scheduled a tracheotomy for later in the evening to help him breathe better. Champlin had earlier argued against the operation on humane grounds, not wanting the pa-tient to go through the trauma of another procedure. He felt the man's time was limited to hours, a day at most. But attending physicians on the various wards have the last word, and the opinion of this one was that the patient could last longer. Champlin, who has seen every transplant who subsequently de-veloped pneumonia, would have liked to agree with the prog-nosis but couldn't.

As we left the unit his face bore the same grieving expression it had shown on the day he spoke with the young man's father. "He knows what's going on," he said on the way to the elevator. "Usually they're quite sedated, and it's easier all around."

When Dan came in to see Linda at 6:00 P.M. she was still re-ceiving the marrow but without further complications. His first thought on seeing her was how tanned she looked, and he tried to figure how she had managed to get some sun; then, with a shock, he realized it was from the radiation the night before. When he walked over to her bed to kiss her he passed close to the bag of marrow, and he had another shock. His father is a meat cutter, and the scent from the bag reminded him of the way his shirts smelled when he came home from work. It was hard to accept that this reddish goop was the salvation, the mir-acle, that they were looking for. When Linda told him there had been a bit of a problem in the transfusion he had a sinking feeling; this was only the beginning, and there was trouble al-ready. But he kept his thoughts to himself, and he and Linda were talking about the radiation when Champlin came back to check on her.

"Did I throw up last night?" she asked Dan.

"Yeah, but you hit the pan. But you had diarrhea in bed."

"Thanks, Dan," Linda said with a playful glare. "That's what I've always loved about you—your class."

The transplant was completed at 7:30. Linda's blood pressure was back to a normal 120/70.

"You are rescued," Ellen said, disconnecting the bag the marrow had been in. "You want the bag as a souvenir?"

Linda looked at her and gave a weary smile. "No, I'll remember it fine."

On November 13, the day after her operation, Jennifer left the hospital. She would be staying in California for several weeks so, among other things, she could donate platelets to aid in Linda's recovery. She had been up and around a few hours after she woke up from the anesthetic, to loosen up from its effects, then had spent the rest of the day and night in bed. She was in mild discomfort, which was to be expected. The pain was somewhere between a charley horse and the aftermath of the caesarean she had undergone to deliver her boys. That, however, scarcely concerned her. More than anything, she was relieved to know her marrow was finally in Linda. She envisioned it, she said, as a butterfly flying to a flower. She didn't spend long with Linda before leaving for home, but it was a happy visit for them both. They each felt that now the worst was behind them. Linda had helped Jennifer so many times in their lives. Now Jennifer was able to return some help of her own. Her only concern when she left the hospital was the same as every donor's: She hoped that her marrow was good enough to save her sister.

Linda was up and walking around and in good spirits, too. She was introduced to a young man from Colorado who had

had a transplant three months earlier and had been released from the hospital a month before. He had come back to the ward to say hello after his weekly outpatient checkup in the clinic on the third floor. He was particularly happy because he had just been cleared to leave Los Angeles. He had become friendly during his stay with Suzana Raymond—she was scheduled to be discharged the next day—and the three of them walked down to the library-lounge on the floor for use by families and ambulatory patients. They were joined there by Nellie Tapia, the eighteen-year-old Arizonian who had checked in that morning. Each represented a very distinct period in a bone marrow transplant patient's course. The young man had successfully negotiated the procedure and recovery and the tenuous first month out of the hospital; his most immediate dangers had passed. Suzana had done as well as one could in the hospital; now she would have to go slowly and carefully, living at home without constant medical attention. It would be a psychologically difficult period as well, because it is the first time in months that the patient is confronted with leading a reasonably normal life again, complete with the attendant problems that have been put aside while in the hospital. As for Nellie, to the surprise and disappointment of everyone, she was not in remission as thought, but had relapsed. The doctors would have to try to wrestle her leukemia into submission for a third time before a transplant could be performed. Even so, Linda was the most medically vulnerable. In two days her white blood cell count would fall below 500 per ml (5,000–10,000 is normal; Linda's was 5,000), and she would have to go into isolation (meaning she had to stay in her room, although visitors could come in with masks on, and she could have no fresh fruit or flowers in the room because of the bacteria that might infect her) until her new marrow engrafted and produced sufficient cells to raise the count past 500 again. That usually takes about two weeks.

The four—at twenty-seven Linda was the oldest—sat on the sofa and in club chairs in the comfortable room and chatted easily among themselves in the intimate manner in which strangers who share an extraordinary experience can. The talk turned to hair. Linda wore her bandanna, some wisps like Angela Hope's sticking out. Suzana and the young man were completely bald. Nellie, who had been given chemotherapy in Arizona, wore a wig, one that she would refuse ever to remove during the seven months she would end up being on the ward. (It was so real-looking that even after she had been there a couple of months a nurse forgot the obvious for a moment and asked her what she had shampooed her hair with that morning. "Woolite," she answered with a laugh.)

Suzana said she could feel new hair growing in and added with mock indignation, "What got me is that two weeks before they discovered the leukemia, I paid sixty-five dollars for a California Curl. Sixty-five dollars!" She rubbed her scalp. "I was thinking of going back and saying, 'Look what you did to my head!' I might have got my money back, but it would have been cruel."

Over the weeks that a bone marrow transplant recipient is in the hospital he relies at one time or another on nearly every department in the medical center: the pharmacy, the operating room, the labs, X-ray, and the talents of various specialists, to name a few. But the blood bank-pheresis unit is arguably the most important and crucial of the lot, because fresh, healthy blood products are the difference between life and death during the weeks of recovery and engraftment. The pheresis unit is where specific blood components (red cells, white cells, and platelets) are collected from family members of patients on 10 West and from other donors.

Pheresis stems from the Greek word for separating. A pheresis machine takes blood intravenously from one arm of a donor, collects it in a bowl, and separates it into component parts by centrifugal force. Red cells, filled with hemoglobin, are heaviest and sink to the bottom. Next heaviest are white cells, then platelets. Plasma, the combination of proteins, minerals, salt, vitamins, and water in which blood cells are suspended, rises to the top. When about a pint has collected in the bowl, the nurse operating the machine draws off whatever component is needed, mixes the remainder, and transfers it by another line from the bowl to a pint bag with a small amount of anticoagulant in it above the donor's head. She then lets the blood flow into yet another line that feeds into a vein in the arm from which the blood was not taken. It is an almost continuous process that generally takes two and a half to three hours and seven passes, or bowlsful, to collect one bag of platelets or white cells. Apart from the discomfort of lying on a large reclining chair with a needle in either arm, the process is more boring for the donor than anything else (although family members of patients are grateful to be doing something to help). The only thing the donor is asked to do during the passes is to tell the nurse whether he feels any tingling, especially in the lips or face, which is an indication of paresthesia, a reduction of the calcium in the blood. The anticoagulant used to keep the blood properly composed binds with the calcium in it to prevent clotting and thus ensure unblocked lines. But too fast a return to the body lowers the level of calcium in the blood and interferes with the electrical charges of the neuromuscular system. Slowing down the return flow to a rate where no tingling occurs solves the problem.

While the pheresis unit provides a vital medical service, as do the other departments, its staff also has the unique opportunity to offer friendship and moral help to the families of transplant patients. On 10 West the nurses speak with the families and provide what support they can, but because the patients require so much care there is generally very little opportunity to spend chunks of time with family members. One thing a nurse doing a pheresis procedure has is time with the donor, who by necessity must lie still for up to three hours. It is the one place in the hospital where family members have the opportunity to talk freely about their anxiety and the difficulties they are going through. Perhaps because they are giving something from their own body for a loved one who needs it, family donors tend to talk a great deal about the patient. Thus the nurses must be more than just capable technicians; they must be able to understand the pressures donors face and be able to provide some emotional support as well.

A central reason that families of patients confide in the pheresis staff is that the nurses make the place so relaxed, both personally and in the unit's decor. The walls are covered with posters brought back by vacationing nurses, there is a color TV, and coffee and a comfortable chair are available for people waiting to donate. The nurses are efficient but they are also a pleasure to be around.

"Whenever someone leaves for another job, we want to be sure that whoever replaces her is crazy enough," one nurse said. "We're willing to laugh and we want to create a good mood. We don't disregard the seriousness of what is happening, but there is room for laughter. We don't want to be stoic, stonefaced people who are all business. Working here is not drudgery because we get so much out of it, and we try to pass that back to the donors. We don't want the unit to be a place of dread, a place where they come to have needles stuck in them."

The nurses' attitude is contagious, and family members generally look forward to going to the unit. Moreover, they sometimes anonymously donate blood products for patients outside their own family whom they have heard about or come to know. "Sometimes," a nurse said with a laugh, "their blood works better than that from the patient's own family."

The pheresis nurses also know the status of the 10 West patients, and many families look to them for signs of progress or setbacks they may not have heard about on the ward. When Dan donated, he felt he could sense how Linda was doing from the look on a nurse's face.

It takes a special aptitude to work on the unit, and even then the emotional skills take time to learn, as Patricia Williams, forty, the mother of eighteen-year-old and thirteen-year-old boys, learned. She worked as a psychiatric nurse and as a drug counselor before coming to UCLA, but even with that background she found that "it was initially hard because I had never dealt with sick people or death—one patient committed suicide, and that was it." She also learned the difference, in the opinion of the 10 West doctors, between the patients she had worked with and the patients she now encounters, who are in the hospital for a disease that is beyond their control.

"Winston Ho is a lamb," she said one day, "but when I told him I worked with heroin addicts, he came about as close as he ever comes to blowing up. 'They do it to *themselves*,' he said. I've learned to appreciate life so much more. I feel like I'm doing something worthwhile."

Still, the job exacts an emotional toll. "You deal with leukemia and parents whose children are sick or husbands whose wives are diseased," she continued. "It's especially difficult when we know a child is not doing well. A child once died while I had his father on a machine. I cried a lot the first six months I was here. It was Winston who helped me separate myself. He's totally unsexist, unchauvinist, and he's real kind to the families. Doctors don't always give families what they need. But Winston does. They suffer as much or more than the patients, and Winston knows it. He knows how hard it can be for us, too. I was going to resign after being here only a while. It was such a downer at first. He urged me to stay and told me how good I was with the families. He also told me not to worry about sobbing with them, as I did one day when a mother told me about the day she discovered her child had leukemia. When you're dealing with humans like this and react in a human way, that's okay. But you have to keep it so it doesn't take too great a toll. Winston is good at that."

The pheresis nurses, like those on 10 West, have to get close to patients and families, but not too close to too many. They become very involved while the patient is in the hospital and stay in touch with some who are cured, but they can seldom emotionally afford to do so after a patient has died.

"We keep contact with some families, but we have to be careful," she said. "Sometimes they call us. One family wanted to have a picnic for us after their daughter died. The daughter, who was in her thirties, asked her mother to put some money aside for a celebration of her life. She was ill for almost a year. She had no donor. When the time came, nobody really felt like a celebration, and none of us could go."

It is an occupational hazard that there are some patients and families who are so compelling that objectivity is lost. One such person was a twelve-year-old who had a great effect on both the 10 West and the pheresis nurses. Patricia was especially involved.

"I was really unnerved by his death," she said, her voice sad at the memory. "When he died I thought I was going to die. Winston talked with me, told me not to identify with the family so much. But he was the age of my son. I don't know that I could ever separate myself totally. The day he died I went home, and my son had a basketball game going in the living room. How can you get mad at that? He was so healthy and happy. I've learned to appreciate my own kids and my own life and my own health. I'm much calmer than before I came here. I haven't had a moment of self-pity since I started. I've learned what trouble really is."

I asked her how she felt when patients pulled through. She brightened and let out a sigh of relief and said, "When people do well—oh, that's wonderful."

The high regard Patricia and the other pheresis nurses have for Winston Ho is shared by the 10 West nurses. Of Gale and his two co-directors, Ho and Champlin, Ho, because of both his position and his temperament, has the best skills for dealing with nurses, patients, and families.

"Winston is the most caring person I know," Nurse Jeanette Leslie told me one day, "even in the little things he does. For example, at least every other Saturday he brings bagels or something in for us. When we thank him and tell him how nice a gesture it is, he tells us that he does it for himself." She paused and said sarcastically, "Sure."

Ho's personal history is exotic. His grandparents were Chinese who emigrated to British Guyana, where Winston was born in 1943. His father was an Anglican priest whose work was in the jungle and who visited the city, where his wife and children were, only a couple of times a year. As a student, Ho became interested in medicine in a country where the medical facilities were rudimentary and understocked with even the most basic antiseptics and drugs. He took his medical training in Israel on a World Health Organization scholarship and when he returned home, the doctors he worked with, recognizing his potential, urged him to leave Guyana not only for further study but to work in a country where he would have the resources he needed. He had married and converted to Judaism while in medical school, and so he returned to Israel. When he finished his residency he decided to go into hematology and oncology because there was no doctor in that field at the hospital he worked in. The place to study that was America, so he sent out several applications. How he ended up at UCLA and in bone marrow transplantation is a story similar to Gale's in its randomness and serendipity.

"I was thinking of going to Georgetown University because I was born in Georgetown, Guyana," Ho told me one day in the pheresis unit. He is a short (about five foot three), thin man with straight black hair, Asian features, an unassuming manner, and an easy smile. "But I came to California because I was told that the climate was like that in Beersheba, where I had lived for seven years. I didn't know anything about bone marrow transplantation. When I came in 1975, Bob had started the unit only eight months or so before. I was interested from the outset. There was no pheresis unit like this, but there was a leukapheresis unit for white cell transfusions. Bob was running the program plus doing what I'm doing. I took over. He was glad for some help while I was studying to become a hematologist."

Ho realizes the special position he holds. "All the patients who are transplanted identify me as being one of their doctors. All the donors know me" (which is not the case with other doctors, who don't deal with every patient). He continued, "We supply blood products, but our support here is more subtle. It is also very important. Donors are family members, and they relieve their tensions here. Upstairs the function is to devote time to the patient. For the two or three hours they are here, they can tell their fears and problems. But our nurses are very careful in not overstepping their bounds. They are not psychologists. Still, they do a lot of good."

As do the other doctors in the hospital, Ho wears a long white coat over his shirt and tie. Its side pockets are filled with a stethoscope and other medical paraphernalia, and the breast pocket has a two-inch-thick pile of colored three-by-five index cards, each one with the details and course of treatment of a particular patient for ready reference. One day I noticed that some of Ho's cards were for patients who had recently died. I asked him why the cards remained, and he just flashed an I-don't-know grin. But then he said, "Dying, you don't get over it. Every patient gives you the feeling of wanting to do the best for them. You don't want to give up. What helps us is the successes we have. We always use the term 'failure' when someone dies, even though the patient had a killer disease. But once we start to interfere, people die because of things we've done; we've interfered with the normal course of the disease. That particular death wouldn't have happened; they would have died of something else. I guess that's how we rationalize it. They died because we tried to prevent that. It's very difficult not to get intimately involved. There is a thin line between being concerned and being intimately involved. I'm there with every patient. You replace everyone who dies with a new one." But the others linger, and on more than an index card.

A few weeks after my arrival on 10 West I was talking with a nurse in the pheresis unit, where I had gone to donate white cells for a cancer patient with my blood type on the fourth floor. She asked me whether I had, as she put it, "been grossed out" by anything I had witnessed on the ward. I recalled the young man who had died my first day there and his autopsy the second day, but told her I had them in some kind of perspective. What had bothered me the most, I told her, was Linda's total body irradiation because I couldn't shake the notion that I had watched a neutron bomb explode over her. Yet I knew that however horrifying the process was, the outcome of it was the hope that a bone marrow transplant offered.

"I'll show you something," she said. "See that?" She pointed to a long, liter-size plastic blood bag hanging from a hook on the wall over a sink in a corner. It was filled with a murky, off-white liquid that looked like *café au lait* with an eighth-inch of raspberry sauce on the bottom.

"What is it?" I asked.

"White blood cells we pheresed off a CML [chronic myelogenous leukemia] patient in blast crisis," she said. "The red is from the few red blood cells and platelets that weren't removed."

I remembered the pint bag of my own white cells that had gone off to the ward a few minutes earlier. They looked exactly as white cells should look: a nutty gold, clear liquid much like a good beer. These looked like sludge, and the idea of them in a body was both repellent and unbelievable. They displayed the body's own betrayal of itself that is the essence of leukemia in a way no textbook description of the disease ever could.

"We took off another liter yesterday," the nurse said. "The patient is a twenty-five-year-old woman from Michigan, and there's nothing that can be done for her. Pheresing off white cells from the peripheral blood helps reduce some of the pain she's in from these cells packing her bones, but it doesn't help all that much. A CML patient in blast crisis has a white count up to two hundred fifty thousand compared with the five thousand to ten thousand that is normal. The white cells are so numerous that they clump together and block small arteries in the eyes, brain, lungs, and kidneys. The woman has had the disease for a year. She had spots before her eyes, which is a good indicator of the disease. But she had no other symptoms and was feeling good until a week or so ago. Then she went into blast crisis, where the bone marrow is so packed with white cells that there is excruciating pain from the pressure, like your bones are breaking. Also, some will accumulate in a joint, or in the skin, and cause a rash from their infiltration. It's a very ugly way of dying—hemorrhage or infection. There is no room for the bone marrow to produce platelets. The white cells cause a fever. They could infarct the brain like a stroke, or jam the lungs and cause pulmonary failure."

It is hard, even for a nurse who deals with the disease every day, to remain detached in the face of so clear a manifestation of a disease. We both stared at the bag for a few moments without saying anything, and I thought of Linda and the other patients on 10 West whose transplants offered at least a chance of escaping a similar death. The aggressive medicine practiced there fell into a perspective I'd not had before.

Then the nurse spoke, more softly than she had before. "The

hard thing for me," she said, looking at the bag, "is that this will happen to almost everyone who comes here."

Ho walked in as we stood there. I told him that this was the first time I felt I had seen a disease.

"You should see the patient," he said, and asked if I'd like to. I wasn't sure that "like" was the appropriate word, but we went to the fourth floor to see her. "This is a disease more often seen in older patients than in someone her age," Ho said as we walked down the hall. "A sixty-year-old man is the most common patient."

All that the nurse had told me was clear when I walked into the room. The patient was feverish and somewhat delirious. She was being given morphine to reduce her pain, which was considerable. On her chest and face was the rash from white cell infiltration—there were so many of them in the body, they were being forced out through any opening they could find. A month ago this young woman had been a graduate student. In three days she would be dead.

Dr. Ho stopped by the pheresis unit after we left her room to retrieve one of the bags of white cells to use in a lecture he would give to medical students. The bag was the size of a large salami. "There are about fifty billion white cells in this bag— five times ten to the eleventh power, or about one tenth of what's in the body. Today you gave about five times ten to the ninth power cells, or one percent of your supply," he said as we rode in the elevator. "It all started from a single cell," he added, and then shook his head. "It doesn't mean a thing. Numbers, numbers."

The doctors on 10 West, like most clinical researchers, endeavor to treat and to defeat human illness with an almost superhuman effort. Gale's daily schedule of starting before dawn and working until late at night is not only the norm for a clinical researcher, it is a prerequisite. The underlying philosophy of Gale and others like him is that people don't have to die from illness, that the workings of the body can be known and used to man's benefit. Psychologists use the term "rescue fantasy" to describe that attitude, and to a certain degree it is an apt one. But many 10 West patients are in fact rescued, and without the drive that is behind the notion that diseases can be cured, medical science would not have come very far. A successful clinical researcher is a complex, driven person, possessed of an inquiring, logical mind and goodly amounts of both hubris and chutzpah. He has the nerve and vision to believe, in Gale's case, that leukemia can be overcome, and the solipsistic attitude that a patient's death from the disease is a personal affront.

Doctors like Gale and Champlin and Ho operate on the frontier of medicine. The techniques of bone marrow transplantation practiced on 10 West have evolved in recent years from being considered highly experimental to being considered in many cases the treatment of choice. Still, much of what takes place on the ward is research, and Gale and his team must always weigh what is best for a patient against the research value that may come from a certain new treatment. The ethics of clinical research are no different from the basic ethics of medical practice: The well-being of the patients is paramount. The difference on 10 West is that where a doctor knows that insulin is the best treatment for diabetes, the best course against complications in a bone marrow transplant is still cloudy. What the doctors know is that they have a patient with a fatal disease and that their job is to do all they can to enable the patient to live.

In the past five or six years the federal government has mandated the establishment of human-subject protection committees to decide whether a treatment that has shown promise in the laboratory can be tried on a consenting patient. It is an idea with both merit and drawbacks. There is no argument that patients should be protected, but every responsible doctor protects his patients. The question is, who can properly decide what constitutes proper treatment? At UCLA, and at any other hospital where federal funds are used for research, a committee must approve a proposed protocol before a doctor tries it on a patient. It is a sane and noble idea that is easy to applaud but difficult to implement, and it is an issue that Gale has very strong thoughts about.

"What is standard practice and what is research?" Gale said one night after he had skirmished with the UCLA human-subject protection committee. "I guess the first thing you have to say is, are there standard practices in most diseases? To be so, they would almost always have to be successful. But cancer is something else. If a woman comes into my office with breast cancer, I might recommend a modified mastectomy while someone else would recommend radiation without surgery. But they are all research in the sense that we don't as yet know which is best. Or take childhood leukemia, where there is now a sixty percent recovery rate. We give cranial radiation to all patients as part of the treatment. But in maybe ten percent of the survivors there are learning and personality problems which are probably caused by the radiation, yet no one knows if cranial radiation is necessary in all patients. Except insulin for diabetes and penicillin for pneumonia, almost all treatment has some experimental aspects. It's not easy to define these terms. There are even variables for the same procedure. At UCLA, a bone marrow transplant is standard for people with aplastic anemia who have a donor, but at, say, Our Lady of Lost Sheep Hospital, it might be very experimental.

"The committee's job is not an easy one. They're trying to protect people, but if it is not a committee of experts, how are they going to know?" The UCLA committee, like others, is comprised of clergy, teachers, psychologists, and doctors, almost none of whom know the intricacies of bone marrow transplantation or of any other medical specialty related to it, such as hematology, oncology, or immunology.

"Generally the committee is made up of people of goodwill who are faced with complicated medical issues they're not entirely qualified to assess on their medical and scientific value," Gale continued. "Theirs is not an easy job. But ours is not an easy job, either. Just because a committee has the title Human-Subject Protection doesn't mean they're the exclusive defenders of human-subject protection. I would call the physicians, fellows, and nurses that. They're all there on the ward to protect human subjects. I think there ought to be some sort of oversight committee, however. What if someone said, 'I wonder if arsenic can cure cancer?' There ought to be a way to regulate totally inappropriate studies. But the problem is, how can a committee pass judgment on the scientific value of what a group of experts has determined to be appropriate? We have a division of twenty faculty members, only a few of whom have a personal interest in bone marrow transplantation. Ideas get generated, and we argue them out among ourselves. Can a committee of nonexperts improve on this?"

An underlying issue is that of informed consent: Does a patient know what the doctor is proposing to do to him, and has he approved it?

"No one in this society can argue with the idea of informed consent," Gale went on. "Treating a patient without it is assault and battery. The doctor should and must tell the patient all risks and benefits. This is not the case in most European countries, but we do it because we believe it is important that the patient know what he's entering into. But research that's been done shows that, in fact, patients usually don't understand all the information. Informed consent forms are written for people with a college education, and only about 30 percent of the people who read them understand them. In that case, consent forms have become a rite, not a right. A key example of this is an instance where women with breast cancer were put into two groups. Half took an experimental drug, half took a placebo. They were told in advance that this was the case, but no woman knew which group she was in. Yet, when asked later, two thirds didn't know they were in a trial. They said their doctors had put them on chemotherapy. Fifty percent of all patients say when they sign a consent form that it is because the doctor and hospital are trying to protect themselves, not the patient. If, as in the case of the women in the breast cancer study, there is a sixty-six percent error rate in comprehension, are we simply trying to clear our own conscience with consent forms? Do we do it so that when a patient who is just about to die of graft-versus-host disease says he doesn't know what's happening, we can show him a form he signed that says he knew the risks? Or are we just trying to cover against malpractice?

"We have a sheaf of correspondence between ourselves and the human-subject protection committee, in which they're constantly changing words in a fifteen-hundred-word document that are all legal considerations, not patient information. You get the distinct impression that they're protecting the hospital or the university. If that's the case, okay, but get a lawyer. Don't do it under the guise of informed consent. We're on one end. We get all these people who are terribly ill and need immediate treatment. The other end is a lawyer changing 'could' to 'might.' It is not the document that is important. It's Dick Champlin sitting down for an hour with a patient and telling him what can be done, and what are the risks and benefits. Committees don't protect patients, physicians do. A doctor who mistreats a case of pneumonia is more at fault than a physician who tries an experimental method as a last resort, with the patient's approval."

These issues are a major part of modern medicine. As Gale says, "Who shall comment? By what forces shall they intervene: Morally? Ethically? Fiscally? Who controls physicians' activities? Is it the patient/doctor relationship? The doctor and his peers? The hospital? Or the state, which holds the power to li-

163

cense doctors? Or is it the federal government, which has no direct legislative powers over doctors but does have the power of fiscal statutes; to get federal money you have to do certain things. All of these issues are as yet unresolved."

Life on 10 West was relatively calm in the few days following Linda's transplant. The Vietnam vet with the herpes infection recovered and was sent home to Phoenix with the understanding that he would come back for a checkup in three weeks. Suzana Raymond went home. The patient who had had the isolation psychosis and claimed to be seeing people in his room had improved greatly but continued to be depressed.

"He's clinically stable," Bob Gale said during rounds. "He's afebrile [without fever], on antibiotics, has some chest pain. I've seen him over the past ten days, and he looks better—but he's not convinced." The man seemed to be in a chronic depression, which contributed to his shutting out the light in his room. He had also developed the unfortunate habit during a bout of mucusitis of spitting on the floor rather than in a basin. But at least for the day, that had stopped.

"If he's not spitting on the floor, he's not depressed," one of the nurses said.

"He's a real hocker," another added.

It looked as though he could be discharged in three or four days if he kept on as he was, but the news didn't seem to thrill him.

"But I've got pneumonia," he told Gale. "A dying man can't go home."

The one unhappy circumstance was the young American-Chinese in the RCU. Janice came back from a visit with him and told the other nurses, "He's putting it together. He asked for all the nurses to come down and see him."

Because the tube in his throat to help his breathing took away his ability to talk, he communicated with nurses and doctors and his family with a notepad and pen.

"He wrote down that he's ready to die," Janice said. "He asked the doctor if there was any hope, and he said, 'some,' so he's giving it one last chance. The family wants to move him back up to Ten West, but a respiratory therapist would have to be at his bedside and that can't be done."

Nellie Tapia, whose leukemia the doctors were trying to get into a third remission so they could perform a transplant, had taken the news that she was not still in remission with equanimity and courage. The second remission that she had achieved in Arizona shortly before coming to UCLA had come at great cost to her; she had been in a coma for ten days from the chemotherapy and subsequent infection she had developed. She knew that she faced a difficult and painful treatment but was determined to succeed. Her donor was one of her sisters, who lived in New York and who had come to the hospital with her the day she checked in. She decided to wait in Los Angeles for a while to see if another remission could be swiftly achieved and the transplant done soon after. Meanwhile, her husband was taking care of their children. Nellie particularly enjoyed disco and rock 'n' roll music, and a tape was always playing in her room. While the doctors evaluated her case and decided on what treatment to undertake, she stayed dressed in street clothes, a cowboy hat on her head.

FIVE

While I was on 10 West I often wondered what life is like after a patient has had a bone marrow transplant and has gone home to begin normal life again. I met a variety of patients who had left 10 West as long as six years earlier, who were doing well in most cases and not so well in a few others. They ranged from a man who showed no physical signs whatsoever of his transplant, and who throws a birthday party for himself every year on the anniversary of his transplant, to a man who had developed chronic graft-versus-host disease. Although his life is not threatened, his skin has drawn exceptionally tight, causing painful cracking and flaking and arthritislike symptoms. Most people I encountered fit somewhere in between. Many had gone back to work but had minor skin problems, or continuing problems with regaining their appetite. In other instances, former patients have developed cataracts as a result of the high-level radiation they had to have to destroy their leukemic marrow. A concern of transplantation research is what long-term effects there will be from radiation and drugs. At present, transplantation is still too young a science to know.

The first successful transplants were done only ten or so years ago, and the effects may not become evident until twenty years post-transplant. Still, patients are aware that they were given the only treatment known to save their lives at the time and that without the transplant they would not be around to worry about its effects years later. As one with troublesome but not major side effects puts it, "It's better to have these problems than to be dead and have no problems."

One of the most lasting yet invisible effects is psychological and emotional. Several people I spoke with went through periods in which the enormity of what they had experienced loomed up.

"It plays on your nerves sometimes," one said. "All that you went through sinks in, and you realize that other patients who were there at the same time died. It makes you wonder, 'Why me? Why did I survive?' "

A former patient I grew to know particularly well was Richard Lee. He received his transplant while in second remission from AML, and a couple of things about him made me take an interest in his case and progress: He was thirty-seven years old, which is much older than the average 10 West patient; and his wife, Pam, moved into his room with him the day he arrived and stayed there until he left at the end of his treatment five weeks later. A year and a half after he left UCLA, I went to Jenner, California, a small town on the ocean a couple of hours north of San Francisco, to see how he and Pam were doing.

Richard is a tall man, six foot one, lean, with sandy-colored hair. Pam is of medium height, with bright eyes, long dark hair, and a high, soft, almost breathless voice. They live in a wooden cabin overlooking an inlet from the ocean, a home they have largely rebuilt and decorated themselves. There are beautiful stained-glass windows and lampshades that they have made, and textile crafts done by Pam. Their lives today are placid and almost rustically idyllic, the result, it turns out, of what they learned from Richard's leukemia and transplant.

"We were on different tracks before," Richard explained over a dinner that included his special homemade french fries, which he has every day. "I was moving up at the company I worked for and at thirty-five felt it was time to buckle down. Pam wanted a performing career. My company was in Berkeley, which was fine for me, but Pam had no opportunity there. Her idea of success conflicted with mine. The leukemia ended that. It yanked us both off our separate paths and put us on one together."

His leukemia struck with different symptoms than Linda's, but the result was the same. He had a fever every afternoon and chest pains that were first diagnosed as a transitory pulmonary embolism. Several specialists examined him during a diagnostic stay in a hospital but couldn't decide what his trouble was. Finally a hematologist took a look and diagnosed the leukemia within the hour. There were no normal cells that she could see on his blood slide. The disease was so advanced he could have died that day. She had never had to tell a young person that he had leukemia, and she paced in front of Richard's door with a nurse for some time, wringing her hands, wondering how to tell him. Finally she decided on a direct approach. Richard, who had no inkling that whatever he had might be fatal, greeted her easily.

"You have leukemia. You will probably die within four weeks if we don't treat it immediately," she told him. Then the nurse gave Richard a shot of Valium as he stared at the doctor in amazement. He and Pam had no children, and his first thought was to go to Los Angeles and make a deposit in a sperm bank. The doctor thought that was a terrible idea.

"You can go to L.A. and put your sperm in a bank and most likely die, or you can start treatment," she said.

Richard tried to make the decision about what to do on his

own, but it was hard. "I was adamant that this was my body and that the disease was my cross to bear, that I was going to make the decision," he explained. "But there was so much pressure from my family and Pam to take the chemotherapy. I was let out in the afternoon to go home and tell my family, but I had to be back the next morning to start."

Unlike Linda's case, the first course of chemotherapy did not put his leukemia into remission, and a second was required. In addition, he had to have consolidation therapy for ten or fifteen days every three months for a year. But secondary infections developed each time, and he was in the hospital for nearly five months of that year. Pam spent every day and night there with him, often over the objections of the staff.

After being in remission for two years he became concerned about the odds he faced. He knew he was in a very select group of survivors. He had had a bone marrow exam every three months that showed he was still in remission. Then came the result he knew would have to come. Fortuitously, it came while he was at UCLA, looking into the possibility of a bone marrow transplant. Winston Ho took one look at his slide and wasted no words: "Mr. Lee, there's nothing we can do for you. You're not in remission, and you must be to have a transplant." He suggested that Richard start chemotherapy the next day. Richard said he wanted time to think about whether he wanted to go through the chemo again and have a bone marrow transplant. Ho said he could have two weeks at most, and added, "Left untreated, you have an automatically fatal disease. There has been no such thing as a spontaneous remission. I can't tell you how long you have, whether it will be a year or next week."

Richard and Pam went on a fishing trip to think things over. It was a hard choice for him to make. "I had no physical symptoms like the first time, so I didn't want to do it, or even go through the chemo. I had to go through a rational exercise to see things clearly—you have to do this torture if you don't want to die."

Pam added, "I told him, 'You can decide whatever course you want; it's your body and your choice. But don't die.' " They both laughed.

The time Pam spent with Richard on 10 West was extraordinary even by the standards of the ward, where family members or spouses are encouraged to stay with patients, and it allowed them to adapt to Richard's illness and the effect of it on their lives in a more comprehensive way than most couples do. They talked about that after dinner, sitting near the late 1890s Beckwith cast-iron fireplace that serves as the house's heater.

"Pam was with me every night in the hospital from the time of the diagnosis," Richard said with admiration and a trace of amazement. "I would want to do the same for her, but I don't know if I could. I do know that she's taken years off the time she'll have to spend in Limbo."

Pam, who is, at least outwardly, always cheery and optimistic, said, "I did lots of handcrafts and beadwork; I designed sweaters. I tried to get him involved."

Looking back, Richard saw why, even if he didn't at the time. "It seemed only like one more thing she wanted help with. I was feeling very sick and wanting to lay back and say leave me alone, and she wouldn't let me."

"He has a good brain, and he needed to use it," Pam said with a shrug. "Plus there was something else that is really important. This might sound funny, but without the leukemia I don't think I would ever have known how much Richard loved me. I have divorced parents, and not ever having a loving home life, I didn't know what it was. Richard always took the opportunity to tell me he loved me. I think in the hospital I finally believed it. I never could before."

"Just because I stayed alive when she asked me to," Richard said, and they laughed again.

Pam continued. "Most people don't get the opportunity to know the depths of that kind of love. It turned my whole head around. I could spend so much time with Richard because he never was a complainer. He believes that complaining doesn't make you feel better. It made it easy to be around him, to take care of him. It was sharing the load. What he was going through was so catastrophic, and I loved him so much, there wasn't anything else for me to do."

"She said, 'I knew if I was standing there, you wouldn't die,' " Richard added.

"It was totally selfish on my part." She paused and then said, "I became very attached to his toes. They've always moved independently of his body. When he was out, I'd squeeze his toes."

"Pam knew as long as they were wiggling, I was all right," Richard said. "Sometimes I was so sick and nauseous I didn't want to be kissed or hugged or to be touched. But she always had my toes. I spent at least nine months in the hospital over a period of four years. I blanked out a lot of this. There's a tendency to bury it. If you don't think about it, it seems it happened to someone else. There's no way to go through a life-and-death experience and come out of it the same."

It is precisely that notion of life not being the same after a bone marrow transplant that contrasts with the idea of living a normal life. Life for a transplant recipient can be normal in terms of a functioning body and the ability to work, but it is never wholly the same afterward for any of them. Life before was something to be taken for granted. Life afterward for a successfully transplanted patient is in large and small ways an almost constant celebration, and it simply is not carried out in the same manner as before. Richard and Pam, for instance, dance in their kitchen every day. Years ago, they visited an island off the coast of Maine, and they went to a dance where nearly every couple was seventy or more years old. But, regardless of age, they waltzed away. Pam made Richard promise that when they had a home of their own, they would dance in the kitchen. After Richard came home from UCLA, the dancing changed from a promise to be kept to a bit of daily joy. Sometimes they get a piece of dry ice and lay it in a pan of water and dance through the clouds on the floor. ("That's the closest the statement 'Better living through chemistry' comes to the truth," Richard said with a big laugh. Then he added, "We always found sex important and worried that the transplant would affect it. I'm relieved that it hasn't.")

"We still haven't got back to being real goal-oriented," Pam told me as Richard put some more wood on the fire. He picked up her thought.

"I was long-term-goal-oriented, and so was Pam," he said. "The leukemia and the transplant had a tremendous effect on our daily life. We're picking every moment for what we want to do. We're not hedonistic; it's just like Huxley's here and now. That's a phrase that came to me all the time during the illness and transplant—here and now. So many things change. Before all this I was having a feud with Pam's mother for Pam's attention. It was very hostile and, I might add, we were blatant, outfront enemies. That just lost all its importance when I got sick. It was a positive change. I don't have time to hate or have a feud, and when Pam and I have a petty argument we'll stop in the middle of it and laugh and say, 'Do we want to be spending our time like this?' There are too many important things to take care of. I look at things in a very short fashion now, and I think that's good. It's difficult to make plans that involve next year, even at this point. I had shortened my 'want span' down to a month, and occasionally, when I was feeling well, to two."

He gazed at Pam and then went on. "These are the best years of my life, however ironic that is. I was sick with what was believed to be a terminal disease, and it's the best period of my life—although there were some side periods off in a time capsule. I don't usually talk about this. I don't concentrate on it at all. I flash back on it almost daily, both of us do, but internally; in a personal sense I'm aware of it every day. I can't believe I'm still here."

In the first week after her transplant Linda progressed, or in a sense regressed, as expected. On Saturday, three days after the transplant, she was put in isolation because her white cell count had fallen below 500 per ml. Her red blood cell and platelet counts had also fallen, as expected. All this was evidence that the chemotherapy and radiation had done their work—Linda's marrow was destroyed. She received transfusions of Jennifer's platelets (the donor's platelets, or those from someone in the immediate family, are generally the most effective) and random donor red blood cells to keep the clotting and oxygen-carrying capability of her blood at acceptable levels. In two weeks she would have a single bone marrow aspiration taken to see if her new marrow had engrafted. For the time being, however, all she could do was wait, a fairly uncomfortable proposition, because, like most transplant patients, she still suffered considerable nausea from the treatment and was now on intravenous liquids rather than solid foods.

For all that, it was a calm period for both Linda and her family. They were all optimistic; there was a general feeling that the hardest part had passed, that there wasn't much to do now. Linda was by no means cured, they knew, but they felt she was well on her way.

And for the first time since Linda was diagnosed as having leukemia, Dan felt that he could do something tangible to help her. For the first few weeks following a transplant, a patient needs many transfusions of platelets. The best source is from the donor, since that blood is such a good match. Jennifer gave platelets but could not do it as often as they were needed. Dan, and John when he was there, filled in the rest. For Dan, giving them relieved the sense of helplessness he had felt for so long, and he donated as often as he could.

It was still a hard time for him. Each morning when he awakened he told himself to worry only about getting through this one day and not to be concerned with the future. He hoped that when he talked on the phone with Linda, and then saw her later in the day, she would be doing well. More than anything, he wished that one day he would wake up and it would be the day that Linda was coming home, so that they could get on with their lives again. In the meantime, Jackie was a comfort to him on the nights when she was there. When he was by himself, the loneliness he felt sank to his bones.

That Saturday evening Hillary Rivera, a twenty-year-old man who had been transplanted eight months earlier and who in the first six weeks following had nearly died so many times that the nurses stopped counting, checked back into 10 West as an emergency patient. He had been doing very well in the six months since his discharge but was suffering now from what looked to be the beginning of pneumonia. He was given antibiotics, among them Amikacin, an effective but kidney-toxic drug that has to be carefully monitored during administration. Nurse Ellen Cummings did peaks and valleys—taking blood samples immediately before and after the dose—to monitor its therapeutic range. Cultures were also taken to try to determine exactly what was going on in his lungs. If it really was pneumonia, he would be in for a difficult time. If, as was less likely, it was only a fungal infection, the outlook would be much brighter.

When patients leave 10 West after their transplant, they are still bald from the chemotherapy and radiation and are usually quite thin from living only on intravenous fluids while their nausea abates. Hillary, however, looked, as one of the nurses told him, like a male model. He had thick black hair and a neat

175

mustache. His body was trim rather than thin, and rather than looking wan from being in a hospital room for six weeks, he was ruddy from leading a normal Southern California life. The nurses who knew him were concerned that if he had pneumonia he might well die. They were also afraid that a patient who had survived a terrible ordeal and then left the hospital with functioning new marrow, looking for all the world like a successful transplant, would prove otherwise. Hillary seemed the least concerned of everyone.

"I was delirious for ten days in the RCU," he said in his room. "I don't remember a thing. They tell me I thought I was Elvis Presley. I watched my best friend there die in the bed next to me. My feeling about all this is that when your number is up, it's up."

He is a Chicano who grew up in a fairly rough neighborhood, and his experiences influenced what he would accept in his treatment. Because he had seen too many of his friends involved with and hurt or killed by drugs, he refused to use marijuana against his nausea even though he was in great discomfort.

"I didn't want marijuana even though I was really nauseous," he said. "I swear my mother and father could die right now if I'm lying, but I never had any drugs before I came here. I just didn't think it was right. Even though I felt real bad, I didn't want people coming into my room and have it smell like a marijuana factory."

He asked Ellen several questions about what he was being given, which she answered, as 10 West nurses do. At the nurses' station she added, "When you're ill you really need someone as an advocate for you. You normally don't find out anything as a patient. You need family members to ask a lot of questions if the patient can't. My mother was in a small community hospital in Florida last summer. They were very closemouthed."

Late in the evening, as they and others had off and on during the day, a couple of patients came out into the hall for a walk. It was a period in which, with one exception, everyone was doing quite well, and it was a pleasing sight. "I feel like this is a rehab floor, with all these people up and around," Ellen said with a grin.

The exception was the young American-Chinese. He died about 6:00 A.M. on Monday, November 16. Nurse Cheri Shilala arrived at the hospital for the morning shift just before 7:00 and met his parents in the elevator. They had been summoned to the hospital but had not yet been told the news. The weekend had been hot and windy and, as is often the case that time of year, huge tracts of Southern California were aflame. Cheri was in a bad mood, and the young man's death was the cap on it. Her reaction was a good example of how the nurses have to cope with a death and yet keep their perspective so that they can continue to do their jobs.

"My Himalayan kitten died over the weekend," she complained, looking very sad. "He had been fixed on Friday and just died on Sunday, probably of heart failure. And the fires came very near my house. It was just not a good weekend. And then I come to work and start off in the elevator with two parents who are about to learn their son is dead." She was quiet for a few moments and then added, "It's only a cat," but she was affected by all the loss.

The good news at morning report was that Hillary's infection was fungal after all and that he would be fine and able to go home in two or three days.

Also during report Winston Ho announced that on Thursday Debra Phillips, a twenty-five-year-old woman with CML (chronic myelogenous leukemia) would be admitted. She would be the first CML patient to be given a transplant at UCLA. Doctors at the Fred Hutchinson Cancer Research Center in Seattle had recently reported favorable results with CML patients having transplants. After rounds, Ho explained the disease and why CML transplants had not been tried before.

177

"Any new therapy shows good results because no one reports failures," he said, repeating an axiom of published medical research. "Everything revolves around the immune system," he continued. "Of course, any specialist will tell you that medicine revolves around his specialty.

"Bone marrow cells are made by a pleuripotential cell, a theoretical cell we feel must be there because everything starts with a single cell, but no one has put a finger on it yet. It is the great-granddaddy cell all other cells are derived from. Now, pleuripotential cells can multiply and produce cells like themselves, or they can produce progeny which are different—differentiated stem cells, which produce five different kinds of blood cells. One kind is lymphoid cells, which produce lymphocytes, and which separate early and go through the lymphoid system. Acute or chronic lymphocytic leukemia happens in those cells. The other four stay together. They are myeloid cells, erythroid cells, megakaryocytes, and macrophages. Myeloid cells produce white blood cells, erythroid cells make red blood cells, megakaryocytes make platelets, and macrophages develop into monocytes—a type of circulating white cell.

"We think that some damage occurs, which interferes with the normal maturation of cells. The further back the damage occurs, the closer we come to a leukemic situation, because leukemia is caused by a proliferation of immature white cells. At the same time, if the damage occurred at the stem-cell level we would never get a remission because there would not be enough cells to grow back. We also think that leukemia is more acquired than genetic, at least in the majority of cases. So in leukemia there is some damage in the early stages that interferes with maturation. Wherever that happens, all cells further along the line are affected by the damaged cells.

"Now, CML is associated with a specific genetic abnormality called the Philadelphia chromosome. It is produced in the majority of patients and is a marker for the disease. If it—the marker—disappears, the disease is generally eradicated. At first we thought the disease was an overabundance of seemingly normal white cells, more than twenty thousand per milliliter. Most cases are between fifty thousand and one hundred thousand. The disease is generally in adults or older people and is asymptomatic at the time of discovery; usually it is found during a routine checkup. The platelet count is in the high to normal range—three hundred thousand to five hundred thousand, but occasionally as high as a million."

Unlike AML, which can be put into remission, CML cannot be turned back by chemotherapy or radiation. On the other hand, the disease advances very slowly and without any discomfort to the patient, often for three and sometimes for as long as five years. That raises an interesting problem for any doctor trying to do something about the disease.

"Most physicians want to treat CML even though the patient feels well, in the hope of preventing the patient from feeling ill," Ho continued. "The usual treatment is pills called Busulfan or Myleran, which decrease the production of white cells. They cause few problems and help maintain the white count in the twenty thousand to fifty thousand range. The patient goes along fine for a long time until blast crisis, a proliferation of immature cells. The blasts are similar to acute leukemia and look like the myeloblasts present in AML, but where AML can be treated with chemotherapy there is no effective treatment for CML. A few will be helped, but almost all will be dead three to six months after blast crisis starts."

He took a piece of chalk and drew a graph on the blackboard. The vertical line went from 0 percent to 100 percent. The horizontal line went from one year to five.

"We generally look at what is the half-life of things," he said as he made a dotted line out from the 50 percent mark. Then he drew a line from the 100 percent mark at an angle until it intersected the dotted line. The point was three years, the half-life of

CML: 50 percent of all CML patients die within that time. Twenty-five percent of the remainder die per year, so that after five years perhaps 10 percent might still be in the chronic phase, where some stay forever.

"What can we do?" he asked, not waiting for an answer. "Keep the counts at the best level we can. Physicians don't like to have people die without doing *something*. You can argue the ethics of that, but that's the way we were trained."

He returned to the problem of finding the ideal time for a CML transplant. "Some people show signs that blast crisis is imminent," he said. "It's called the accelerated phase, where an increasing number of blasts can be found in tests. It is difficult to do, but if you can time it right, the beginning of the accelerated phase is when you are ripe for a bone marrow transplant. The problem is, it is almost impossible to find that point. That leaves us with doing something in the chronic phase, when we are treating ourselves, really.

"The ideal transplant is between twins, because they are immunologically identical. The success in Seattle between twins in CML is very encouraging—eight or nine in ten. GVH is eliminated, the marker disappears. It is an ideal situation. But, of course, few people have twins. The second best is a transplant between HLA identical siblings, but with that come the attendant problems of GVH or interstitial pneumonia. But the figures of transplants in patients with AML in first remission give hope for bone marrow transplants in patients with CML.

"The question is," he repeated, "when do you take CML patients for transplant? We've chosen eighteen months post-diagnosis. It's ambitious but not unreasonable to offer it if there is a matched donor and the patient is aware of the risks. But it's still an investigative approach, not accepted therapy." (Recently, doctors have suggested that, in some cases, a transplant be done when the disease is diagnosed.)

He plotted two other graphs on the board, one that showed the survival curve of AML bone marrow transplants, the other showing the survival curve of AML patients without transplants. They clearly showed the advantages and drawbacks of bone marrow transplants. Between four and six months posttransplant, 40 percent of the patients die. But of the remaining 60 percent, only a very small percentage die each year posttransplant; the overall survival rate for the eight years of AML transplants is around 50 percent. For nontransplanted, conventionally treated AML patients, 50 percent die in the first year postdiagnosis and 30 percent of the remainder die per year, so that after three years only about 10 percent of the original population is alive. However cold and actuarial the graphs are, they are what must determine whether or not a treatment works, at least in aggregate. Individual cases are something else, as Ho pointed out.

"The curves show why it is ethical to transplant," he concluded, "but there are the 40 percent who die several months earlier than they likely would have if they had not had a transplant. We *are* killing some people. Some physicians would disagree with that; they would say that these people were already dying of leukemia. I guess that's how we rationalize it. But, as I've said before, I feel that once we start to interfere, people die because of things we've done. We've interfered with the normal course of the disease. It makes for a hard decision for the patient. We've decided it is practical to do transplants in CML patients, and we have a woman who has had the disease for five years without incident. Statistically, she is about out of time, but she could be one of the few percent who stay in the chronic phase forever. We just don't know. What we and she know is that she feels fine now. We're offering her a life-threatening procedure that will make her sick because we believe she has a better chance in the long run that way. But you've got to be in her position to be able to say what you would do."

Debra Phillips was a beautician and she had a five-year-old daughter. Her leukemia had been diagnosed in 1976. She had heard about bone marrow transplants only recently and, having thought it offered a new hope, was glad it turned out she had a donor, one of her brothers. She was, as she put it, "ready for it." Her donor-brother and his wife accompanied Debra and her husband, Rod, to UCLA. Her parents and two younger brothers were driving across country to be with her, and one morning in rounds there was a discussion of where they might stay. Cheri Shilala mentioned the young man who had complained about the three phantoms in his room. "How about putting three of them in his room?" she asked. "Instead of three imaginary people in the corner, he can have three real people from Pennsylvania."

Although the rooms on 10 West provide considerable privacy, it is still possible to hear louder than normal conversations in adjoining rooms. Debra was in the room next to Linda's, and when the TV wasn't on Linda was party to much of what Debra and the doctors talked about. She heard, too, when Debra cried from time to time out of anxiety.

On November 19, Linda was in as grumpy a mood as she had been in since coming to the ward. It is common for patients to develop a fever during the first couple of weeks post-transplant, because their immune systems are inoperative. Linda had not done so, but she was feeling pretty low. She overheard the doctor telling Debra about the Foley catheter she would have inserted in her urethra during the Cytoxan treatment three days hence, and she said, "The Foley was such a big deal at the time, and now it seems so long ago."

Cheri Shilala was her nurse for the day, and she had been in earlier to tell her that she would have to take some potassium because the level in her blood was too low. The doctors wanted her to take it orally, but Linda had had it before and knew how unpleasant-tasting it is. Except for transfusions she had been free of the I-med, an electronically monitored intravenous feeder used for all substances going in through the Hickman catheter. Being attached is something like suddenly finding oneself with a Siamese twin. It would not have been so bad if Linda had had to stay in bed. But she was able to spend part of the day sitting in the chair in her room, and didn't relish dragging a machine around. So Linda had the choice of drinking the thoroughly unpleasant liquid or spending several hours with a machine on wheels as her counterpart. She didn't like either choice.

"If I'm going to die from not having the potassium, I'll consider it," she said. "They know how much I hate being hooked up, but I told them I'd rather be hooked up than drink it." Later, she was hooked up.

She was thinking that day of complications that could arise and how little control she had over them. She sipped tea as she talked.

"If you've ever had one of those chest colds that settles in forever, that's how I feel about GVH or pneumonia. There's nothing you can do. I'm not going to wish that away."

Nor was she going to wish away Cheri, who had come in to take her temperature. Because the hot tea had changed the temperature in her mouth, Cheri told Linda to put the thermometer under her arm. The device was a disposable plastic strip with rows of brown dots, each representing a tenth of a degree. The dots turn blue up to the patient's temperature. After a few minutes Linda took it out and looked at it.

"Any blue dots?" Cheri asked.

"Some." Linda looked closely. "A lot."

"Want me to be brutally frank?" Cheri asked.

"What now?"

"I think you're going to start a fever. You've been pukey the last couple of days. You might start tonight."

"Thanks a lot. What's my platelet count?"

"Eight thousand. That's why I wasn't surprised when you didn't jump out of bed today."

"I thought it was low." Linda was more interested than angry now. "I went to blow my nose and was very careful, and even so there was a little blood."

"Don't forget that the air is very dry, too, from the Santa Ana winds. The smog creeps in, too."

"Eight thousand," Linda repeated. "Gosh, that's low. How much longer do you think I'll need platelets?"

"You're just beginning. Probably a couple of weeks." Cheri was very matter-of-fact. "What does your thermometer say?"

Linda looked at it again. "Gosh, it's gone over to the other side."

"Don't look at it right away or you'll get upset." Cheri went over to the bed.

"This dot on the line is where I am?"

"Yeah, 99.5 Fahrenheit."

The next day Linda sat in bed eating a red popsicle, which she had chewed away at the bottom of one side; it looked like a miniature Easter Island statue. Her mood was as pleasant as the look on the face of one of the statues. She had been troubled the past few days with mouth sores from the radiation, and now a rectal fissure was causing more pain. Also, her mother had complained earlier over the phone about Dan's housekeeping, and Linda muttered, "If I get through this and have been saved from the grave, it's not for cleaning house."

A soap opera had recently discovered bone marrow transplants, and one of the characters was going to have one, provided her younger sister and only HLA match would agree to be the donor. The continuing drama of all this had been a source of both amusement and anger to the patients on the ward, because the procedure was not properly explained, and the prospective donor had been told marrow would be taken from her leg. To compound all the hand-wringing, the girl, who was an aspiring dancer, was told that donating marrow could permanently injure her. "If this doesn't work," she whined as the music swelled, "I won't be able to dance anymore. My career will be over before it started." Linda groaned. The girl decided to run away from home.

Linda's temperature was only slightly above normal, but she had a ruddy look, and the consensus among the nurses was that she would spike a fever that night. If she did, she would be treated according to the protocol for every patient who develops a fever: antibiotics, a chest X ray to see if the lungs are clear, and blood and urine samples for culturing. If the infection is bacterial, the antibiotics should control it within twenty-four hours. If they don't, it means the problem is probably viral and more difficult to treat.

But by the next day nothing had happened. Linda's temperature was unchanged, and so was her mood. Her hair was noticeably falling out, the delayed result of the radiation. Ironically, as she cleaned it off her pillow she could overhear the radiologist explaining total body irradiation to Debra. Debra was apprehensive, and Linda appreciated what she was going through.

"It sends a shiver up my spine just to think of that stuff," she said as she sat up in her bed. "It was creepy. I'm just so glad I'm past that point. If the option were available, I'd do it all again. It doesn't mean I'd have to like it. I don't regret having done it, but I'm glad it's over. Although it's not really over. It's just beginning. It's curious to me that I feel this sense of relief. I guess now it's out of my hands, and what's going to happen is going to happen, where before [during irradiation] I had to fight back nausea and worry if I'd get to the bathroom in time for the diarrhea. Now the burden is off me." She looked forward to getting out of isolation and being allowed to eat fresh dairy products again. "I'll be so glad to have a vanilla milkshake—even though

I'm usually not crazy about them. You just want the thing you can't have."

An obvious subject for someone in Linda's position to think about is living or dying, not only from leukemia or a bone marrow transplant but from other random acts as well. That evening was one of the occasions when it was on Linda's mind. There had been a tragic fire at the MGM Grand Hotel in Las Vegas two days earlier; it had got her thinking about how to get out of the hospital in such an event, and she talked about premonitions. "I have this sixth sense sometimes," she said. "When I was pregnant I went through a corner in our truck very fast and banged against the door. It made me think about falling out. Then one day not long after, I got in the truck—we have a real steep driveway—and got to the bottom and turned, and my door came open.

"I had another about Angela. I had her in the back of our Celica. I got this feeling about the car being on fire—how would I get her unstrapped and get her out? Soon after I was in the truck again, and I had Angela on the seat beside me. It smelled like the heater was on but it wasn't. Pretty soon fumes were filling the car. The hydraulic line to the brake for the horse trailer looked like it was on fire, it was so hot.

"I also had a premonition about the oak tree falling on the house. A day or two later an earthquake came. The tree didn't fall, but it sure shook." Then she described some others that would later be interesting.

"In OB I had this several times," she went on. "It was a *Little House on the Prairie* kind of thing. I'd be lying there dying and telling Dan, 'I want you to marry again'—very melodramatic. But also something about being alive a long time from now and the feeling I have about Jennifer and all she's done for me. And maybe the good that will come from people reading about my case, that I'll be a symbol of hope for some people. I'd do that a lot better alive than dead."

She paused a few moments. "Maybe I'm afraid that it will be the *Little House on the Prairie* ending. I want people to read that as of such and such a date Linda Galbraith is alive and well. Not that, unfortunately, on January 8, 1981, Linda Galbraith died. There are times when I thought I was being punished. God, was I *that* bad? Did I deserve to get this terrible disease? I had this conversation with Dan not long after I found out. I knew why it was me. I'm strong enough that I can go through it all and be a better person, whereas someone else might not have the will or endurance to go through all this, and it would serve no purpose."

"Endurance" is a necessity in a bone marrow transplant, as it is in any drawn-out, serious illness. From the moment that the patient's life is irrevocably changed by the sudden diagnosis of a killer disease, normal life is impossible. Between July and this point in late November, Linda and her family had been forced to focus their attention on really only one thing: Linda's possible recovery. The joy and exhilaration of being a new parent was mitigated by her disease. John and Jackie had come from Georgia to help out. Jennifer had traveled from Samoa, her two boys in tow. In almost every respect, each of the people involved was in an unnatural and difficult position. The stress the experience puts on a family is immense, and at some point it is expressed, if only obliquely. Linda's family was no exception. Jennifer was staying with her sons in a house thirty miles from her mother, with no phone, and it was a struggle to handle the boys by herself. Linda's mother was staying with Dan and Angela Hope; her father came back and forth from Georgia as best he could. Dan was having to work and do what he could with the baby and drive three hours round trip to the hospital every day. Added to all this was Angela Hope's catching a cold, preventing her from seeing her mother for fear of infecting her. In the way all family members do, they sometimes complained about one another—though when they told things about each other to Linda it was in an effort to talk about something other than the problems of her transplant. But rather than accept it with the perspective she normally did, Linda ended up feeling as if she were being blamed for being sick, a common feeling among patients who try to compensate in some way for the guilt they feel about upsetting so many people's lives.

By Friday, November 21, her frustration was about at its peak. About 8:30 P.M. Dan called. One reason Linda had opted for the bone marrow transplant as quickly as she did was so she and Dan and Angela Hope could go to Georgia for Christmas with her parents and family.

"Did you get the tickets to Atlanta straightened out?" she asked him on the phone. Her eyes opened wide as he answered. "Eight hundred and four dollars? That's what they're going to cost? Gosh, tell my mother not to get me any Christmas presents." They talked a while longer. Apparently her mother had made spaghetti for dinner. "Friday's always spaghetti night. I had a taste for spaghetti tonight, too," she told him. But then her frustration began to show. "I told my mother that I was sorry to be in bed sick and that I didn't like it either," she said. "She gets so frustrated being there and takes it out on me."

After she hung up she was still upset. "I'm sick of all this," she said. "All I hear is complain, complain, complain. Shit," she said, swearing for the first time, at least in my presence, "I didn't ask for this. It isn't convenient for me to be laid up in this hospital."

Linda had, as well, been getting phone calls from people at work, some of them bringing her their problems, as they often did. But she was in no mood for things as usual.

"In my work people come to me with problems, and I feel obligated to do something," she said. "And I feel the same way here. But there's not anything I can do about it."

Dallas came on the TV, and it took Linda's mind off all the trouble, at least for a while. "She's the dumbest thing," she said of one of the women on the show, "but she has a body like a well-seasoned grape."

As I drove home from the hospital that night I thought of Linda's fantasies and premonitions. Suddenly a car came across several lanes of traffic directly at me, but I managed to avoid a fifty-mile-per-hour collision. I told Linda about it the next morning.

"You lie there and spin *Little House on the Prairie* endings, and I go out on the highway and nearly have them," I told her. "You can't die young," I added. "The way things are going, you'll have to write your own story."

Her spirits were much improved. "I'm starting to feel almost human," she said. "Not on the brink of death, or wishing I were. I really dwelled on the negative aspects. After being confronted with all the horrible things that can happen to you, signing consent form after consent form with all the dire things that could happen—and you could go through all this and still die. If someone told me that I would go through all the Cytoxan and the sores and the discomfort and then be okay, that would be something. But with this there are no guarantees, expressed or implied. But I don't dwell much on it now."

She turned her attention to her Hickman catheter, which she had had to clean every day when she was at home between her induction therapy in August and her return for her transplant. (The catheters can be left in place almost indefinitely, and so Linda kept hers in while the decision was made whether to have a transplant.) The procedure takes several minutes. Betadine and alcohol are used to clean the skin around the tube, and heparin, an anti-coagulant, has to be flushed in and out of the line. It is a messy and unattractive process.

"The first time I had to clean it, I thought I'd get sick," she said. "I couldn't accept this tube hanging out of my body." She told a story about a family horse who had been severely cut, and because he kept pulling out the stitches, the wound would not heal. "The vet said, 'You're going to have to put your hand in the wound and wash it,' " she continued. "It was very unpleasant, but it had to be done. I measured his progress by how far I stuck in my arm. At first it was like sticking your arm in a jar, then just fingers. People really got grossed out when they saw me do it. Proud flesh and blood and gunk would run out—but it had to be done. And like the Hickman, when I first did it, it made me sick to my stomach. But I knew I had to do it. Now I guess I've accepted it as part of myself. You wouldn't believe how well that horse healed up. Just a little scar. It shows what you can do if you have to." Her problem with the Hickman now was one of vanity. "The trouble with the Hickman," she complained, "is that you can't wear anything tight or low-cut."

During the evening report by the day nursing shift to the night staff, Linda's condition and needs started a discussion. "She told me, 'It feels like all my orifices are violated except my ears,' " Ellen Cummings told them. Because of the rectal problems, which were as yet undiagnosed, the nurses were required to take a seventy-two-hour stool sample for Dr. Oscar Krits (as I'll call him), a bacteriologist whom the nurses had taken to calling "Dr. Shits" because he wanted the collections (usually twenty-four-hour) from so many patients. The nurses, however, weren't really sure just what he was looking for. A request that he give them a lecture one morning on his research was acknowledged, but he said he wouldn't have time to give it until early December. Nobody was very happy doing work that was unpleasant for reasons that weren't known, but they did it anyway and compensated for it with grumbles and jokes.

"Linda's stool is in the refrigerator," Ellen reported, and several nurses exclaimed, "Hers? In her room?"

"No," Ellen said, laughing. "In the supply room. It's so disgusting," she added. "You know, there ought to be a direct rectal line from the bed to the lab."

SIX

You can do something dozens of times, and each time will seem the same as the last. Then suddenly it will all seem different. That happened to me after visiting Dr. Gale's lab on the fourth floor nearly every day for a couple of months. One day I came down after spending some time with Linda and, as I often did, I went into one of the lab rooms where various experiments were being done to find optimal ways to grow colonies of human cells. The cells were in petri dishes an inch or so square and grew in a bright pink tissue culture solution. Each dish contained bone marrow cells from a patient or donor. One was labeled "Linda Galbraith." The relationship between the ward and the lab suddenly became clear to me. While the Linda upstairs in bed was obviously the most important immediate concern of Gale and his staff, the Linda Galbraith and the cells of all the other people in the dishes were what this was all about. The basic problem was not Linda's leukemia or her bone marrow transplant and the attendant hopes and risks that went along with each; what would happen to her would be within the realm of medicine as it is understood today. What the experiments with these cells would result in, it was hoped, was a knowledge of how the problems of graft-versus-host disease and other complications of bone marrow transplants could be overcome. The underlying necessity in preventing those diseases is to understand the nature of cells and how they work.

Gale politely understood my epiphany when I said this to him—he had obviously seen this distinction many years earlier—and he told me, "We really have two basic interests in the lab. The first is, how do lymphoid cells recognize other cells? Graft-versus-host disease results from one cell recognizing another cell as foreign; one surface is not the same as itself. There are implications in this beyond transplantation. Why, for instance, don't your own lymphocytes eat your liver? How does a cell know when to stop growing? If you cut off half the liver, it grows back to normal size; how does it know when to stop? What does a cell do to kill a foreign cell? How does it arm itself? Does it release a factor that you could detect? It is the issue of self and nonself.

"The second is of basic hematopoiesis [the formation of blood cells]. What are the progenitors or ancestor cells? What controls their growth? How many times can they multiply before they become senescent? We all come from one cell. The basic question is, what determines cell maturation and differentiation?"

To try to answer those questions, Gale works with a staff of fifteen researchers and with a statistician. The computer terminal in his office and the statistician on his team are two of the more visible signs of the changes in medical research over the past decade. For better or worse, a clinician/researcher today must not only know medicine and chemistry but must understand computers and statistical probability.

"Data management and computers," Gale said as we walked out of the lab. "How do you keep track of what you're doing? It used to be that you just did A and B and compared it to C. If someone was dying from pneumonia, you gave him penicillin.

You didn't need a computer. Now you need mathematical proof. How do we know it's better or not better? We can no longer do that by hand. We need to collect and store and retrieve information. Yet the people who do this have no idea of medicine. That's a problem. They can prove a lot of silly things because they don't know medicine.

"I spend an hour at my terminal every day and two hours a week with the computer people. That's standard. Before we start a trial we sit down and say, okay, half our patients get graft-versus-host disease. We're going to introduce a new therapy. We think it will knock GVH in half. If that is the case, we need to know how many patients we need to show it in a double-blind experiment, where no clinician knows which is which. Two years later you break the code. It takes months to set a trial up, to figure the right number of patients. Also, you need a critical statistical review to get a paper accepted [by a medical or research journal]. You can do the greatest work in the world, and no one will accept it without statistics. No longer will people take the word of a clinician because he's respected."

For a clinical researcher such as Gale to carry out his work, he must compete with other scientists in several ways. The most important of these is for financial support of grants from the National Institutes of Health and from specialized nongovernmental associations such as the Leukemia Society of America. Research requires a staff, and a staff must be paid. In order to get a grant, your work must show results. In order to show your results, you must have them accepted for publication in a respectable journal, such as *Science*, or *Nature*, or the *Annals of Internal Medicine*, or *The New England Journal of Medicine*. Taking care of patients and conducting experiments, which is what a clinical researcher does by definition, is only a part of what he really must do. Besides the daily computer time and the weekly time with statisticians, another several months of work a year go into writing grant proposals and, in the case of government grants, preparing for visits by teams of other clinical researchers in which the doctor goes through the equivalent of orals for a Ph.D. as part of the evaluation of the proposal. Gale estimates that a modern academic physician spends up to half his time scrambling for grants.

If he's any good, he gets much of that money from the National Institutes of Health, a $3-billion-a-year arm of the U.S. Department of Health and Human Services. There are thirteen specialized institutes that make up the whole, among them the National Institute of General Medical Sciences (NIGMS), the National Institute of Allergy and Infectious Diseases (NIAID), the National Heart, Blood, and Lung Institute (NHBLI), and the National Cancer Institute (NCI). Each institute (except for NIGMS) is a physical place with investigators at work on the NIH campus in Bethesda, Maryland. All institutes support their research through the funding they receive from Congress, and they also support research by scientists such as Gale. Of all the institutes, NCI receives the most, about $1.1 billion a year. Heart, Blood, and Lung is second, about $800 million.

Money is distributed either through contracts or through grants. A contract is awarded if an institute feels something is important and they want someone to look into it. It is rather like the Department of Defense ordering an airplane; the idea comes from the institute, the contractors provide the services, and eventually the job gets done. It is a practice that has never been held in much favor, however. It was in vogue about ten years ago, but today contracts amount to about 10 percent of the funds given.

Grant money is awarded through competition. A scientist submits his idea to a body called the Division of Research Grants. They read the title and an abstract of the application and decide which specialist committee should consider it. Those committees meet four times a year and are composed of experts from across the country. They decide on a grant's merits without paying attention to its cost. The standard grant request is around $100,000, but some are in the millions. For a large request like that, several members of the committee and a ten- to fifteen-member advisory board consisting of basic and clinical researchers from around the country will visit the applicant's institution, where they can question the applicant. Any large grant has several components, and the site-visit committee suggests, on the basis of the science alone, which areas should be funded and which should not. Those recommendations are accompanied by a fifty-or-so-page report that evaluates the application line by line. The report of the site-visit team is presented to the specialist committee at its quarterly meeting. The committee considers the report and the quality of the competing requests and assigns a priority score based on how important the research is in the context of things being studied, and how good the underlying science in the proposal is. A perfect proposal would have a score of 1, a worthless proposal would be rated 5. Everyone on the committee assigns a score, and they are averaged. An excellent grant would be about 1.4. Average should be 2.5, with two thirds of the proposals between 1.3 and 2.7.

Gale explained all this to me one day shortly before a site visit to consider a four-year $3.2-million grant he and his team had applied for. It had been a busy period, for not only was a lot happening on the ward, but he had also spent part of each day rehearsing various researchers on his team in the presentations they would make to the site-visit committee. They were all also reading recent articles published by committee members so they would know what their questioners knew. As fair and impartial as the system of grant giving is, there are still human factors that count. A researcher who can clearly present his results and his hypotheses is likely to be more impressive than one who can't, even if their basic science is the same. Other things count, too, Gale explained.

"After the science is established, the committee gets into whose purview the proposal falls under," he said. "I applied only to NIH, but different institutes have differing dollars. The title could be crucial. The panel could send your grant to an institute that has no money, so I could get a 1.7 and it would not be funded. One aspect of grantsmanship is knowing how to get enough into the title and abstract to get it to the right specialist committee and an institute with adequate funding. Keeping track of words is important. 'Immunotherapy' was a key word ten years ago. Now it's 'biological response modifiers.' In many regards, it's the same as immunotherapy but a new, trendy name. These changes in the perception of what is interesting are something one must be aware of. In some regards, institutions are as susceptible to fashion as individuals are. Also, some numbers are not good. Nine hundred and ninety thousand dollars sounds better than one million."

The concept of peer review—of scientists judging the worth of other scientists' proposals—is the keystone in the arch between the NIH and clinical researchers. The site-visit teams are large enough to override any individual animus or jealousy that may be latent in one or two members, and no one is put on a panel that judges the merit of a proposal if he is competing for the same money. The scientists who are asked to serve on them—Gale is among them—do so because it is both an honor and a responsibility.

"It's a very fair system," Gale continued. "It's very high-minded—and also very expensive, flying these guys all over the place. But the time is voluntary, to all intents and purposes; we're given an honorarium of one hundred dollars a day for the visit itself, which in theory is a major loss to a physician. And I usually spend two or three days preparing for a visit, and a day afterward writing a critique. You're just expected to do your fair share. Not all grantees serve; NIH just tries to pick the best scientists in the country."

I wondered, considering most scientists at Gale's level and specialty know each other from conferences and site visits, how it is possible for a panel member to put friendship or enmity aside and consider a project on scientific merit. Gale argued that the generally high-minded principles of scientists and the seriousness of the venture make everyone behave as scrupulously as possible.

For instance, he said, "Ten of the site visitors coming here are either good personal or professional friends, but none of us would tell the other the outcome of the panel's discussions. Panel members sometimes pass a hat around after lunch so that it could not be said we gave them anything. And even though a colleague on the panel might visit here next week, he would never call me for dinner during a site visit. Everything possible is done to keep the deliberations on science alone. If a proposal arrives in Washington in a pretty binder with fancy pictures, it is dismantled and photocopied so that they all look alike. The only drawback to the process I can see is that scientists tend to react logically, so really wild ideas generally don't get funded. Unfortunately, many scientific discoveries occur serendipitously. Even so, when I go on a site visit and someone says, 'You never know unless you try,' I give very serious thought to their proposal. That's not what science is about. Science is about testing hypotheses."

A hypothesis Gale and Champlin had been working on for some time was that a fetal human liver could be a suitable source of bone marrow cells for a patient who needs a transplant but lacks a donor. The reason is that in early development a fetus's liver is not the organ an adult has but is rather the blood-producing apparatus until bones form and are sufficiently large and mature for the cells to colonize and reproduce there. The advantage of fetal cells over adult donor cells is that those of the fetus are immunologically incompetent: They have not matured enough to know self from nonself and thus they would eliminate the risk of graft-versus-host disease. Experiments on mice and dogs have been successful, and the question now is whether it will work in man. To try to answer that question, some of Gale's team had spent the past several months attempting to get fetal liver cells to grow in the lab. Finding the proper conditions and solution in which to keep the cells alive and reproducing would be a major breakthrough. (The cells used in the experiments, and those that will be used therapeutically if the experiments prove useful, are from stillborn or aborted fetuses in the second trimester—the period when the liver is the source of blood for the fetus, yet before the time when the white cells—lymphocytes—have developed their immunologic capacity.)

The answers to this and other questions Gale and his team are trying to solve go beyond the treatment of leukemia and aplastic anemia. Bone marrow transplantation has potential uses against other diseases as well. It has recently been tried in the treatment of other cancers that don't involve the bone marrow, such as breast and lung cancer, which have proved resistant to conventional therapy. In treating cancer, the higher the dose of an anticancer drug or radiation given, the greater the number of tumor cells killed, but beyond certain doses, the bone marrow is destroyed. If a patient has some of his own marrow extracted and frozen, he can be given much higher doses of anticancer drugs and radiation and then be rescued from bone marrow failure by an infusion of his own marrow. (Because it is the patient's own marrow, the risks of graft rejection and graft-versus-host disease are eliminated.) The procedure is called an autologus transplant, and many have been done on 10 West.

Theoretically, bone marrow transplantation could also precede other organ transplants. The organ donor could provide marrow, and the organ could then be transplanted without fear of rejection. Although this has not yet been attempted on man, bone marrow transplants as a prelude to other transplants have been done successfully in laboratory animals.

Bone marrow transplants have been done to correct inborn abnormalities of the immune system, such as severe combined immunodeficiency. In the future it is possible that they can be used to treat other diseases of the immune system, such as lupus erythematosus and rheumatoid arthritis. This has already been done in animals. Transplants also provide the most effective means to introduce new genes into the body, and there seems little argument in the medical community that as genetic functions are more clearly isolated and gene therapies approved for humans, bone marrow transplants will be used to correct abnormalities in the patient's natural genetic makeup. One disease that might be treated by genetic engineering through marrow transplantation is sickle-cell anemia. Victims of the disease have a mutation of a gene in their genetic makeup that produces deficient hemoglobin in oxygen-carrying red blood cells. Isolating the normal gene, cloning it in bacteria to make a sufficient amount, then inserting the cloned normal gene into the blood-producing system could provide a cure.

The work being done by genetic engineers will have a significant effect on the future of bone marrow transplantation. In the past few years, they have made extraordinary gains in mapping the genetic constitution of cells. The biotechnology industry is based on identifying gene sequences in order to make a protein for a product—such as interferon, or insulin, or growth hormones. Involved in that is finding the signal sequences that turn a gene on and off, that tell it to act or not to act. With that knowledge, scientists may be able to unlock the secret of malignancy, which is very likely the product of abnormal regulation of genes.

Bone marrow transplantation is a new and wondrous endeavor. It is also in its technical infancy. The massive doses of cell-killing drugs and radiation are the only alternative today, but in the true sense of the word, they are overkill. As the functions of cells are better understood, transplantation technique will be greatly refined, as any medical advance is.

"We'll look back in a few years at what we're doing now," a researcher said one day in the lab, "and it will seem like the days when we put leeches on people to cure them."

At least once a week Gale meets with his researchers to go over progress in various experiments. I joined him for one session with Champlin and two others in which the status of the fetal liver-cell experiments was the topic. The researchers have worked with Gale long enough to need very little direction from him. The boundaries of the experiment are set up, and they go off to find what they can. The meetings are short and serious insofar as the presentation of data is concerned; the researchers come with tables and charts neatly made up and copied, and the talk is about scientific procedure and results. But there is also room for banter and bad jokes. For example, after one of the researchers reported that she had about fifteen million liver cells in one group that seemed to be performing better because they were first chopped rather than puréed, Gale nodded his head and asked, "Do you find that onion or egg white makes a difference?"

Champlin turned to me and explained, "The idea is to find a solution in which normal cells can grow without becoming neoplastic [tumorous], or whatever."

Gale, still considering the data he had been given, which was promising, wondered why the cells weren't doing still better. "Maybe they're unhappy because there are no lymphocytes," he said.

His anthropomorphization of the cells caught my attention. Scientists the world round are spending billions of dollars trying to understand minute, incredibly ordered and complex particles that hold the key to our lives. Gale has spent the past ten years looking at them, like an archaeologist studying hieroglyphics, hoping to find the genetic equivalent of the Rosetta stone. To any lay person, cells in a petri dish look like a drop or two of purple water; under a microscope they appear not much different from bits of moving bubbles. The notion that trillions of them comprise and run our bodies is intellectually understandable but, when you come to think of it, hardly believable. Yet to Gale and his co-workers these cells have not only personalities but likes and dislikes, are even capable of being unhappy because there are no lymphocyte playmates for them.

The experiment in question concerned the growing of cell-forming unit colonies, or CFU-C, and the results to date brought out the pragmatist in Gale. He urged his team to write up their results for publication so other scientists could see what they had come up with and try to confirm it. Publications are also important in terms of getting grant money, and for adding merit badges to a research team's credentials.

"If you feel confident that you have derived a system of keeping CFU-C alive for six weeks in this type of solution or twelve in another," he told the researcher, "unless you want to read Malcolm Moore's article in *Nature* [announcing similar results], I suggest you write it up. CFU-C don't come out of the woodwork. You have an experiment that shows that they are there or they aren't there. I suggest you get this written, because the next step is harder. And *Nature* takes only short manuscripts. It's important to know when to stop as well as when to start. There are four important phases in any experiment—starting, stopping, analyzing it, and publishing."

The meeting broke up soon after, and as he walked down the hall to rehearse two of his staff for their presentations to the site-visit group, Gale said, "It costs forty thousand dollars to put a major proposal together. It puts you to the limit in reviewing what you can do—and puts others beyond the limit and into private practice. There has to be some other motivation than just money." He stopped in a lab along the way for a moment and then added, "I'm like someone trying to manage a five-million-dollar company. I didn't train to become a corporate executive, but I had no choice."

On Friday, November 28, Linda was still in isolation, but her white count was slowly rising. Her spirits were rising, too. Her main complaint was continuing nausea, something common to many patients. Jeanette Leslie came into the room to give her half a marijuana cigarette (which was all she usually wanted) to help ease her stomach, and Linda said in a jocular tone, "You have to be more careful with the marijuana cigarettes with someone like me. I've singed my eyelashes lighting them."

"Why don't we get you a pipe?" Jeanette asked.

Linda laughed. "You guys have got me to go pretty far as it is."

Jeanette left, and Linda unloaded her other gripe. Friends were continuing to call and talk about their problems along with other things they talked to her about. Normally Linda was happy to counsel them, but her patience had worn thin now. It was hard, however, for her to tell them not to bother her with their troubles, that she had enough of her own.

"I'm the world's psychiatrist," she said. "You take two psychology classes, and everyone calls you. I lean on myself. I'm the only one I really trust. I never really had to lean on anyone," she said with some ire. But then she added, "Well, sometimes."

Her outburst was over quickly, and she talked about Thanksgiving, which had fallen the day before. Dan and Jackie had gone to Dan's parents' for dinner, where they had spent a reasonably festive evening; John was in Atlanta with his other children. They all missed Linda but looked forward to her being with them the next year. Linda had talked with them on the phone and had been visited by Dan and spent the day in relative peace. Because any holiday marks the passing of time more clearly than ordinary days, it made Linda think of the time she had spent in the hospital.

"Later on, when you go home, it's like lost time," she said. "I went into the hospital to have Angela, and it was beach weather. I got out after chemo, and it was fall. What happened to the summer?" Her unspoken question was, "What has happened to the fall?"

She had self-imposed timetables to meet: Christmas with her parents and brothers and sisters in Atlanta; back to work in January. She didn't have much time to dawdle in a hospital room, no matter how serious the illness. For the first time in a couple of weeks she talked about going back to work.

"I told the company I'd be back in January," she said, as if it were a matter of fact. "It's a super-busy month, and I'd feel bad if I couldn't be there at least part of the time. I enjoy the work so much—especially when it's part-time." She laughed and went on a little dreamily, "Then I would have time to spend with the baby. Not get there until nine or so, like before I came in to have her. I didn't have to get up at the crack of dawn and could get back before Dan and get a little dinner started or take a nap. Plus, before, when I was at work, I had this transplant staring me in the face. The only time I didn't brood about this was at work, where you really have to use your brain. But I didn't work too hard. Some days I'd go to lunch with the girls, some days not. I really felt I was leading the life of Riley."

In speaking about the past and the future, she used the past tense, as if going back to work would have the same beneficial effect that it had had before, when all the horrors of leukemia and a bone marrow transplant, and the possibility of a quick death, were pushed aside.

Then she started looking only ahead.

"I think they are prepared for the fact I may not come back full-time, at least at first. It will be nice to have a little time to pull myself together. The company has been real good—I've been on full salary. I feel an obligation to them. Dan's looked out for me, and so have the people in the office. Let's face it, they'll certainly have a loyal and dedicated employee after this. One thing's for certain," she said with another laugh, "I'll never quit. I'd lose my insurance, and no one else would take me."

Somehow the conversation turned to how one makes use of time after he's told he will in all likelihood be dead in a certain, short time. I told her about the novelist Anthony Burgess, who many years ago, while a teacher in Malaysia, was told he had a brain tumor and would be dead within the year. Burgess quit teaching, wrote six novels within that year, and has just kept on going.

Linda thought for a few moments and said, "I don't know what I would do if someone told me I had only so long to live. It would take an awful lot for me to be convinced. But if I did know I was going to die in x months, I'd probably not work because that's an investment in the future. I'd probably spend time at home with the baby—or take a cruise; that's something I've always wanted to do. It was terrible when I was making the decision to have the transplant, knowing that it could cost me the last year of my life, that I could be dead in a month. That's a heavy thing. But I didn't want to be sitting and worrying about the relapse and knowing that the chances of a second remission are slim.

"I knew a guy who was discovered to have a brain tumor and was told he had six months to live," she continued. "He was like me. He had everything in the world seemingly going for him. The first reaction is disbelief—not me. But the cold finger of death has come out of the crowd and tapped him—and it could be you."

I sat in on the evening report when the nurses changed shifts at 7:00 P.M. All but one of the patients were faring reasonably well. The exception was an eighteen-year-old Hawaiian with aplastic anemia whom I will call Luke. He had no donor and therefore could not have a transplant. Instead he had been given antithymocyte globulin (ATG), the only other choice. A couple of days earlier it had appeared that he had developed a blood clot in his brain, and he had been intermittently hemorrhaging. He was a bearlike kid who looked as if he belonged on the beach, and everyone liked him; a couple of the nurses were particularly attached to him. He hid Kit Kat bars, which were no good for him in his condition, under his bed or mattress and ate them in spite of doctors and nurses trying to stop him. At this point no one was trying to stop him very hard; other things were more important. His white cell count was only 800, and his platelets were an almost invisible 9,000. He was taking antibiotics and being given platelets, but nothing seemed to be of much help. He was also diaphoretic, a sweatiness that is induced by reaction to something rather than a sign of fever; in his case it was from Tylenol. He had abdominal pains and said blood transfusions hurt him, but he refused any pain medication. In fact, he laughed and joked around with anyone who came in the room. But he was so seriously ill that the doctors had declared him a DNR—do not resuscitate—and it seemed that he could bleed out at any moment.

Linda was diaphoretic, too, perhaps from the Darvon she had been given for some pain she felt, and she was switched to Dilaudid. But the nurses agreed that it looked as though she was brewing a fever. Her temperature had been mildly elevated all day. Still, all signs were that she was improving. Her platelet count was 35,000, and her white count was up to 400; at 500 she would be out of isolation, probably in two or three days. Her lungs were clear, which meant there was no need for concern over possible pneumonia.

Dr. Krits, who was still Dr. Shits to the nurses because he had yet to explain why he wanted so many twenty-four-hour stool samples from patients, walked into the room after visiting a patient, as the nurses were finishing. He had a towel in his hand, and Cheri Shilala called to him, "You have his small bowel in the towel, right?" Everyone laughed, even Krits.

Another doctor came in then, and the conversation shifted to the more serious subject of giving nurses credit for work they had done. In this case, Cheri was upset because she and two or three others on the 10 West staff had collected data and written up an orientation and protocol handbook for nurses new to bone marrow transplantation. Recently some nurses from another hospital had visited and taken a copy for their own information—and then published an article under their own names using much of the UCLA material. Cheri was furious, but the doctors, whose grants and success are based greatly on published work, didn't see what the fuss was about. Since nurses' jobs don't depend on whether they publish, it didn't appear to them to be of much consequence. What the doctors overlooked in this discussion was the ego satisfaction for the nurses in seeing their work in print, regardless of the scientific or grant-gaining value.

"It is the same as if someone had taken your research material and published it as his own," Cheri told the still unconvinced doctors. "It took us years to figure these things out."

That evening I went to a UCLA basketball game and ran into Patti DeLone and her husband, who was then getting his doctorate and teaching in the graduate school of business. It had been Patti's day off, and she asked how things were on the ward. I repeated as best I could what I had heard during report and told her that Linda seemed to be doing all right.

"I have a good feeling about her," she said. "I think she's going to make it. I really do. We're owed one."

On Saturday the twenty-ninth, two of Linda's co-workers at Petoseed came by to see her for half an hour on their way to the

USC-Notre Dame football game. Dan was there, and while the four old friends had a pleasant visit, Dan seemed to them to have an underlying air of worry and depression. But not Linda. She was very happy. Her nausea had lessened, and she looked good, too. Her only trouble was with the death of the young American-Chinese. It was hard, she told them, to be on a ward where she knew people were dying.

Even though patients are in private rooms, each knows the status of the other patients on the ward. When they are well enough, some visit with others, and they share, among other things, what they have heard of everyone's progress. The nurses do not give information unless asked. But with what they hear from their families, other patients, and the nurses, there are few secrets that patients can keep from each other. A patient who is doing well, or is sent home, brings hope. When a patient does poorly or dies, however, the fact that the same could happen to anyone on the ward is unavoidable.

The fever that the nurses had been anticipating developed late in the afternoon, and that, combined with a minor but aggravating rectal problem, made Linda ask for a pain pill early in the evening. She was asleep soon after dinner.

Happily, her fever abated during the night. When I went in to see her the next morning, she had been up for hours.

"I woke up at five thirty because of the pain pill yesterday," she announced as I sat down. She was being given an infusion of red cells that hung from a pole on her I-med. Usually the cells are in a clear plastic bag and they flow easily through the Hickman at a rate set on the machine. But these were in a pressure bag that helped squeeze them through the tube because for one reason or another, the cells were thick and sluggish. Linda was sticky from sweating out the fever, but showering while attached to an I-med is hard and not allowed during a transfusion anyway.

"I wish this room had a bath," she said. "When I was pregnant it was the first time I ever had any trouble sleeping. I got up and took lots of baths then."

She had several things on her mind that morning, and she jumped from one to the other. The first was her morning platelet count, which had just come in. It had dropped from the day before, and she was going to need more.

"They were only fifteen thousand, even though I got some from Jenny yesterday. But a lot were probably burned up by the fever, and it was her lowest yield, too. My platelets were the first to come back after chemo, but that was my bone marrow, not Jenny's."

She belched a couple of times, and I asked her how her stomach was doing. She shook her head. "I'm burping a lot whether I eat or whether I don't. Whenever I change my position, too. I roll around at night—burp. It's so gross. But my hair is doing okay. It's going to be a mess at all these different lengths. There were a couple of days where it was coming out by the handful, but not now."

The most important thing on her mind, however, was getting out well in advance of Christmas so she could do all her shopping before going to Atlanta.

"My goal all along has been to be out by December tenth," she said firmly. "The fifteenth would be okay but no later. I have a lot of shopping to do. I wouldn't go to any place really crowded, though, because I know I'm supposed to stay away from crowds until my immune system gets a little stronger. But I can't remember a Christmas when I didn't go to Northridge, which is about half an hour from home. There's a big mall there—a Broadway and a May Company and a Bullock's and a Sears. I always go there for Christmas, mainly because they have a nice Bullock's. One year I found a candle with angels on the outside, one holding a harp, another holding something else. I got it for Dan's aunt. It burned down on the inside only, then you could refill it with votive candles. It was just perfect.

Every year there is a special find. But I guess I'll give it up this year. It's always jammed. There are umpteen zillion parking places, but you have to park out in the north forty whenever you get there."

This would be the last family Christmas in Atlanta. John and Jackie had decided before Linda's leukemia was discovered to move to California again, and this year's celebration was being planned not only to cheer Linda's recovery but also to say good-bye to a special place.

"The South is really my home," Linda went on. "I'm glad I grew up there even if I wouldn't want to live there now. I'm really glad I could walk alongside a creek by big trees with coons in them. I'm really glad I got to grow up like that. It's a big change from the concrete jungle here. Dan grew up in a small town, but it's not the same. Everything is so much slower in the South. I took him back there a couple of years ago. We saw some cloggers dance. We'd never seen anything like it. Toward the finale they sang 'Dixie,' and I could feel the tears welling up in my eyes. If I had been alone I probably would have bawled, but Dan was there and so were my parents. You could feel the roof coming down. You know, when you go to Dodger Stadium and they play 'The Star-Spangled Banner,' only about half the people make any noise. But everyone there just sang at the top of their voices."

At the nurses' station Patti DeLone and Mary Anne Bright were writing their patient notes and listening to the radio. "Breakfast in America" by the group Supertramp was playing. Patti looked up at Mary Anne and said, "You know who this reminds me of? Dave Scott."

"It's hard to believe he's dead," Mary Anne told her.

"That's because we didn't see him die."

Mary Anne turned to me and said, "He was eighteen years old, and he had a face like a god."

Patti looked over, too. "It took a year for him to say anything."

"Then he talked about everything. He wasn't afraid of anything. He just didn't want to be in pain."

"I really liked him. He was one of my favorites."

"It still hasn't hit me," Mary Anne said. "He had, like, a 1954 Chevy . . ."

"Not that old—a '64."

". . . his brothers would drive it here and park it under the window, then he'd watch as they drove it around."

"He had parking tickets outstanding all over Orange County," Patti said with a laugh. "He was one guy who would have appreciated the marijuana study."

"He didn't smoke, did he?"

"Yes, he did. I used to roll them for him. You know who looks like him? Debra Phillips's brother. I saw him, and for a split second I thought I had seen a ghost. But not as good-looking. I'm glad he didn't have to come back in here. I used to smuggle him pudding from the kitchen. I went in there once with it, and Winston Ho was examining him. Whoops." They both laughed.

"He was a little hotshot," Mary Anne said sadly. "A neat kid."

Mary Anne Bright had worked on 10 West for two and a half years at this point. She found the job challenging and liked her co-workers, but she was eager to change from nursing to a job in the medical-business field and had tendered her resignation, effective in two months. She is a tall, attractive woman whose face matches her surname.

"I'm leaving because, ever since I was a kid working at thirteen, I've been afraid of being in a rut, and I feel I'm getting in one," she explained. "I'm a little more ambitious than some of the people here. I want to be more financially stable and have a more prestigious job. But I'm leaving with no spite, and I may never be able to say that about another job. I just don't see what I'm doing as terribly ambitious. Most people I know are making four or five thousand dollars a year more than I am." (She was back on the ward a year later, however, after finding that the rewards of the work on 10 West exceed the rewards of simply more money.)

She was one of the most capable and articulate of the nurses, no small achievement in what is by nature a capable and articulate group. Her being on the cusp of involvement with the ward and looking ahead to other work gave her a perspective different from that which anyone wholly focused on 10 West could have. One evening after she had put in a twelve-hour day we walked to a restaurant near the hospital. She echoed a familiar refrain when she explained how she came to the ward in the first place.

"I had no intention of working in bone marrow transplantation," she said over dinner. "In May of 1978 I was a little hot-shot nurse from a critical care unit in Cleveland, Ohio. I had received a letter from UCLA saying there was a job for me in the intensive care unit. But I got here and they said, sorry, the last day job has been filled, but there are openings for nights. No way, I said. Work and sleep are all you can do when you work nights. But there was a job on 10 West. The first thing I saw when I went to interview with Janice was a bald, skinny kid with a Hickman hanging out of him. My idea of a bone marrow transplant was like anyone else's who isn't familiar with them— take a femur out of someone's leg and see if it grows. Nurses who float up [who are assigned for a day when there is a staff shortage] think we're a surgical ward."

The job, however, looked interesting, so she took it, to her great satisfaction. "Ten West came close to being the most ideal nursing I've ever had," she continued. "They're a gung-ho group, close for the same cause. There's no ladder climbing. It's a very healthy atmosphere. I had never wanted to pursue relationships connected to work, but it was an easy thing to do on the ward."

One of the reasons for that is that the work is so specialized, the course of treatment so rigorous, and the emotional demands so great, that lay people are generally frightened away by stories of the ward. Most people just don't want to be made aware of daily life-and-death struggles. Thus a 10 West nurse has to find other ways to exorcise herself of the intensity of the job. One is through a strong sense of camaraderie that allows the nurses to speak to each other with full understanding. Mary Anne had that but needed more.

"There is a support system at work but not much of one away from it," she said over dessert. "I have several close friends who are not nurses, and we got together one night to watch a movie of the week called *A Perfect Match*, which was about a bone marrow transplant and which was quite accurate. Most got up and left during the show. They didn't want to handle it. The rest said after, 'Oh, is that what you do at work?' I've found that writing poetry helps me to put the work in perspective. It's very easy to write poetry about the floor. Most of it is very sad stuff. Sometimes I write twenty poems in a night and will be up until four in the morning resolving things. I've written two hundred and fifty poems in the past three months. But it has been a most wonderful learning experience."

Still, there is a price. "I could go to a gym and work out for two hours and feel less tired than I did tonight when I finished. But we've learned to cope with the work; we've done it over and over. It builds a strength inside.

"The biggest thing I've learned is that whether someone is dying or not, they're alive. You have to treat them like anyone else. In other hospitals I never sat on the bed to talk with a patient because we were told you could contaminate the bed with your uniform. Well, so what? Getting close is more important.

In the critical care unit [CCU] they're hooked up to machines and in four days they're dead—or alive and out. I used to love it when they called a code [for resuscitation of a patient with a cardiac arrest]—it meant we might save a life. But in the CCU you monitor machines. Ten West takes people away from machines and brings out their personalities. The CCU becomes very automatic. If someone has a pulmonary edema, you know what to prepare for—just like on Ten West—but you never get to know the person, only the body."

Death is an event and a subject a 10 West nurse has to come to terms with to be able to function well on the ward, and off it, for that matter.

"When I first started here I was worried—what if a patient wants to talk about death? Well, the death process is as natural as the birth process. You learn not to fear talking about it. It's not such a terrible thing to die. I'm not afraid to die—not that I want to now. But I've had a wonderful twenty-six years. One day some of the nurses sat around, and we talked about which leukemia we'd want if we had to have the disease. I chose basal cell; it's the least rapidly progressing, least malignant cancer."

For all the hope that 10 West offers, it must be remembered that it is still a research unit, that the staff treats patients with state-of-the-art medicine but also develops much of that medicine on the ward through generations of patients. A patient who comes to 10 West is told this, and signs a form stating that he understands that certain medications or procedures may be experimental and of unclear value, that they are only believed on the basis of laboratory evidence to be the best course. The great strides bone marrow transplantation has made in the past decade are the results of this balance of established medicine and experimentation. No patient undergoes experimental procedures if any conventional therapy works. But if all those fail, the nature of disease and the approach of the ward dictates extraordinary measures. Every patient who comes to 10 West comes because he is willing to try any way he can to defeat his leukemia.

This dual nature of the ward can cause problems for the nurses, who appreciate the long-term results but must also administer and see firsthand attempts at cures that are not yet proven. It is one thing to administer protocols that cause immediate discomfort in return for long-range health; it is another to administer them when the results are uncertain but the discomfort isn't. The only guarantee a 10 West patient has is that the doctors will prescribe whatever course they feel will benefit the patient; and when every common course is tried and proves a failure, they will ask the patient if he is willing to submit to a promising but as yet unproven one. In the end, it falls to the nurses to carry out the doctors' orders.

"A couple of times I've felt that we acted in the death of a patient," Mary Anne said. "It was in a phase-one study, where you administer a drug to measure toxicity [whether the drug or the dose is harmful or fatal]. A phase-two study measures effect. Anyway, we gave this guy the drug over a couple of days. Six days later he had a GI bleed. He bled out in a couple of days. You have to ask yourself, 'Did I do this guy a favor?' I don't like the idea of thinking we could contribute to someone's dying faster than he might have."

The other side of this, she pointed out, was in the case of the young American-Chinese of whom everyone had been so fond. "His father feels he tried his damndest, and therefore died a dignified death. His mother thought we did our all, and therefore he died a dignified death. I would have liked to know him on the outside. I shared a lot of his personality. It's strange when every tape someone plays is one you have at home."

As with every nurse on the ward, Mary Anne had to learn to balance the need to be generally emotionally detached yet always professional against a natural pull of friendship toward some patients. One woman in particular had demonstrated to

Mary Anne how strong the bond between nurse and patient can become and what effect a nurse can have.

"I've become haunted by some of the words I've said to people," she told me. "There was a twenty-four-year-old girl who had a bone marrow transplant, and we talked about what would happen if her graft didn't hold and she had to come back on Ten West. Sure enough, a few months later she was back in relapse. She was in very bad shape. I talked with her family about what to say, and we decided to tell her that it was okay to die. I grabbed her hand and said, 'I'm really sorry to say good-bye to you, kiddo'—and bang! She died. If *that* doesn't influence you about getting close to your patients . . ." Her voice trailed off and then she continued. "After her death her mother found a box with my phone number and some writings she had done about leukemia and dying and she brought them to me. You learn you have to distance yourself. Another patient like that would have destroyed me. I'm still in touch with her mother. She and the father were divorced a week after the death. It had been in the works, the papers were signed. Their daughter just asked if they could tolerate being together at least until her death. She was my best learning experience as well as the best friend I've developed since working on Ten West. But I could never do it again like I did with that kid, I think."

The value of the ward for the patients and for the families— whether or not the patient lives—and for the nurses as well, Mary Anne added, is that "in a sense we offer the hope—in a strange way we offer the excitement of it all—that at least we tried everything and everyone pulled."

All she talked about made her think of Linda, whom she had taken care of that day. "Linda feels alone, I think," she said, and shook her head. "Here she is, a new mother, a planned pregnancy. In the midst of crises I'm very selfish. How can these people go through so much? Isn't it amazing? Look at Linda, who's so strong. I can't imagine giving birth to that wonderful

Gerber baby and waking up the next morning to chemo for AML."

A question I asked everyone on the ward was whether he or she would be willing to undergo a bone marrow transplant, knowing what they do. They all agreed that no one can say unless actually faced with the decision, but about half of the nurses felt they wouldn't. Mary Anne was one. "Would I have a BMT? No, I would die," she said, and then laughed. "I'm too stoic. There are a lot of reasons why I wouldn't. I've nearly died three times. I have control of my life, and I feel good about it. I want the same thing in my death. I don't want the donor feeling guilty if it doesn't work, and the family full of anxiety. I would rather be out mucking around for two months than wondering every day and being evaluated on paper."

Although the relationship between doctors in the hospital and the nurses on 10 West is good, there are occasions when communication breaks down, sometimes with frightening implications. Mary Anne ran into such a case on the afternoon of December 1. An anesthesiologist came up to the ward and screamed at her for not watching and recording a patient's vital signs over what he felt was a long enough period. Mary Anne listened with both annoyance and perplexity as the doctor unloaded. She was still mad an hour later when I arrived.

"I asked him why he needed so much information just to implant a Hickman," she said. "He said, 'A Hickman? I thought he was supposed to have a gastrojejunostomy [an operation in which part of the stomach is resected and about ten feet of the lower bowel are removed].'

"What a jerk," she said, walking away.

That was about the only drama on the ward that day, though. When the night shift arrived at 7:00 and both groups of nurses sat down for evening report, a day nurse said, "It looks like an easy night. Nothing exciting is happening."

Report went by quickly; the status of the patients was generally good. Linda and Debra Phillips were at either end of a cycle that day. Debra went into isolation, her white count having fallen according to schedule. Linda's count had jumped to over 1,500 per ml, and she was taken out of isolation. Her graft was doing well. Her problem was continuing nausea. Her nurse for the day reported that she had been given some Dilaudid (an antinausea drug) through her Hickman but still lost her breakfast, and then some Hawaiian Punch she tried after a marijuana cigarette in the hope that that would calm her stomach. Her reaction, however, was not uncommon. Nor was the generalized body rash she had developed. Her skin was warm to the touch, her face flushed, and her palms red. It was possible that she had a minor case of graft-versus-host disease, but it was too early to tell. It was also just as likely that her intermittent fevers had made her body hot and irritated. An electrocardiogram and chest X ray had shown nothing worrisome; the only thing to do was wait and see what happened next. At the moment, though, it looked as though she could go home in about two weeks.

The most impressive news was of Luke, the Hawaiian with aplastic anemia. He had improved markedly and was jokingly uncooperative with the nurses. If he could hold his own for another two days, the doctors thought, they would have done all they could and he could go home, even though it looked as though the therapy had been a failure and he would not live long. But staying at UCLA would not lengthen his life, and being at home would make him happier. (As things turned out, he did go home two days later and once there made what appeared to be a full recovery; ATG takes as long as six months to work.)

Mary Anne was his nurse that day. In ending her report she told the woman who would be his night nurse that he had passed a waxy red thing out of his nose earlier.

"It's probably one of those Q-tips he lost," she said, to general laughter.

By 8:00 P.M. the night shift had settled in for what looked as though it would be a quiet 12 hours.

The night shift on 10 West, or anywhere in the hospital, is very different from the day. The place is, first of all, far less crowded. Doctors and families and visitors are at a minimum, the patients are usually asleep, the corridors quiet. Usually, between 2:30 A.M., when 10 West nurses finish the nightly drawing of blood for tests, and about 4:30, when preparations begin for the transition to the day shift, everything is still, and the urge to sleep is great. Nurses do charting and paperwork and gossip and wait for the slump to end just before dawn.

This night was no different from most others. Ellen Cummings and Sharon Anthony chatted with Peter Belauskas, the one male nurse, and worked on their patients' charts. Sharon, who at thirty-one was the mother of a thirteen-year-old girl, sat beneath the glass-doored bookcase. One of the things in it was a handmade clay statue a couple of inches square at the base and two or three inches tall: "World's Greatest Nurses—10W" was etched on a slope below a bed with a patient in it. The patient had a sheet up to his chest, his head on a pillow, a smile on his face, even a little Hickman catheter where it ought to be. Sharon was recording the bacteriology report on one of her patients, but I interrupted her to ask who made it.

"Jimmy Knautz," she said, putting down her pen and looking fondly at the statue. His was a name I had heard often since coming to the ward. He had been one of those special patients, one who was cared for by everyone who came in contact with him. His death six or eight weeks previous had devastated many of the nurses, and each had a different story about the twelve-year-old boy, who was clearly a remarkable child. Normally, children who receive bone marrow transplants are treated on the third floor by the pediatrics staff. But Jimmy was mature beyond his years, and that, combined with special medical considerations, made it better for him to be on 10 West. He had been a patient there three times, actually, over the course of a year. Sharon had been particularly close to him.

"He made the statue here, after his second admission," she said. Peter and Ellen looked up from what they were doing to listen. "He was always doing things like that, making little puzzles or games, getting involved in one project or another. He was so cute. I was the first person he met when he came here. He always said, 'You were the first one I met.' That really tickled him. He was so mature that he liked it up here. We didn't treat him like a peds patient at all.

"His leukemia was discovered after he fell on the handlebar of his bike one day and was taken to the emergency room at a hospital in Chicago. He had hurt his throat, and they took a frontal X ray, which showed only tissue damage. But two weeks later he had a respiratory arrest, and they discovered a mass around his windpipe, and then that he had leukemia. They gave him chemotherapy, but he kept relapsing, two or three times in only a few months. He had just turned eleven when he first came here, supposedly in remission, to have a bone marrow transplant. But it turned out that he had relapsed again, that there was leukemia in his spinal fluid. The doctors gave him four weeks of chemotherapy, including injections in his spine, and sent him home, thinking he would die. But after he got back to Chicago he was given another bone marrow test, and it turned out he was back in remission, so they shipped him right back here and did the bone marrow transplant. It engrafted, and he was sent home, only to come back the third time with graft-versus-host disease.

"Anyway, when he came the last time, he was my only patient one day. I went in, and he was very up-tight, and I just said, 'I'm not leaving.' He relaxed right away. I'm a mother, and so is Patti DeLone, and he responded to that mothering sense. His mother was also there, and she reminded me that he had already died once, when he had respiratory failure in Chicago. My daughter is only a little younger than Jimmy was, and I could appreciate what she was feeling."

She paused for a moment or two, obviously caught by the emotional recollection. She took a deep breath, then continued. "One night a couple of weeks before he died I went in to check on his Hickman. He was asleep when his I-med beeped [indicating a need for an adjustment]. It beeped only once before I shut it off, but he woke up anyway and said, 'It's a good thing you were here.' I said, 'Yeah, I know, I'm so perfect I can't stand it.' He just started giggling. It was just one of those moments late at night; kind of silly." She shrugged, then quickly went on. "Jimmy had a little girl friend on his last admission. She was thirteen. She had aplastic anemia, and I'm not sure what became of her after she was discharged. I know she wasn't here when he died, though. She was an only child and lived with a single parent, which is the case with my daughter. I think if I had got to know her . . . I feel so for her mother. They were so cute. They'd send notes back and forth between their rooms. If one wasn't feeling well and couldn't visit the other, they would say, like, 'Be sure and tell Jimmy that I wanted to see him but didn't feel well today.' "

Sharon sniffled and looked to be fighting back tears. "There was a TV show about kids with leukemia at the time of his transplant," she continued. "Two of them were from UCLA, and one was, strangely enough, named Jimmy; he had taken a lot of steroids and had a moon-type face. I watched the show with Jimmy and his family. It was very realistic. They showed about six children and what they had gone through—chemo, BMT, the whole thing. At the end of the show they showed who had lived and who hadn't. [Something of interest to a detached viewer but a terribly difficult thing for a transplant patient to see.] He was depressed for several days after that." Sharon's sniffling picked up, and her tears could no longer be held back. "It's just unfair," she said through them. "I just couldn't believe he would die. You know better, but you just don't believe it. You really don't.

"The night he died his mother went downstairs to stay with him. He had developed severe breathing problems and was on a respirator in the respiratory care unit on the fourth floor, and had asked her to stay with him. Anyway, they called a code blue [the code for cardiac arrest that is sent out over the hospital PA system] to the unit, and it was just like a shock. I was in charge of 10 West, so I sent Peter downstairs to check. When he had heard the code called he had said, 'No, it must be the other patient across the room.' After he had left I kept saying to myself, 'No, it's not Jimmy.' Then they called us from the RCU and said, 'Your patient has just coded.' I said, 'No, no, it can't be.' I had to go into Jimmy's room on the ward, where his father was sleeping, and tell him. I kept thinking, What do I say, what do I say? How do you keep from crying when you feel so close? I woke him and just said, 'They need you in the RCU.' I kept thinking that I wanted to be down there with the family, but I was in charge of the floor, and I thought Peter could handle things with them better than I could. It turned out he was crying along with them. They coded him for about an hour without success, and finally the family came upstairs, and we all went into Jimmy's room and just cried. The last thing his father said as they got in the elevator to go was, 'Just keep giving that love to your patients.' The thing is, that kid was easy to love." She paused a long while, then said softly, "He was just such a nice . . . he never complained." She shook her head and paused again. "You'll have to ask someone about his brother. He was eighteen. Jeff. He was always out here making us laugh."

She paused yet again and collected herself, and then said, "Everybody here works hard to give our patients every bit of success. But sometimes our patients feel we're doing things to them, and they have an attitude of 'Just leave me alone.' There was one patient who was whiny and pouty, who overexaggerated things so you never knew how she was. She was also addicted to her Demerol and would get mad if you came in at 9:31 instead of 9:30. I understand the effects that medications can have on you, but we had to be very stern with her. I just told her, 'We go through this, too; not in the same way you do, but we go through your illness, too, and it hurts. We're human, too.'

"Saying this reminds me of my first leukemia patient. He was a Mexican who couldn't get into a second remission. He wanted to live so much. He was taken to the emergency room once with some bleeding problems, and there was another Mexican kid there who had overdosed. My patient went over and started yelling at him, 'Here I am trying to live, and you're throwing your life away.' "

She straightened the bacteriology report in front of her and then looked at me. "It's not that often you get involved with someone as I did, as we all did, with Jimmy, and it's not that often that it's so obvious that your being there makes a difference, that even if they don't live you feel like you've done something. What it comes down to—when people ask, 'What do you get from it?'—is love. It's like having an intimate relationship with someone. What can be more intimate than their dying? It changes your life-style. You think in terms of now instead of the past or the future. You appreciate every day of life, of health, and of your children's. That's what it comes to."

She stopped talking and went to work on the report again. Then she smiled a little smile and pointed to Jimmy's statue.

"I'll just leave that up there," she said.

A few hours later, when the morning report had ended just after 8:00 A.M., all the nurses, whether they were on duty or not, gathered in front of the window by the elevators on 10

West to have a picture taken for the Christmas card they send each year to ex-patients and their families, and to friends of the ward. Everyone wore a standard green uniform with some red added for the season—a sweater or a ribbon or a belt. It was a rainy day, but inside there was laughter and teasing and grumbling, especially by the night shift, who wanted to go home and sleep, and for a few minutes, at least, the cares of the ward were put aside. The finished card had "California Christmas" and a little palm tree printed on it. It was, like most amateurly taken, family-type group shots, a rather goofy but sweet picture. The cards brought in responses from twenty-five or thirty people who had been on the ward, or from their surviving families, all full of good wishes and cheer and thanks for everything the staff had done for them. One, from a young woman transplant patient now leading a normal life in Hawaii, had a stamped, self-addressed envelope enclosed to encourage the nurses to send more news of themselves.

SEVEN

On December 3, three weeks after her transplant, Linda had her first full day without nausea. She was out of isolation, but the strain of all she had gone through was showing in a way it never had. When I went in to see her at 8:00 P.M. with Ellen Cummings, her nurse for the night (and the nurse who had administered the transplant), she was lying in her bed and looking very tired. A copy of *The First Twelve Months of Life* was folded open on her bedside table.

"I started reading at five-thirty this morning, when I couldn't sleep," she said. "I'm finding out what my kid is up to." She managed a little grin, but she missed not being able to see the baby. She was a little testy, too—actually a sign of improvement. Ellen asked how she was feeling, and the two of them began a long conversation.

"They took a bone marrow this morning," Linda told her. "My resistance is down; it hurt. I'm just worn out by the whole thing. I don't have the power of concentration I used to. You really have to concentrate on something else when they're working you over, and for the first time, I couldn't do it. Then one of the doctors came by and said he wanted to do a proctoscopy. I said, 'In my behind?' All this is for research, and I owe my life to it, but enough is enough. I said, 'Can't you wait just a couple of days until it's healed?' He said they should have done it two days ago. I finally consented to a biopsy of my colon, I think it was. That's just little, but a proctoscope is a big old thing. I'm not going to be Miss Cooperative Patient when I have to suffer like that. If I were strong it would be one thing. But I'm really worn out. I don't need to have my butt ache like that. I need to go home. Once that isolation sign comes off the door, I feel it's time to go. I've never been in a hospital without being in isolation; but maybe because of that, it hasn't bothered me to have my door closed all the time, because that's the only way it's ever been."

"Why don't you start asking to go home?" Ellen said. "Sometimes that helps."

"I have," she replied, and perked up a bit. "I haven't smoked any marijuana today. I ate my dinner—the baked potato and sour cream and all the fruit salad and iced tea, plus I had half a bacon, lettuce, and tomato sandwich for lunch."

"Think of this as a vacation," Ellen said with a little grin. "When you get home you'll have to start working, all the pressure will be on you. But you'll have a cleaning lady, right?"

Linda grimaced. "I hate cleaning the shower. I *hate* cleaning the shower and the sink, scrubbing the shower, and Dan's whiskers in the sink."

"Why don't you tell him to clean it up?"

"After five years I've given it up. But I've told Dan I've not gone through this to go home and clean the shower. I'm destined for greater things than to be a maid. But you know, when I had leukemia I never missed a day of cleaning, even though toward the end I couldn't wash all the dishes at one time or do all the cleaning and vacuuming without a break."

"You were working full-time, too, weren't you? Do you think Dan would like you at home and not working?"

"He likes the money I make," Linda said with a laugh. "But, yeah, I think he would like that. It's hard to get to his real feelings. He's not like me. I'm like a blackboard with everything on it. This has changed our lives a lot. We've talked about a lot of things. He took this very hard. He really did. In a way it was a help for me because one of us had to be strong. It was days before I broke down. I probably would have earlier if he hadn't been such a mess. But one of us has always been there when the other was down. There's never been a time—well, I guess down in OB when everyone said I was going to die—but neither of us ever really lost hope even though we were both afraid I would die."

"Did you ever discuss death before?" Ellen asked.

"I don't know." She paused. "Once we did. Dan and I went to his grandfather's funeral in Santa Paula, where his family is from. I said, 'I bet you want to be buried here.' He said yes. I said, 'Don't you dare put me in a hole in the ground. I want to be cremated, and I want to be let loose. The world is for the living. It's not meant to be messed up with tombstones and monuments for the dead; they're gone. Their spirits have gone, and their bodies only clutter it up. This dwelling over what was—they're better off. The grave isn't doing them a bit of good; and a freeway or something will come through eventually anyway.

"It's like a release," she went on. "Your soul has left your body and gone on. It's free of this body, not bound by it anymore. All that embalming turns me off. I go to funerals and respect that they serve some families' wishes, but they don't serve mine.

"It's ironic, but the day the hematologist drew blood to see what was wrong with me, there were two old ladies—and I mean *old*—in the waiting room, and they were swapping their medical ailments and problems. They were so old and had so many problems that I thought, I hope I don't get that old." She grinned. "Well, I'd like to get a little older than I am. Sixty, seventy. Then you get bogged down in all your problems. As long as you're healthy, it's one thing. But frail, unh-unh. But I don't

227

want to die at twenty-seven. That's a little *too* young. Little did I know as I was making that wish not to grow too old how close it would come to coming true."

We were all quiet for a moment, and then Linda changed the subject to something more mundane and of the present. She rubbed the hundreds of strands of hair on her head and said easily, "I'm glad *all* my hair didn't fall out. I've kept a lot. It's stubborn like the rest of me. I can feel it coming back, too. It hurts when it starts coming out like it does. You always like to think that you're not the norm, that this won't happen to you. It's a way to deny it. You always think you're special. But I had been expecting it." She sat up straighter in bed. All that she had said seemed to have given her new resolve.

"Tomorrow I'm going to start bugging them to begin weaning me off the hyperal [hyperalimentation—liquid IV nourishment]," she said. "I know it takes a while, and I want to get out of here next week. I have so much to do before Christmas."

At 2:00 A.M. the next morning, Ellen went quietly back into Linda's room to do the nightly routine that is performed on all patients. She spoke softly to Linda, telling her to keep her eyes closed. Ellen took her vital signs, then cleared her Hickman catheter. She flushed the line with heparin, then drew 5 ccs of blood from it to evacuate the hyperal and any extraneous medications. She pulled from her pocket several five-inch-long glass vacuum tubes with colored rubber tops and filled each with blood from the line for various tests—the green top went to virology, the red to serology to check for intestinal amoebae. Purple for blood count, another red for liver function. A final red for the blood bank to type and screen. It took twenty minutes in all.

When she had finished, she went to the medication room at the nurses' station. A sign on the wall said, WHEN IN DOUBT, THROW IT OUT. Ellen held up a pill she had not used and said to Sharon Anthony, who was assembling the proper medications for her patients, "This is a codeine pill. Will you watch me throw it out?" Narcotics are closely monitored.

Each patient's prescribed medications are listed in a book. Linda's read like a pharmacopoeia, but it was little different from any bone marrow transplant patient's: Norulate, a birth-control pill given to all women to help control bleeding; nystatin powder, used under arms and on the groin to eliminate fungal infections; Ketoconazole, an antifungal drug thought to be superior to nystatin; Polysporin, an antibacterial agent; Nupercainal, a topical ointment of cocaine and lidocaine to ease itching; Prednisone, a steroid used as an anti-inflammatory agent; Methotrexate, given to every patient in a small dose every week for three months in the hope of preventing or re-tarding graft-versus-host disease; Carbenicillin, an intravenous antibiotic; Amikacin, a penicillin derivative for use against fe-vers when the white blood count is below 500 per ml; codeine and Demarol for pain; Seconal for nausea and vomiting, also for sleep; Compazine, in the event marijuana wasn't wanted; Dilaudid, a pain narcotic; Bactrim, which all patients take pre- and post-transplant as protection against interstitial pneumonia and which is also effective against urinary infections and as a GI sterilizer; folinic acid, to combat the suppressive effect Bactrim has on the bone marrow; Vancomycin, Polymixin B, and Colistin, GI antibacterials for when the white blood count is below 500 per ml; Cimetidine, a drug useful in preventing ulcers. And these: Sudafed; Tylenol; and milk of magnesia.

A piece of paper that looked as though it came from a biblical fortune cookie was taped on the glass at the receptionist's area of the nurses' station. The quote is from Galatians: "And let us not be weary in doing well: For in due season we shall reap, if we faint not."

In the afternoon of December 4, Patti DeLone and Cheri Shilala chatted while taking a break in the chart room. The pace on the ward had been slow the last while, and both of them commented on it.

"Things have been real quiet for three weeks," Patti said with a hint of disbelief in her voice. "The last six months, there was always someone sick. I can't remember the last case of stomatitis [a painful infection of the mucous glands]. I don't know what they're doing to people now."

Patti's observation got Cheri thinking about the early days on the unit, when there was never a quiet moment, and of how treatment has evolved through experience.

"People were already in isolation even before you did anything to them, which pretty well guaranteed that it wouldn't go well," she told me between sips of a Coke. "We were treating people with steroids before radiation, and it was a terrible combination. People were burning; they had big faces. We had a bad reputation among other nurses. People who floated up here were not only going to a place totally foreign to any experience they had had, but also to a place where people weren't being discharged out the front door. Those who were admitted to the RCU were in such bad condition that most didn't make it out. Now we seem to be doing what we are supposed to. It's amazing how things have just stopped, like fungal infections. It seems almost routine to start people out on Amphotericin [an antifungal drug]. It would be nice if it stayed this way. It's not as challenging as it used to be, though. You had to gird your loins every night before coming in. But if it does get boring, you can always transfer somewhere else."

The feeling of calm was compounded by the impending discharge of Luke, the Hawaiian with aplastic anemia. Later in the day he was out of his room for the first time in about two weeks, and he stopped by Linda's open door while taking a walk in the corridor with his father. Linda was feeling all right but not great and did not particularly want to talk with another patient, especially one who was about to go home. They talked about milkshakes and other staples of a patient's life at greater length than Linda would have liked, but she said nothing to stop the conversation. At the end it was his father who said the most interesting thing, and then inadvertently.

"Luke was going to end up in a hospital anyway. He was going to be a physical therapist." He used only the past tense. The present was too uncertain.

One reason his present was so uncertain was the danger of his developing an uncontrollable nosebleed on the flight home. The pressure in an airline cabin is about the same as at 10,000 feet above sea level, and that lessening of pressure combined with his diminished platelets could be catastrophic. That evening Peter Belauskas put together a kit for Luke's father to take with him on the plane.

"I'm ordering a bunch of Adrenalin-soaked cotton balls," he explained. "Adrenalin is a vasoconstrictor, but you really need to apply pressure to stop the flow because it won't really stop or clot. If they're on the ground, they can get help, but on the plane he needs to know what to do. So we'll give him these and let him pack his nose with Adrenalin cotton balls and hope there's a doctor on board who's not afraid of being sued. There's stronger stuff, silver-nitrate stick," he added, "but it could blow off half his nose if it's not used right."

"A neurosurgeon in medical school said there are only two reasons to be a doctor," Dr. Robert Figlin told me one afternoon on the ward. "One, to make a shitload of money and, two, to know who to send your family to." He was in a generally foul and cynical mood because a patient he liked a great deal was in relapse and none of the treatments tried had brought her into remission. He couldn't help dwelling on the risks of the treatments themselves, and he was looking for a little perspective.

"The science of it makes it acceptable that you're destroying some of these people because it's the science of it that's ultimately going to save others. I'm thirty-one years old. I've gone through four years of undergraduate work, two years to get an MA in chemistry, another four of medical school, and three more on top of that in internal medicine. There has been a concomitant commitment to teaching people how to take care of patients—I was chief resident for another year. Now I'm in the middle of a three-year fellowship in cancer. All together, that will be seventeen years to get to a point where you can take care of a patient with cancer with some competency. Seventeen years." He grunted. "I don't even want to think about that."

The patient he was so upset about was Nellie Tapia, the eighteen-year-old with ALL who had come just after Linda and who was found to be in relapse, making a transplant impossible for the time being. Acute lymphocytic leukemia is difficult to put into a second remission, and Nellie's getting a third one looked less and less promising. About her only hope was an experimental drug reputed to have terrible side effects. Still, she had been cheerful and stoic through the various regimens of chemotherapy she was given and that, combined with her winning personality, had made her a favorite of the staff. Of mine, too.

From the start of my stay on 10 West I had appreciated the difficulty the nurses had in explaining their work to their families and friends and the necessity of keeping a safe emotional distance from their patients. Daily reports of life-and-death struggles don't make good dinner conversation with one's husband and children, and most people not involved in medicine don't want to be reminded of their mortality by hearing news of a fight for life so close at hand. I noticed after I had been on the ward awhile that my own friends began to distance themselves from my experience. They would ask a few polite questions about how things were going, but the moment I went into any detail, they became uncomfortable. This made conversation difficult at times, because in pretty short order nearly all my attention and thought were on and about the people on the ward, whether I was there or not. I was convinced that after all Linda had got through she would get through the transplant as well. Thus the gravity of what she faced was not omnipresent. Yes, she was in a critical situation, but everyone—Linda, her family, the 10 West staff—believed she would pull through. The specter of killing complications was an intellectual concern with her, not an emotional one.

In Nellie's case, however, I found I had no protection. First, from the time she came to UCLA her prognosis was very unpromising; there was not the sense with her that there was with Linda that she would be all right. Second, my relationship with her developed not as the subject of a story but simply because she was someone I was drawn to.

"I've been here for three weeks and three days, and I'll probably be here for another forever," Nellie said resignedly as I walked into her room after talking with Figlin. In a way she was right. She would eventually get a third remission but not until February, by means of an experimental drug whose side effects were so damaging to her that she could not take the last two of the six doses prescribed. That she achieved a remission surprised everyone, for it came several days after the medication had been stopped and while the doctors were trying to decide what next, if anything, they could do for her. But although she was in remission, her liver was too damaged to undergo immediately the requisite radiation before a transplant, so she stayed on the ward to heal. As she recovered, she was able to spend days out of the hospital, although she had to be back for the night. She and I spent some of those days together, and I took her to meet several of my friends. Her convincing wig covered the only residual exterior sign of all her therapy, and no one who met her could believe that this apparently normal teen-ager was in such desperate condition. She went to movies with nurses and played on the beach and shopped in the local stores, taking one day at a time but convinced that she would have the transplant and be all right. By mid-March she was in good enough shape to begin the radiation—in her case small doses would be administered over several days—although not in optimal condition. Statistically her remission wouldn't last much longer, and if she relapsed again, all hope would be lost. So she and the doctors pursued the only course they felt they could.

The toll on her body from the leukemia and the drugs proved too great for her to have a transplant, however. Before the end of the radiation treatments it was clear that her liver was too damaged to go on. Through April and May she struggled against one complication after another. Without the remission she achieved, she would have died at the beginning of the year. When it came, it gave her hope and a month or so of comfort and a partial return to normalcy. But even though you may beat leukemia one way, it often ends up getting you in another. I sat with Nellie and her mother and one of her sisters while her life deteriorated quickly toward the end of May. She lapsed into a coma in the respiratory care unit. I spent hours there with her, looking at a brave young woman with tubes plugged into her, her body moving only to the beat of the respirator she was attached to. I tried to see the smiling girl who had come onto the ward seven months earlier in her cowboy hat and with her tape deck blaring as I wiped the dark foam of blood and saliva that crept out around the tube that went down her throat, and I listened for her cheering on one team or another while watching a football game on TV. Instead I saw a young woman dying before she had had much of a chance to live and heard only the chug of the machinery that kept her technically alive. After she died I arranged for her cremation and the shipping of her ashes back to Arizona, and I said to myself after seven months on 10 West, "Enough."

But all that unhappiness was yet to come. It was mid-December now, and Christmas was on everyone's mind. The tenth came, the day Linda had set to go home, but she was not near being able to do it; she was farther away, in fact, than she had been a week earlier. Graft-versus-host disease had been recently confirmed, and now her liver was in poor condition as well. Acknowledging that she would spend Christmas not with her family in Atlanta but in bed on 10 West was a terrible blow.

Linda's worst problem was simply that her liver was not able to do its jobs properly. The liver is the body's largest glandular organ; an average one weighs three pounds. It is a marvelous piece of equipment that performs more than five hundred functions. Most have to do with breaking down fats and proteins for digestion and absorption and with filtering harmful substances from the blood, among them the drugs Linda was taking. Because her liver could not break down and carry out the refuse properly, it was accumulating in her peripheral blood. Her bilirubin (red bile) count was three times normal, which in turn increased the likelihood of her developing jaundice. Under normal conditions, the hemoglobin of old red blood cells is converted into bilirubin, removed from the bloodstream by the liver, and eliminated by the body in bile that passes through the intestines. Put bluntly, her body was piling up garbage.

Linda's graft-versus-host disease and her liver problems were serious setbacks, but they were not critical, at least at this stage. The doctors were hopeful of stabilizing her liver, and GVH occurs in half the transplants done. She was in a good deal of discomfort, however, and her spirit was shaken by the necessity of spending Christmas in the hospital. For several days she had been in no mood to talk with anyone while she sorted out her disappointment and struggled with her pain. She also made a difficult admission to herself.

"All the talk I've done about death is intellectual," she told Janice Campiformio in a rare conversation during that period. "Now I realize that I actually *could* die."

Nellie and Linda were not the only ones having a hard time. Ellen Cummings came to work looking tired, and with reason.

"When I worked at Sidney Farber Hospital in Boston," she told Peter Belauskas, "I dreamed about kids I knew with ALL who didn't respond to regular treatment. They gave them some experimental drugs, and some died really horrendous deaths. I couldn't sleep last night thinking Nellie could do that."

To add the final emotional twist of the day, a sweet-faced nine-year-old Chicano boy was brought up to the ward for a day or two until there was room for him on the pediatrics ward, where he would have a bone marrow transplant. A nurse who was in the midst of a tough emotional period—she had been very close to Luke and was also already very attached to Nellie—was assigned to take care of him. When she went in late in the evening to see if he was asleep, he bombarded her with questions about what was in store for him. He called the procedure a "bone transplant" and asked what floor they would do it on.

"They'll do it in your room," she explained. "It's just a transfusion."

"Will they take it from my sister?"

"They'll take it from inside the bone. It's not blood, but it looks a little like it, only darker. But there's a lot of other stuff in it."

"Will my sister have enough after?"

"Yes, it will replace itself in a couple of weeks. They'll probably give her some iron pills, too."

"Will the Cytoxan make me sleepy?"

"We'll give you something."

"Do you have the Hickman a long time?"

"As long as you're here and maybe longer. A lot of our patients leave with them. The doctor will make a hole in your vein, a little hole, a needle hole, to put it in."

"Will they put me to sleep?"

"No, but you won't feel it. They'll give you a lot of medication."

"They gave me a shot today for the bone marrow, but I felt it . . . how long do people stay here?"

"Six or eight weeks."

"My doctor in Fresno said I might have to be here three months."

"That's very uncommon. We have had someone as long as a year, but usually you have a transplant and it takes two or three weeks for it to take and then it goes into your bloodstream and makes you strong again."

"How will they know it's working?"

"You'll have a bone marrow sample taken every week or two and then maybe a few after you get out."

"Will I be here for Christmas?"

"You'll be here for Christmas."

When the nurse returned to the report room she shook her head and said, "He's a nice kid, but I'm glad he's going downstairs. Real glad. I'd get too involved with him. He's a real button."

Between the seventh of December and the thirteenth, when she began to show some improvement, Linda retreated into herself. Not being able to go to Georgia had ruined all her plans and expectations. For someone who had never doubted getting through the transplant according to the schedule she'd set up, the realization that she actually might not survive was devastating. She was irritable and unhappy and did not want to see anyone. Any intrusion made her feel almost as though she were being harassed. The withdrawal was from everyone—nurses, doctors, friends, family, Dan, even Angela. She needed the time to prepare herself for whatever lay ahead. She told her parents and Dan not to come to see her; even talking with them on the phone was something she wanted to avoid.

Her withdrawal put a great stress on her family, but they had seen it before. During the last days of labor she had been this way, in need of time to toughen herself mentally, wanting only to concentrate on the problem at hand. Even though they understood why she was doing it, they felt as if she were rejecting them and they called Dr. Ho for advice.

237

"She's drawing into herself, but she needs her family," he told them.

So they went to see her in spite of her retreat, not every day and not for long, but enough to keep contact, to show her that they loved her and were pulling for her. When Dan was with her he made sure he kept the conversation on light matters, such as news about friends or co-workers, or about little things that Angela had done. However much Linda felt that only she could get herself through, her family believed Ho was right, that she needed them, whether she admitted it or not.

For one of the few times in her life, Linda was facing the possibility of defeat. In the past, she had always been able to summon the mental and physical resources to reach her goals. Only three months earlier she had overcome incredible odds to have her child. But this time her body wasn't responding to the importunings of her mind, and she felt a mixture of shock and loss, and however unfair it was toward herself, failure.

After a week, though, her body and spirits rallied. On the thirteenth she was ready to see people again. When I went in that evening she was out of bed for the first time in days and was sitting in a chair by the window. She looked like someone who has come through a long ordeal and is resting after it. She smiled when I gave her the roses I had brought, and said hello. Her dinner tray was untouched on the table near her. I asked if she wanted it moved closer so she could eat.

"It's cold," she said. Then: "I need a joint." She was quiet for a minute and then explained. "I'm trying to be real easy. I was eating great guns last week when everything hit me so hard. Today was the first day I've eaten in a week. I had half a cheese sandwich and some cream of mushroom soup for lunch. I'll eat this rice," she said, pulling over her dinner tray, "and maybe a little of this chicken. Who knows about this liver of mine," she said between bites. "It could be twice as bad tomorrow, or half, or the same. And this diarrhea I have is like broth."

However disgruntled she sounded, at least she was talking again. The last week had been physically and mentally hard on her. So hard, in fact, that in the morning when her doctor had asked her what day it was, she didn't know. By evening, however, she was in real time again.

I stayed only a few minutes with her but stopped by again about 11:30 P.M. Her spirits were still down.

"I just smoked a joint for the cramps I've been having," she said, propped up in bed. "They're like a bellyache. The marijuana doesn't work as well on them as it does on nausea, but it gives relief for an hour or so. I'm also starting to sleep better. They're giving me a real sleeping pill now, not that Benadryl crap." Her tone became irritated. "They tried to give me a Benadryl last night. I said, check your order."

Most every patient on 10 West goes through periods like Linda's, where frustration and annoyance, and fear as well, leave them unhappy and short-tempered. The nurses and doctors expect patients to go through them and try not to take patients' short responses to heart.

Linda was not the only one on the ward with low morale. The nurses as a group were frustrated and somewhat depressed; everyone seemed unhappy. Much of it could be traced to two favorite patients—Linda and Nellie—doing poorly. Some of the rest had to do with their feeling that Bob Gale was not paying much attention to their concerns. The topper came at about 2:00 A.M. when without warning Gale had a young man with terminal testicular cancer admitted to 10 West. His name was chalked up on the blackboard and DNR (do not resuscitate) was after it. The nurses were furious. It was bad enough that the patients they had slaved over were in trouble; now strangers were being sent to the ward to die. He was like the patient in white, the character in *Catch-22* who is brought to the infirmary while the other patients sleep and who lies wrapped head to toe in white gauze, motionless, speechless. Forty-eight hours later, the young man was officially brain dead, but his heart, young and strong, kept going for another six.

By fortunate coincidence Gale's monthly staff meeting with the 10 West team was later that day. No one liked him that morning. The nurses were still mad about the middle-of-the-night admission; the fellows were mad about how they were being treated. Gale took one problem at a time.

"Look," he said of the patient, "I was called at eleven or twelve Friday night; the doctor was in distress. He had a patient with ten thousand platelets, no granulocytes, and a crit of seventeen. It was an obviously life-threatening situation, and the guy had to go to a hospital." The nurses already understood that, but after being assured that this would happen again only in an emergency, they calmed down. Then Janice Campiformio brought up the fellows. "They complain that they're being abused by the service," she explained. "They feel that they're overruled no matter what they say. They feel like interns."

Gale took a split second to compare the years he had put in on the unit to the weeks the fellows had and he answered, "They are." The nurses laughed loudly. The tension was defused, but one of its underlying causes wasn't.

The problem was Linda. The bad turn she had taken over the last ten days had shaken the nurses and was threatening to interfere with their ability to give her the treatment she needed. Their professionalism was being eroded by their compassion and empathy, and they had the good sense to admit to themselves and to each other that it was an effort to go into her room. So they asked Dr. Wolcott, the psychiatrist available to the ward, to come and meet with them. He had no magic cure, but over the course of a two-hour session he helped them to try to get a better perspective. His advice essentially was for them to try not to combine all the sadness of the floor with Linda. And he added that Linda's recent withdrawal was her way of coping. All the nurses could do was just keep offering.

No one agreed more with that than Linda, who didn't know about the trouble the nurses were having or their meeting with Wolcott, but who told me, "I'd like a little less sympathy and a little more expertise. I sure hope the GI guys they're bringing up to see me can figure out what's wrong with me." Her greatest complaint was a constant upset stomach, and her annoyance with it and with the inability of anyone to do something about it was evident in her sarcasm.

"Here I am in the UCLA hospital," she said. "A place where they have and develop wonder drugs, but where they have nothing for an upset stomach."

Bob Gale was frustrated, too. As a physician, it is his sworn duty to do all he can for his patients. As a researcher, it is his duty to look for ways to attack incurable diseases, although not at additional risk to a patient. It is a frustration that always lies just below the surface, but now it was evident for the same reason it was in Dr. Figlin: Nellie Tapia. She had not responded to any antileukemia drug given her, and the experimental drug from the National Institutes of Health that he and Figlin were considering was the only treatment left. His dilemma was that he had a patient who was not responding to conventional treatment, but who wanted to try everything she could to achieve a remission for a transplant. Yet she was physically miserable from all the drugs she had had so far and was now faced with even harsher side effects.

"People sometimes ask, 'Why do you torture the patients?' " Gale said one night at his house after dinner. " 'There's a ninety percent chance of failure, of having them die as a result of receiving the drug rather than from their disease. You cannot do this to human beings,' they say. They cannot handle the concept of no way out. Nellie's prognosis is clear. Think how much easier it would be for the doctors and the nurses not to treat them. The easiest thing is to do nothing—easiest for everyone

Eric Lax

except the patient. It's hard for a doctor, especially, to deal with external criteria—if only ten percent benefit, how can you subject the other ninety percent to this treatment? Intellectually that makes sense, but actually every patient has the same chance. They are the one who is either cured or not cured. We are all sensitive to this criticism. You harbor some guilt. Nellie will probably die because she has leukemia, but she could die from something we did. In the extreme you create a new disease, graft-versus-host disease. It's hard to react rationally because you already feel guilt."

Giving up on a patient, however, is something Gale seldom does. But giving up, or at least diminishing expectations, is something he feels doctors do often.

"I call it the hanging of the crepe," he said. "Some physicians tend to paint the bleakest picture to the patient and to the family so that if anything but the worst happens, they won't have committed themselves. If the patient dies, it was predicted. If he lives, the doctor's a hero. I'm fairly optimistic, I think, but when I see the handwriting on the wall I tend to become realistic. Yet, you never know. I once had a patient who had been on antibiotics for weeks, was growing two microbes in his blood, had low blood pressure, weighed about ninety pounds, and although he was thirty, looked to be about eighty. I started to prepare the family for death because I anticipated he was going to die. They took it as a personal insult. Then for some miraculous reason he turned the corner. When he got well he realized he had almost died and got mentally sick. He wouldn't get out of bed. Finally we threw him out of the hospital. You sink or swim, we told him. Now he's five years post-transplant."

EIGHT

There are times when the strain on the family of a transplant patient is greater even than on the patient. Christmas was such a time for the Peters family and for Dan. For months they had all planned on this being the biggest and best Christmas ever. The holiday was always celebrated with a huge tree—sometimes two, because the children liked a green tree and Jackie liked a flocked one—and preceded by Jackie's baking fruitcakes for neighbors and Linda's making a gingerbread house. Over the years Jackie and Linda had collected ornaments and decorations that each had sent the other. This year Linda's youngest brother had surprised the family by spending a week's pay on a gigantic tree for the Atlanta house, and he and his girl friend sent Linda a big green arrangement with candles ten days before Christmas, with a note that said how much they looked forward to her coming home.

When Jackie realized that Linda would have to be in the hospital, she sank into despair. Linda's reaction to having to stay in was to retreat into herself and, in a way, to ignore that Christmas was actually coming. So she said no when Jackie asked if she would like to have a little tree in her room. Particularly hard for Jackie were the doubts she began to have for the first time about Linda's being able to recover. Even though the doctors were not yet pessimistic, all seemed hopeless to Jackie. What convinced her might seem a small thing, but it was full of portent to Jackie: Linda had stopped taking a shower and putting on a clean robe every day. To her, it was a sign that Linda had given up. She was able to hide her feelings from Linda, though not from herself. A few days before Christmas she went shopping with Jennifer, who was not going to return to Samoa until after Christmas, to buy gifts for Angela. She knew that Linda had planned to get her a cradle gym, something filled with attention-grabbing and dexterity-promoting devices, so she bought one and forced herself to buy presents for others in the family; they had to have at least one thing to open Christmas morning, even if the joy of Christmas had vanished. As Jackie walked up and down the shopping center to various shops, tears rolled down her face.

On the twenty-third, John Peters and two of his children left Atlanta in his plane to come to California, where everyone was now gathering. They planned to be able to get halfway across the country before stopping for the night, but an ice storm pinned them down in Memphis. On Christmas Eve another storm grounded them in Amarillo. It was the first Christmas in thirty years that John and Jackie were apart. Things were going poorly in California, too. Dan had the flu and couldn't go to see Linda. And Linda took an ominous turn. Fluid began to accumulate in her lungs, and if it went unchecked, she could develop pneumonia.

On her first Christmas morning, Angela Hope had only one present that her mother had bought her, a cloth doll in a rosebud dress that Linda had bought in October. She called her daughter Angela Rosebud or Little Princess, and the crib she had bought in September had a canopy and sheets with pink rosebuds. The doll matched the sheets.

In the afternoon, Jackie put Angela into a Christmas dress and set off on the drive to UCLA. It was a cold, cloudy day with intermittent rain, and she drove especially carefully. Even so, after going ten miles she ran into trouble: the car's oil-pressure light came on, and she was on a deserted state highway miles from a gas station. When she finally did find one they had neither the filter nor the gasket it turned out she needed. It was dark by now, and Angela was hungry, so Jackie found a roadside restaurant and got her some milk. She also started calling friends, all of whom were out somewhere else for the day. She finally reached Dan's stepfather, who drove to meet her at 8:00 P.M. The two of them drove around looking unsuccessfully to find the replacement parts for Jackie's car; they finally had to give up the search. It was too late by then to go to the hospital, and Jackie was terribly upset. The only good thing about the day was that John was finally able to get the plane to California, arriving at 10:00 P.M.

The next morning the Peters family all got to the hospital at last. They brought some festive decorations for Linda's room and had something of a celebration. Linda had asked that the packages be saved until she was home and they could celebrate properly, but they brought a few presents anyway: a gold bracelet from Dan that he asked John to bring; a robe from Jackie. No one dwelled on the family's not being able to be together the day before. Linda's only comment was a brief "Don't worry about it." Jackie had a picture of the big tree that was in the house in Atlanta to show her, but the fun was gone.

"It was the saddest Christmas I hope I ever spend," Jackie said later.

In the days between Christmas and New Year's, Linda's condition worsened. Her liver continued to deteriorate, her lungs did not clear, her diarrhea (a symptom of graft-versus-host disease) did not abate. When I went in to see her on the morning of December 29, she was not only mad and unhappy, she had begun to despair of getting well.

"I've lost all confidence in my doctors," she said immediately. "I think you could treat me better. I think they care but they don't know what to do. Do you know what they did when my diarrhea started? Nothing for a week. They took cultures. Do you know what they want to treat it with now? Aspirin. Aspirin!" I had never seen her so angry. "If this goes smoothly, fine. But I wasn't prepared for weeks of pain like this. I'm spent. I came here prepared to either get through this fine or to die quickly. But not to go on like this. I've never felt such pain—my stomach, my gut, my knees. I'd never recommend this to anyone. Remember how I came bouncing in here two months ago? The only way I'm going to get out of here is with God's help."

She looked away for a minute or two, and when she spoke again, it was more softly.

"The one thing they didn't prepare me for is that I could have gone through this. If only I could have a couple of days where I improved, it would help."

December 31 was such a day. It was also the day Jennifer and her boys were to go back to Samoa. Linda had not shared with her family the bulk of the depression and concern about her ability to come through the transplant, and she was in good fettle when she and Jennifer visited before Jennifer went to the airport. She and her husband were due to come back to California in March, when his contract was up, and she and Linda talked about things they'd do then. Jennifer had, understandably, mixed feelings; she was glad to be going home but sorry to leave her sister behind in the hospital. She was confident, however, that Linda would be all right; otherwise she wouldn't have left.

And Linda was encouraging. She talked about being back at work before Jennifer returned.

But Linda was not as confident as she wanted people to believe. She felt her doctors had lost control of her ailments. Worse, she felt more and more as if she had lost control of herself. She noticed she was not breathing as easily as usual, and she wondered if this was the precursor of pneumonia. Shortly after dinner she asked for a painkiller and slept through the end of a year that because of Angela couldn't have been better, but otherwise could hardly have been worse.

The other patients on the ward rested that night as well, at least they all did except Nellie. She was up and around, dressed in jeans and cowboy boots. Her liver wasn't very good, she was attached to an I-med, she had to wear a mask over her nose and mouth so as not to pick up any stray bugs, but she didn't care. She sat out at the nurses' station laughing and joking with the night shift, helping them with their paperwork and listening to rock 'n' roll as the new year came in.

At 8:00 A.M. New Year's morning, Bob Gale met with some of the staff of the J Service on 4 East, the ward where general oncology patients are treated and where he would be the attending physician for the next month. In attendance were a fellow in hematology and oncology, who had just been assigned to the floor, and two interns, who had been on the service for a month. Despite whatever festivities the doctors had succumbed to the night before—Gale had been out quite late—hospitals run on a schedule, and rounds are held at 8:00 A.M., year out and even the first day of year in. The purpose of the gathering was for Gale to discuss the status of the nearly thirty patients with the interns who had been largely responsible for their daily care and to make some decisions about the course of their treatment. They sat informally in a rectangular, cracker-box-shaped room off the nurses' station. Each had an index card on every patient, and from time to time in the discussions Gale would make a chart on the blackboard to make a teaching point to the young doctors.

Several of the patients had leukemia, and I immediately noticed differences in approach to patients on the J service and on 10 West. Most obvious, of course, was that on the fourth floor the doctors were trying to control leukemia itself; on the tenth their concern was with the complications in the aftermath of wiping it out. The fourth floor is where what is called conventional therapy is practiced, although it became clear very quickly that conventional therapy includes several approaches, none of which is known to be best. Conventional therapies for leukemia are a crap shoot at best because the disease is so overpowering, and the decision as to what drugs to combat it with and in what dosage is based more on experience and best guessing than by definite procedure.

For instance, one of the first patients discussed—it would take three hours to go through them all—was a thirty-five-year-old woman with AML who had been diagnosed in mid-December and treated at another hospital without achieving a remission. The exact course of therapy she had been given was unclear, however, and the doctors at UCLA were trying to figure out the best one to follow now. The intern responsible for her reported his prescription, and Gale listened quietly. When the intern finished he said, "It's my own personal prejudice, but unless she's one-point-five feet tall, eighty milligrams is grossly undertreating her." The woman had come to UCLA because she hoped one of her brothers or sisters would be a match for a bone marrow transplant. That was not important at the present, Gale pointed out.

"We have a neutropenic leukemic [meaning a patient with a dearth of white cells that surround and destroy foreign bodies in the blood] with a fever [meaning the patient was infected and had no defense]—you understand the rationale of stepping in quickly," he told the intern. "She has a lot of siblings and therefore might be eligible for a BMT, but our first job is to get her into remission, then we can see about offering her something." Identifying the source of her infection was crucial to giving her the proper treatment promptly. "If we can't document the source of infection," Gale continued, "we'll really be flying by the seat of our pants."

One by one, they discussed the patients. For a few, there were clear treatments. For most, there weren't; medicine is a very inexact science. "No one seems to know what he has," Gale said about one patient. "He came here with masses on the left side of his neck, then we discovered them on the right side as well. He was given CHOP [an antileukemia regimen] and thought to be in remission. But now we discover he is thrombocytopenic [having a lack of platelets], and his bone marrow shows two populations of cells, one perhaps myelocytic. He remains a mystery. He is given a regimen of Prednisone and L-Asparaginase [two antileukemia drugs] and shows great response in the neck mass. But he is also obese and has diabetes that is difficult to control." The question was whether he might have AML or perhaps Burkett's cell leukemia, a rare lymphoid malignancy.

"These kinds of dilemmas are not all that uncommon, unfortunately," Gale concluded.

One of the most telling examples of the difficulty and frustration of trying to treat leukemic patients and of trying to be humane when the disease has clearly won was the last patient to be discussed. Gale used her case as a springboard for a small lesson in statistics.

"Here we have a sixty-two-year-old woman, diagnosed in September as having ALL. She was treated with Prednisone, Vincristin, and L-Asparaginase. She achieved a remission but relapsed a few microseconds after that. She was treated again with the same drugs. What do you think is better to have as an adult [post-twenty years old], ALL or AML?" he asked the interns. "You get eighty percent remission with either, but the median survival in ALL is less—about nine months. Age determines survival and the disease. You don't cure many ALL adults—about six percent, not sixty percent as with kids, at least those between two and seven; before two they do very poorly."

The question at hand was how to treat the woman, who was not responding to much of anything but who also wasn't expected to, given the nature of the disease. Still, the woman was determined to try everything she could. She had been given white cell transfusions for six weeks, with lessening effect.

"We have a clear-cut, documented infection, treated with the appropriate antibiotics at the appropriate doses, but she's deteriorating after forty-eight to seventy-two hours here," Gale went on. "We're trying to keep her alive after her second course of chemo with the knowledge that she will do very poorly. She's going to die. She's developing basically intractible leukemia. To complicate it, she has low platelets and epigastric tenderness. She was given an enema before an ultrasound test to try to find out what the trouble is, and she's been febrile ever since. She has a painful crust on her tongue, preventing her from taking antibiotics orally. She doesn't want a bone marrow sample taken because there's not much in it for her; there could be something in it for us, but I respect her wishes. We are thus obliged to do what we can to support her. Should we continue granulocyte transfusions? She had a documented sepsis [a toxic spread of unremoved bacteria within the body] six weeks ago, but what about now? There must be some point of decreasing return. I'm trying to see what's responsible to do," he told the interns. "Having treated her we're responsible for taking care of her. It sounds like we should do reasonable but not extraordinary measures; we should try to keep her alive and try for a remission."

The problem the doctors faced was that although they agreed the woman's position was hopeless, she wanted everything possible done, including whatever heroic measures might prolong her life, even in discomfort, for a short period. Gale asked what the interns thought.

"I think she's a full code because she wants to be kept alive," one who had treated her said.

They agreed that they would use, in Gale's words, "a full court press" in treating the woman, but Gale also summed up the feelings of all of them, who knew the woman was dying, when he said, "I wish she would settle for less."

Settling for less is something not done on 10 West. Every patient there was a full court press because, finally, there was hope on 10 West while there wasn't on the J service. As Gale said to me afterward, "Hope is a valuable commodity of itself." It was the absence of hope in the discussion of many of the J service patients that struck me as I listened, and it was the sense that such is usually the case in the conventional treatment of leukemia that left me so depressed at the end of rounds.

"The tenth floor is actually no different than the fourth floor, and really no different than the other floors, except the stakes are higher," Gale said as we walked back to the elevator to take us to 10 West. He was both right and wrong. He meant it in the sense that anywhere in the hospital, doctors were doing what they considered the best thing for their patients. Ten West's designation as an experimental unit did not mean it was the only place where what could be construed as experimental medicine was practiced. I had seen during rounds on 4 East that no treatment is a sure treatment and that the doctors have to trust their experience and best sense and then try something else if that treatment fails. Where 10 West differed from the other floors was in its opportunity to go beyond the conventional and beyond what was until recently a dead end. I had sat in on rounds on 10 West every morning for two months and listened while the doctors prescribed every course of treatment they knew of. I had watched patients ride a roller coaster of improvement and relapse before either being discharged or dying. It was always terrible when one died, but the sense in the air and the motivation that kept everyone going was hope, hope that one new protocol would work where none had before, hope that instead of a 50 percent success rate, it could be 100 percent. Ten West at times discouraged, but 4 East depressed. In the face of the most distressing evidence, I always felt that miracles could happen on 10 West. They had before. I had seen them.

Linda was full of hope that morning and ready for a miracle as she told me the story of the two fortune-tellers. A brother and one of her sisters had gone independently to see a fortune-teller in the different cities they lived in.

"You know what they both said?" she asked. "You have a relative near death who will make it."

It was as good a time as any for another miracle to happen to Linda; there hadn't been much of one since Angela was born, and Linda was getting sicker. A chest X ray later in the day confirmed what everyone had feared would happen: She had viral pneumonia. A transplant patient can usually handle any one of the complications Linda had developed. But liver involvement—the organ was now three times its proper size—graft-versus-host disease, and pneumonia combined put a terrible strain on the body. Yet, while the outlook could certainly have been better, the situation was by no means hopeless. Nothing was yet irreversible. One of the most important things was for Linda not to give up. For the moment, however, that was a problem.

"Don't count on this working out as we thought," she told her mother in passing. It was something Linda wanted to say but not dwell on, and Jackie, who kept her own doubts to herself, tried to reassure her yet still continue the conversation.

By the next day her resolve was more intact, although physically she was no better. Her younger brother and sister returned to Georgia, he without being able to come and say good-bye because of a high fever. Dan's infection had passed, however, and he was finally able to see Linda after more than a week. During that time doubts about her pulling through had entered his mind for the first time, and when Linda told him a couple of days later, "Do you realize how serious this is?" he became very alarmed. Days before, he had nervously accepted how serious Linda's condition was, but he had tried not to let her see it in his manner or hear it in his voice. He had done that so effectively that Linda, in a way, was mad at him for apparently not realizing how ill she was. For Linda to be upset meant that she had lost the self-control she usually displayed. With that gone, Dan worried about her ability to keep fighting.

"You got the baby," he said to her in hope of offering encouragement. "Nothing could be more grueling than that."

Pneumonia was the complication Dan feared the most all along. Linda had just come to the ward when the young American-Chinese was dying of it, and Dan had seen his degeneration. It was the only case he had seen firsthand, and its memory haunted him. He could only hope that Linda's course would not be similar. It was hard, however, for him to believe that she could beat it.

Linda's inability to eat compounded her problem. It is common for patients who have a major illness such as graft-versus-host disease, burn victims, and those who have recently undergone major surgery to become catabolic. Twenty-four hundred calories a day are sufficient to keep a healthy body even with itself. But one under such attack and stress needs at least twice that to repair itself. What isn't taken in as food is taken from the body's muscle mass. Hyperalimentation through an IV line can make up some of the discrepancy, but the most a body can absorb that way is about 4,000 calories a day. Over the past two weeks Linda had not been able to take in enough energy to help herself properly mend, so her ability to fight her disease was lessened even more, at great cost.

Over the next few days Linda found it increasingly difficult to breathe. She was given first an oxygen tube for her nose and then, as the difficulty increased, an oxygen mask. It was a frustrating time for the 10 West staff, who liked Linda so much but were able to do so little for her. For the first three weeks following her transplant she had responded pretty much as expected in a normal recovery. Then, when it looked as though she would be ready to go home in another ten days or two weeks, she had developed complications that had brought her down to the condition she was now in. To see her decline as a result of the treatment she had been given rather than from the leukemia, which would have been more emotionally tolerable for the staff, pressed very hard on them. The nurses visibly sagged when they came on duty and were brought up to date on Linda's status. Dr. Champlin, who was the attending physician on the ward, hated to see what was happening. There is no solace in the fact that half the patients treated on 10 West survive when confronted with the decline of one who looks as though she will be in the other half. But of course the person this was hardest on was Linda.

"Every patient knows the chances are fifty-fifty," Dr. Champlin said one day. "But almost every one thinks she is going to be in the fifty percent that makes it. Linda is a bright woman. Everything was going well for her, and now it's not. It's hard to convince her otherwise. I try to give realistic appraisals, try to balance hope against reality. The shock and realization of her condition is very hard for her to see beyond."

It was hard for Dan to see beyond much, too. Each change in Linda's condition seemed a greater step of severity to him, and with each his spirits sank lower.

On January 5, Linda asked if she could be transferred to the respiratory care unit. Her color was good and so were her spirits, but breathing by herself had become too hard. During the last day the 10 West staff had told her to say if she wanted to go there; for the moment, anyway, it would be her decision to go as a matter of comfort rather than because of immediate need. Before deciding, however, she asked if her same room would be there for her. She was assured it would be, and late in the morning she was wheeled down to the fourth floor.

It took about half an hour for Linda to be taken down and settled in one of the eight cubicles around the perimeter of the unit. In less time a 10 West nurse stripped the bed in Linda's room, unplugged the refrigerator, and locked it up against the time she would return.

Jackie and Dan came to see her in the afternoon. Linda had called them before she went to the RCU and they had each tried to look at the move as a positive one, although without much success. When Jackie arrived it was with bad news. Angela had caught the flu that most everyone in the family had suffered through over Christmas, and it looked as though it would be a week or more before she could come to see her mother.

John had left in his plane for Georgia early that morning, hours before Linda's call about her move. This time he made the trip quickly and without incident and was already there when Jackie, who was very upset, called him after returning from the hospital. After she told him that Linda was in the RCU and was, in her opinion, slipping, John made arrangements for a commercial flight back early on the seventh. The news depressed him terribly. He went the next day to see the president of his company, who had lost a son three years earlier. He was very sympathetic when John said he needed to go back to Los Angeles for an indefinite stay.

"Go for as long as you need to," he said, and added, "good luck."

On the sixth Linda was comfortable with help in breathing

and talked about going back to 10 West soon. Several nurses from the ward stopped by on their lunch break or on their way to or from work to say hello to her. The number of nurses and the frequency of their visits over the next days were unusually high. Visiting a patient in the RCU is difficult for them because the patient's care is out of their hands, and seeing someone they have grown fond of in such distress is emotionally unsettling. The nurses risked and endured that in Linda's case because their fondness for her outweighed the unhappiness they felt. They tried to be as reassuring to her as they could, even if secretly they feared the worst.

"Your bed is still there," one of them told her. "Hurry up and come back."

"I know that it's better for me to be here," Linda said. "It's so much easier to breathe. But I'll be glad when I can go upstairs again."

Linda's condition was very volatile, and even with the benefit of a respirator, she had periods when breathing was difficult. When they came, so did her doubts.

"I keep having this feeling that if I don't concentrate on breathing, I will just stop," she told her nurse that night. She said little else for several hours, although she was able to sleep only a little. She was thinking a great deal, however, as her nurse heard at 6:00 A.M.

"This death and dying at twenty-seven is happening to me," Linda said quietly, in part to her nurse and in part just as an admission. The nurse comforted her as best she could, and by 8:00 A.M. Linda was calmer. John arrived in Los Angeles soon after and came with Jackie and Dan to see her. She waved when she saw them but, perhaps because of her difficulty in breathing, didn't say much. But part of it was also that Linda had once again pulled into herself.

In the early hours of January 8 her breathing was no less difficult, and she was still unable to sleep. Her nurse was able to offer no solace or comfort. Linda was also in pain from her other ailments, and she asked how much morphine she could have. A lot, she was told. She asked for a lot and was sedated for virtually the whole day and night. No one knows whether Linda remembered or was keeping track, but January 8 was the date she had mentioned dying when she had said in November that she hoped her story would be a symbol of hope, and how inappropriate her not surviving a transplant would be.

On the ninth, however, she asked that the morphine be reduced, and she remained alert. It seemed to some of the 10 West nurses that Linda was almost surprised to be alive. She said nothing about it, one way or the other, but it appeared that some fight had come back to her. Her prognosis was bad, however; that evening for the first time the doctors admitted as much. "We are not optimistic," one said.

John David, Linda's physician uncle from Atlanta, arrived that night and, with John and Jackie and Dan, came to the hospital and spent the night. For the second time in five months Dan and Linda and her family were playing out a similar drama. They waited helplessly while Linda, quietly and by herself, marshaled her strength and faced the possibility of death. There was one difference this time, though. The first time there was the baby to think of; delivering a healthy child was all Linda wanted. Now the baby was doing well. She had seen it form a bond with Jackie, and she knew her child was taken care of. All her family could do was tell her to keep trying and console her as best they could. As Linda's stay on the ward lengthened and her condition worsened, the number of lines and tubes in her increased. It made them sick to see her like that.

It was especially hard for Dan, who wanted desperately to see Linda and spend time with her but hated to see her in the condition she was in. As the days passed, she began to show signs of deterioration. Air began to accumulate under the skin in her neck, swelling it out of size. Dan saw all that was happening to her and once again felt helpless to do anything to help her. Sometimes Linda was too tired to answer his questions and would just squeeze his hand in response.

Dan and John and Jackie and John David fell into a routine similar to the one they had followed while Linda was in labor. They met the doctors immediately after morning report to get the latest news, sat some with Linda, paced the halls, and visited every local restaurant, where the waiters by now all knew them. They became experts on ventilators and the other medical paraphernalia Linda was hooked up to. After dinner they would return to the hospital for the evening lab results and wait around some more, often until the early hours of the morning. When they went to bed it was with a sigh of relief that Linda had made it through another day, and they hoped for a quiet night. But the nights were long for everyone. They woke up, yearning to hear of improvement "but knowing," as John David said, "that you're going to get a beating."

They all knew that they couldn't keep their sanity if they spent the whole time talking about Linda. They had to have distractions to give them a release. They found it in a woman friend of John David's who spent a good deal of time with them, especially during meals. She was in show business and had stories about activities and work that were foreign to the others, stories that were amusing and diverting. She made them laugh often, which they appreciated, but Jackie said what families of critically ill patients often do.

"I feel guilty about laughing," she said. "What have I got to laugh about? What have I got to be happy about amongst all this sorrow?"

By this time, Linda was being treated with just about everything the RCU had to offer. Now she was not so much a bone marrow transplantation patient as she was a typical patient in respiratory distress. Her condition was a side effect of her therapy, but the problems she had were those of any patient with severe pneumonia or advanced liver complications, and she was being treated as would anyone else who came to the unit with similar problems. She was on a ventilator that forced air into her lungs and could be calibrated to range from normal room air to 100 percent oxygen. In her left wrist an A line (which looks like a pressurized IV line) was inserted into the radial artery to give a continuous measurement of blood pressure and provide samples for measuring the percentage of oxygen in the blood; both are critical measurements for a pneumonia patient. In the middle of her other forearm was a Swan Ganz catheter that ran via a vein through the heart to the pulmonary artery to measure the pressure inside her lung and warn if too much fluid accumulated; too much fluid and a pneumonia patient drowns. She had two IV lines running as well, one for hyperalimentation to provide nourishment and another for her medicines, which as time went by became numerous: Donnatal to settle her stomach; Serax, a sedative much like Valium; Septra, an antibiotic effective against pneumonia; Solu-Medrol, a steroid for treatment of graft-versus-host disease; flagyl, an antibiotic for anaerobic bacillus infection; Cefoxitin, another antibiotic; and Intralipid, a fat emulsion given for nutrition.

An NG (nasogastric) tube ran through her nose to her stomach to carry lactobacillus to help restore the normal bacteria in the intestine that were killed off by the antibiotics. The tube cut off Linda's ability to speak.

That, combined with the sedating drugs she was given, made it hard to communicate with her, or at least to understand what she wanted. She had a pad and pencil, but her hands had needles and lines running into the backs of them and writing was very hard for her. On January 11 her family surrounded her bed as she tried to tell them something. She was unable either to speak or write clearly enough for them to understand it, and they desperately tried to figure out what it was she had to say. They called out every question they could think of and asked her to nod her head if one was right; apparently they never knew the right one. Finally, they called out letters of the alphabet one by one. "Does it begin with 'A'?" Jackie shouted. " 'B'?" Nothing worked.

Very little in her body was working by then, either. Her lungs were full of fluid; her blood, even with the help of 100 percent oxygen through her face mask, wasn't carrying enough oxygen to sustain her; her liver could not metabolize the poisonous ammonia in her blood as it normally did, and it appeared that she was sinking into septic shock. In the evening her blood pressure bottomed out at 80/50, and it looked as though she would die at any moment. As the evening progressed, however, she stabilized. Around midnight a 10 West nurse came down and said to her family that there was an empty room on the ward if any of them wanted to use it. The men went upstairs and managed to get a little rest. Jackie stayed with Linda, continuously bathing her feverish face with a cool towel.

She improved some through the night. The oxygen in her blood increased, and some of the poisons lessened. Every time a blood gas report came back from the lab, Jackie ran upstairs to tell Dan and John and John David the good news. Over the next two days they lived in a mild euphoria of hope. It would be tough, but she could yet stabilize.

Whatever the promise, however, Linda paid little attention to what was happening. She was generally conscious, but she had pulled far into herself. Time was suspended. Dan and the three others took rooms once again at the Holiday Inn near the hospital, where they had been during Linda's labor, but they spent most of their time in the corridors and lounges of the hospital. Linda had blood samples taken and tested every hour, and their ups and downs kept everyone fixated on the arrival of the next batch. More than anything else, they gave the best indication of her progress.

"Her heart deserves the California Timex Award," John David said in a corridor one morning at 1:00 A.M. when more news of improvement came along. "It takes a licking and keeps on ticking."

John David sensed a change in his niece in spite of whatever improvement she was showing. He had never known Linda to be defeated or beaten by anything; she had always got what she strived for. Now, however, he felt she was hanging on not for herself but for her family, because they wanted her alive. The will to live for herself, he felt, had vanished.

In the night of the thirteenth, Linda was able to tell her nurse that she wanted to see Dan. The nurse called him at the hotel and he rushed over, hopeful, curious, and frightened, to see her. It took only fifteen minutes for him to get there, but by then Linda was out of touch again. Her test results still showed improvement, though, and he went back to the hotel feeling there was still a remote chance.

Then, on the fourteenth, Linda rapidly declined. She went blind in her left eye, although no abnormalities could be found. In the afternoon she was given a tracheotomy to help her breathe better; the surgical procedure opened a hole at the base of her neck and prevented the trachea from narrowing and thus lowering the supply of air. Her doctors thought that, plus supporting her breathing on a respirator, might allow her to get through the next few days.

Half an hour after they finished I stood in the hallway outside the RCU with her family. They were exhausted but still hopeful. No one needed to say anything, it was all on their faces: a mixture of hope, resignation, and fear. I excused myself to talk with a doctor down the hall. When I returned two or three minutes later I saw through the window in the door of the RCU that they were back in with Linda. I looked up at the TV screen that monitors the electrocardiograms of the eight patients in the unit. Seven of them bounced rhythmically. Linda's was flat.

After a while the family came out into the hall. They were drained and numb. Everyone just stood silently, composing him- or herself. It was her father who spoke first.

"Well," he said, "what do we do now?"

Linda was cremated, her ashes scattered at sea off the point on the Ventura beach where she and Dan had gone so often. On January 17 there was a memorial service for her at the First Methodist Church in Ojai. The place was packed with friends and co-workers. Even two of the 10 West staff were there. Others who had the day off thought of going—something they usually didn't do—but in the end did not want to add to the sadness and loss they already felt. Other patients had to be taken care of, and they had to be emotionally strong to do it properly.

When I returned to 10 West later I went in to see Nellie. I hadn't seen her since Linda died three days before.

"You went to Linda's funeral, didn't you?" she asked me. I told her I had. She put her head against my chest and cried but then stopped after fifteen or twenty seconds. She had herself to worry about, and she knew she needed to spend the strength she had on the living.

That afternoon, two people were discharged from 10 West, well enough to go home.

There is a framed poster in Bob Gale's office, atop the computer terminal behind his desk. It reads:

THEY SAID TUBERCULOSIS WAS HOPELESS.
THEY SAID POLIO WAS HOPELESS.
THEY SAID SMALLPOX WAS HOPELESS.

CANCER IS ONLY A DISEASE.

EPILOGUE

Debra Phillips negotiated the course of her transplant and is home in Pennsylvania with her family. Suzana Raymond is fine. Hillary Rivera is in college. Luke is in Hawaii and appears to be cured. Richard Lee is well.

There has been some turnover in the 10 West nursing staff, but Janice Campiformio and Peter Belauskas, who is now the assistant head nurse, are still there. Doctors Gale, Champlin, and Ho were recently awarded a four-year, $3.2-million grant from the National Cancer Institute for their research.

Dan has remarried. He and his wife, Elizabeth, had a daughter, Melanie Anne, in late 1982. Angela is thriving and has many of the characteristics that Linda had as a child. She also looks very much like her mother. So much so, in fact, that on occasion when she is visiting John and Jackie and she wanders into John's office at home, he has to remind himself when he turns to see who has come in that it is not Linda standing there.

Acknowledgments

The 10 West staff made a leap of faith in letting me become a part of their ward, and the kindness and cooperation I was given made a difficult project much easier. My thanks to Head Nurse Janice Campiformio, and to nurses Joyce Adams, Sharon Anthony, Peter Belauskas, Kerry Berhalter, Mary Anne Bright, Ellen Cummings, Pam Frasier, Karen Hansen, Jeanette Leslie, Gail MacFadden, Marcia Malmet, Cheri Shilala, and Marciel Whittington, and to Patti DeLone and her husband, Bill, who opened their home to me.

Without Bob Gale's commitment and help in all sorts of ways, I would not have had access to most of the material and the people I've written about. Moreover, he and his wife, Tamar, did all they could to make me comfortable and keep me well fed. I thank them both.

My thanks to Dan Galbraith, to John and Jackie Peters, to Jennifer Peters O'Neill, and to John David Mullins for many hours of time, and for recalling traumatic events, often more than once. They endured much unhappiness, and yet were unstinting in their help to me. I regret almost as much as they do that Linda won't read this book.

Eric Lax

Doctors Richard Champlin and Winston Ho spent a lot of time helping me to understand the science I've presented here. The benefit for me in having no medical background is that I could unabashedly ask questions again and again until I finally grasped whatever subtlety of the immune system they were explaining to me. I'm not sure what the benefit was to them. They were excellent teachers, and any errors are mine alone.

The nurses of the pheresis and respiratory care units at UCLA were very helpful to me, and I thank them. I am also grateful for the cooperation of several former 10 West patients and their families, especially Richard and Pam Lee.

My affectionate thanks to John Cushman, and to Jane Wilson and Kris Dahl of JCA for always being there.

This book may never have been had not Jon Carroll, then the editor of *New West* (now *California*) magazine, suggested I go off on their behalf and "do something about modern medicine." Meredith White inherited me and proved both a marvelous editor and a good friend. Louise Damberg somehow found the space for a piece that grew to 20,000 words.

Patrick Filley brought me to Times Books, for which I heartily thank him. Jonathan Segal edited this book with care and vision, and he made me think and dig. May we do many books together, and may Ruth Fecych do them with us.

Many thanks to Dr. Joseph G. Perpich and to A. Scott Berg for reviewing the manuscript, and for their helpful comments.

Friends are always important, never more so than during a hard time. David and Jamie Wolf gave me unending support. Peter Tauber, bless him, handed me the keys to a beach house and a convertible. And Sally Ann Hotson, who hates hospitals, patiently listened as nearly every day I spilled the latest I had seen.

Families are important, too. Thanks, Mom, for all your faith. And thanks to Constance and Stan Midgely for a Baby that needed no diapers.

When I proposed to Karen Sulzberger, I also asked if we could put off the wedding by a couple of months so that I could finish working on this book. We did, but I didn't. I brought a half-finished manuscript into our marriage. She brought support and patience and help, and they show themselves on every page. Sorry, Sweetheart, and thank you.

Eric Lax

July 1983

Los Angeles